UNDER THE RAINBOW

D.A. Hartman

You are the Best Thompson

Day Hartman

D.A. Hartman
Copyright © 2024 by D. A. Hartman
All rights reserved
ISBN: 9798880063000

The characters and events portrayed in this book are fictitious. Any similarity to real persons, living or dead, is coincidental and not intended by the author.

No part of this book may be reproduced, stored in a retrieval system, or transmitted in any form or by any means, electronic, mechanical, photocopying, recording, or otherwise, without the express written permission of the publisher.

D.A. Hartman Author of Round Trip

Sign up for my newsletter
dahartman.com

Under the Rainbow is where the dreams of sapphics burst into reality. It's a place where love breathes life and women explore caverns of different shapes and colors. It's here **Under the Rainbow** brightness pushes darkness away, and with a brassiere of support, all things are possible, and love will find you someday.

Dedication
To all the beautifully flawed women who dare to dream

Under the Rainbow   D.A. Hartman

1 - Hunger Pains

The humming vibration between my legs doesn't soothe me as usual. Instead, it rumbles inside my chest and makes me anxious as I power down my motorcycle in front of Writerly, a trendy coffee shop in the gated community of Amboadia.

When I remove my helmet and peer into the rearview mirror, I gulp at the sight of my smudged makeup and rush to grab sunglasses and a face mask from my saddlebag. Adjusting the shades and mask, I sigh in comfort at being safely tucked under the mundane costume.

My stomach growls and gurgles at the smell of fresh pastries from the bakery next door. I want to surrender to their desperate pleas, but failing at weight loss isn't an option. I, Deviant Wallace, soon to be a supermodel, must dazzle the audience with Chase Janice's latest designs. Sashaying down catwalks in fabulous clothes is what I have worked toward since I became emancipated from child welfare services six years ago.

While grappling my way into the fashion industry, many suggested I marry a wealthy man. But no, I'm not interested in an antiquated fairytale. I value my independence, and frankly, I find sex repulsive.

At least I did before I met a woman with stunning turquoise eyes. During our only date, the adorable yet quirky lesbian gifted me with something nobody else ever had—orgasms.

Bent over the seat of my bike, with my forehead pressed against the handlebar, I close my eyes and envision beautiful tanned skin pressing against me. Her strong leg spreading my thighs apart. Heat flaring from my center, and kissing her bare shoulders as I beg for her to take me.

A toasty California breeze whips the fantasy away by blowing strands of puke-green hair across my sunglasses. It's the color a stylist at Chase Janice insists I maintain until after New York's fashion week. They say the temporary tint will match the strapless dress and the gems in a tiara I'll wear at CJ's new design launch this Friday. My financial struggles are finally over. I'm about to enter a new world where dreams really do come true.

A tap on my shoulder has me springing upward, nearly bumping into a person standing beside me.

"What the fuck?"

The outline of a body glows from the brilliant morning sun behind them, and their face remains obscured in shadow.

"Are you alright?" the person asks.

To admit I'm irked because a woman dumped me after one date might appear too egocentric, but this is Amboadia, aka Sapphic-ville and this stranger will never know who I am under my lame disguise.

I swipe green bangs out of my view, and mutter, "It's just that I met a woman I like, but she prefers we go the friend route. So, I'm kind of bummed."

The stranger steps back, and sunlight reveals stunning fawn eyes hooded by long lashes. She has boxy shoulders, a strong nose, a square chin, and her extraordinary eyes have caramel irises with flakes of vivid straw. Under thick, dark lashes, her expanding pupils pull me in and I'm lost in her.

Shaking me out of my reverie, she taps an orange baseball cap atop her head with *she/her* pronouns embroidered on its bill, and says, "I'm Joleen."

She extends her hand and waits for me to acknowledge her gesture. Still mesmerized by her golden eyes with specks of yellow and black, I'm stifled and dazed. What is up with my stupid ass?

Ultimately, I take her hand and give it a skittish shake.

Joleen turns to face Writerly. "I'm having a crappy day too." She hoods her brows with both hands and peers inside the windows of the not-yet-open coffee shop.

Concealed behind plastic lenses, I squint my eyes in bewilderment. The woman looks about a decade older than me and doesn't know squat about fashion. Her ill-fitting gray Gucci sweatpants and beige silk shirt clash big time. And what's with the blank sticky note stuck to her sleeve? Despite her poor taste in clothing, her confidence to wear them is a turn-on and I can tell by her attire, and Louis Vuitton sneakers, she's rich.

Curious, I ask, "What happened? Did you lose an extra million in the stock market?"

Joleen moans. "My well-meaning parents bought me a nightclub with hopes of magically turning their introverted daughter into a socialite. The grand opening is tonight."

If I was worried about how frivolous my whining over a minor rejection appeared, I'm not anymore. This nepo-baby is ridiculous.

"*That's* your problem? Your parents bought you a nightclub?" My eyes crinkle with laughter.

Joleen raises her hand in protest. "Being petulant over having coddling parents carries more merit than brooding over the loss of some player you recently met."

Telling this club owner who talks like she's reciting a textbook I've been celibate for over a year and this was the first time I ever slept with a woman might be overkill. Instead, I defend my one-night stand.

"She isn't a player. She's sweet, and it's not like I have deep feelings for her. I barely know the woman."

Joleen shakes her head and chuckles. "For a minute, I thought you had an emotional attachment to your one-nighter, which would go against the three-month rule."

"The three-month rule?" I ask.

"Yes, the average time it takes to know someone is three months. It's foolish to have romantic feelings for someone before then. Statistics prove newly dating couples often break up within three months."

This woman is very analytical. Interesting, but I won't explain to her how emotional attachments can't be explained away or predetermined by arbitrary time limits.

"So, tell me, Joleen Hunt, how long do *you* have to know someone before you let them into your heart?"

"I wouldn't know. I've never dated." She deadpans.

I slap my thigh and cough out a laugh. "I get it. I'm twenty-four and have only been out with four men, but now that I know I'm a lesbian, I'm bursting to go out on dates!"

Joleen quirks her mouth. "I'm thirty-seven and I simply prefer my own company to that of others."

Wow, this woman with eyes so exotic they have me spellbound wasn't joking about never dating.

"Okay, so what's your plan, if not to find a soulmate?"

"My goal has always been to become an arrogant ice queen." Joleen closes her beguiling eyes and shakes her head. "Thus far, I've only managed to become a frigid nerd with the grace of a wombat."

This makes me laugh. She's taking my mind off of food and how tired I am.

Joleen wrinkles her nose and stares into the darkness of my sunglasses, then huffs. "Perhaps you and your tryst will make better friends."

"Maybe." I agree.

She walks to one of Writerly's two bay windows and leans on the red brick to peek inside again.

I want to remove these shades and itchy mask, but I can't risk someone taking a photo of my red-rimmed eyes and smeared black mascara. The last thing this newbie model who just landed a three-year contract with Chase Janice needs is to be discredited on social media.

With a weary sigh, I shove the oversized glasses closer to my face. Cheap cosmetics are gross, but I can't open the coffee shop to wash it off yet. The lock to Writerly is set to a timer. "We have a few minutes before I can open." I yell at her.

Joleen returns to my side. "You work here?"

"Writerly's a temp job. It's slow here, which gives me plenty of time to read and write."

"Are you an author?" Joleen asks with excitement in her voice.

"No. I accept advanced reader copies from authors and review them on Amazon and Goodreads. Being an ARC reader is how I read novels for free." I dismount my Honda, adjust the kickstand, and stand near Joleen.

"I've never met an ARC reader before." She takes my wrist and lifts my arm.

I'm about to scold her for touching me without asking, but her hand pricks me with the same sensation one gets from musical frisson. Only hell, this is better than native flutes or the plucking of a harp.

She glances up and down my body. "You're a beautiful toothpick. Your twiggy shape makes garments appear flawless. As you can tell, I have much more meat on my bones." She steps back to show her form but doesn't let go of my arm or her gaze on me.

What does she know about fashion? Her clothes are mismatched, and she still has a damn sticky note stuck to her shoulder.

Joleen inspects my legs and arms, then works her way up to my neck. Her warm touch seeps into the core of my toothpick—I mean being, the core of my being. Now that I've had a taste of what it's like to be with a woman, my libido has shifted into overdrive. Is this what infatuation feels like? If so, I'm a fan.

She lowers my arm and releases her grip on me. I'm empty without her touch, or maybe it's just my stomach that's empty.

Wiping some of the two-day-old makeup off my neck with the back of my hand, I groan. "I need to quit wearing this grimy shit."

Joleen gestures to a white Bentley parked next to us. "I have tissues."

I approach her practical yet high-priced SUV as she opens the front passenger door and flips down the visor.

"There's the mirror." Joleen leans in farther and nudges an unopened bottle in a cup holder. "And here's some water if you need it."

To determine if this atypical woman is sapphic, I ask, "Do you know what year 'Pussy Is God' came out?"

Joleen groans. "Is it a song or a book?"

"A song. I've been researching the hell out of sapphics—everything from music to sexual positions. 'Pussy Is God' has an awesome beat. It's a great dance song."

"Crap, I'm not into women and I can't dance." Joleen dips inside her SUV. She opens the glove compartment, snatches a pen and notepad, and scribbles something. "How about I give you this instead?" She rips a sheet from the pad and hands it to me.

She's not into women. Bummer, but she doesn't date anyway so I accept the consolation prize and read the note, *One free pass to Joleen Hunt's club, The Tenth Muse.*

Astonished, I ask, "You named your club The Tenth Muse? That's pretty sapphic."

She tosses her palms up. "I had no idea Plato coined Sappho the tenth muse when I allowed my friend, your boss, to name my club."

"I didn't realize you and Virginia were close."

"Yes, we attended the same university as undergrads. When she learned my new club was in LA, she suggested I move to this beautiful gated community of Amboadia."

"Ah, okay then, and FYI, the year was two thousand eighteen." I squeeze past the *non-sapphic* and plop my ass onto the passenger seat, making Joleen jump back as I slam the car door shut.

While she walks to the other side of her vehicle to get into the driver's seat, I glance at the sun visor and view the pancaked foundation on my forehead. Ugh, Joleen must think my deteriorating vampire facade is creepy as fuck. Too self-conscious to allow her to see my bloodshot eyes and the rest of my wrecked face, I leave my sunglasses and mask on and wipe my neck with a Kleenex.

The scent of cherry perfume seeps through my mask when she enters the vehicle. I'm not into fruity odors, but I like the smell of this self-proclaimed frigid nerd and lean in to inhale her scent. I guess along with an awakened libido, I've been gifted with a sniffing fetish. Yay me.

Joleen pokes her tongue out. "Back up weirdo."

"And this isn't weird?" I point to the blank sticky note on her sleeve.

She tilts her head, and when she notices the Post-It, she covers her eyes and bends her head in embarrassment. "I have no idea how that got there."

Besides Cain, who pays rent to sleep on my couch, I'm not prone to letting people in, so I'm surprised at how much I want to get to know this wannabe ice queen.

She lowers the window and flops her long muscular arm out of the car. "So, tell me, who sings Pussy Is God?"

"It's not important if your gorgeous ass isn't into women." I wink at her.

Her eyebrows raise, and her body stiffens. Oh shit, I screwed up.

I'm about to apologize for flirting when she says, "Those must not be prescription glasses you're wearing. I'm anything but gorgeous."

"I have 20/20 vision," I say as I exit the vehicle.

When I reach the thick medieval door of the coffeehouse, I open its lock, pull a Medusa handle, and wave Joleen inside. Writerly smells of coffee beans, assorted teas, and croissants. Mm, what I wouldn't give for one small bite of a buttery treat.

Once Joleen enters the coffee shop, I ask, "What's your pleasure?"

"My parents are visiting and I'm out of matcha tea. Do you have ground leaves for sale? My mother likes to steep fresh tea."

"Not for sale, but"—I walk to the Self-Help counter and grab a handful of individual bags— "will these do?" I drop the tea into her cupped hand.

"Yes, thank you." Joleen takes a wallet from the pocket of her sweatpants. "How much do I owe you?"

"Nothing. Everything at the Self-Help counter is free to Amboadia residents." I pull out a seat for her. "What would you like to drink?"

She grips the back of the chair but doesn't sit. "I can't stay. My parents are waiting at home for me. But I have a question for you."

My shoulders sink at the thought of her leaving. "Sure, what's the question?"

"Do you dream, and if so, do you dream in black and white or color?"

Hmm, she's using me to collect data for research no doubt. Maybe she's a scientist. I don't care who she is as long as she sticks around longer.

"Definitely in color. How about you?" I ask.

"I don't dream. If I do, I don't remember them. I'm much like my father in this respect. What do you dream about?"

She is curious about things—about me, which I'm not used to, but her question has a simple answer because I have the same dream almost nightly.

"This may sound odd to you, but my dreams are always the same."

Joleen's eyes widen. "Please describe the scene for me."

"Okay, well, they always start with me on a runway wearing a metallic dress and an uncomfortable scarf. When I get to the end of the catwalk, before making the turn, a faceless woman in the audience offers me a bouquet of yellow tulips. She stretches forward to give me the flowers and I lean over to accept them. When our fingers touch, I lose my balance and fall off the stage onto a dancefloor. The anonymous woman hurries to kneel by my side and laughs—we both do. She tries to help me up, but we're laughing too hard and can't stand. That's when she tells me she loves me. Sadly, I wake up before her face comes into focus."

Joleen stuffs the tea I gave her into the pocket of her Gucci sweatpants and says, "It is said love is a fundamental need. Humans cannot survive without it. This is a myth."

She's most definitely a scientist, a mad one at that. I'm clinging to my dreams. Starting this Friday, I'll wear some of the fanciest clothes ever made, and each time I strut down a catwalk, no matter how many months or years it takes, I'll scan the audience for a woman holding a bouquet of yellow tulips.

Joleen reaches for my sunglasses. "Come to think of it. I don't know what you look like either."

Too vain to allow her to see my messed-up face, I push her hand away. "I could be the woman in your dreams if you had them."

"I doubt that." She smirks and before exiting the shop, she says, "If we meet again, please call me Joel. I'm aware Joel is a boy's name, but I like the sound of Joleen about as much as I like peas."

Again, she makes me laugh and I try to think of something to prolong her stay. Nothing comes to mind. Melancholy settles in my gut and builds. Why do I become emotional when I'm hungry? Without warning, warm tears stream down my cheeks. Shit, this is embarrassing. I really need to eat something.

Joel encloses me in her arms with extreme gentleness. "Why are you crying?"

I snuggle in close, pressing my head into her neck, and the soft give of her chest comforts me.

Through sniffles, I mutter, "I'm sorry. When I fast for too long, my feelings get out of whack."

Warmth permeates my body as Joel holds me tighter. She squeezes me and my weeping ceases. My breathing slows, and my heart swells with fondness. Being in Joel's arms feels natural—as if I belong here. This woman soothes me, and yes, arouses me.

A small scone or an English muffin would help my emotions bounce back into check, or maybe a chocolate bar. But hell, Joel's hug is sweet and nurturing. Her grip is much more welcoming than a dinner plate heaped with mac and cheese.

Her affection travels through every one of my veins, temperate and forgiving. Without fear, I nuzzle into her neck and exhale the stresses of my life. If home is a person, I wouldn't mind this person, whom I've known for all of fifteen minutes, to be where I reside.

A buzzing in my pants pocket interrupts our moment. Believing the text might be from my boss, I pull away from Joel.

Checking my phone, I see a message from Cain. The little turd has the worst timing. I can't wait to tell him about the amazing woman I met, even if she is straight, or ace, or well—not sapphic. But for now, I want to spend every second I can with her. I almost wish I didn't have to leave for Manhattan tomorrow so I could ask her out for lunch.

Joel looks over her shoulder with one hand on the Medusa handle. "Did you know Finland has been ranked the happiest nation in the world eight years in a row?"

Okay, this woman is odd as fuck, but I like her. "No, but now I know where I'll take my first vacation. Thank you."

She grins. "I forgot to ask your name?"

I reach into my pocket to retrieve the free pass she gave me to her club. "I can't make your grand opening tonight. But I'll tell you my name at The Tenth Muse when I return to California next month."

She grins and nods, but her eyes appear sad. Sad yet beautiful.

Watching Joel take off in her SUV through Writerly's bay window, I see my roommate, Cain, standing outside, glaring at her as he slams his fist against his thigh. Since revealing his love for me last month; he's been acting possessive, and it's pissing me off.

I fling open the door and growl at him. "What are you doing here?"

Cain's demeanor changes from angry to giddy in a matter of seconds, and he winks at me. "It's not like I'm spying on you, love. I'm here to visit my favorite roommate is all!"

"I'm your only roommate, silly." A knot forms in my throat as I drag him inside. He is not going to like what I have to tell him.

2 – Joel

At The Tenth Muse's grand opening, I step out of my SUV and grab my textbook on finance so I have something to do while I watch what's happening on stage from the safety of my office. At the door, I'm fumbling with keys when a man jumps in front of me with a tiny but intrusive camera person standing beside him.

"I'm a reporter with WeHo Entertainment," he says, staring at the book in my hand. "What are you reading, Joleen Hunt?"

How does this guy know my name and why is he here? I lift my textbook and both the reporter and camera person burst out in laughter. Looking down at my hand, I notice I'm holding a self-help book on how to date men. What the fuck? I run back to my vehicle but can't get the door to open and the reporter is in my face again.

"Look," I tell him. "I don't know where this book came from. It isn't mine."

Ignoring what I said, the reporter asks, "What advice does your book give about finding Mr. Right?"

This is ridiculous. I push him aside and stand behind my SUV. "Please leave me alone."

But they don't leave. What they do is follow me around and around my vehicle until the book falls from my hands and the camera zooms in on the cover of a praying woman under the title, *Seven Ways to Trap a Man*.

Early the next morning, after my evening from hell, the phone rings. It's my mother.

"Sweetie, your father and I heard about your grand opening at The Tenth Muse. Don't worry, honey. This is a teeny pothole in the road. You can always hire someone to manage the place for you."

Under the Rainbow D.A. Hartman

The pity in her voice makes me wince.

"Mom, a photo of me cowering behind my SUV holding a ridiculous book on how to date men went viral."

"I'm sorry, Joleen. I left *Seven Ways to Trap a Man* in your car when your father and I visited yesterday. You must have picked up the wrong book, dear."

My face is puffy from a lack of sleep, and I go to the refrigerator for ice. "What's with the book on dating? In case you've forgotten, you're married to Dad."

"It wasn't for me, Joleen. You're almost thirty-eight and you've never dated that I'm aware of. I'm merely trying to help, sweetheart."

"Stop worrying about my love life, or lack thereof. I'm fine, Mom." I roll some ice in a towel and dab my cheeks. "Why would the media show up at a nightclub opening? I don't understand."

Mom huffs. "Your dad and I contacted a reporter we know in Hollywood. We thought the publicity would benefit your business." Mom huffs again only louder. "I'm scanning through vicious comments about you online. These trolls are bashing your choice of attire. I'll admit the argyle V-neck sweater you had on was atrocious, but the orange corduroy pants are stylish."

My mom and dad aren't totally to blame for how socially inept I am. They have sheltered me to an extreme, but it's not their fault I'm a loner. I've been taken advantage of a few times. It's what people do to scions of the wealthy. Hence, I'm not interested in love, sex, or friendships. I enjoy the safety of solitude, and a good book. However, I wouldn't mind hanging out with the green-haired barista I met at Writerly again. She didn't seem interested in my money and I'm not sure what it is, but I felt something for the young woman.

"Sweetheart. Are you listening? Maybe you should come home. Pineapple is teaching beadwork, a solo activity you might enjoy."

"Who is Pineapple? Never mind. Mom, I'm hanging up—"

"Think about coming back to Manhattan, Joleen. We'll make more space for your books and fill the hallway with whiteboard. You can write all the equations and trivial facts you want on them. Doesn't that sound fun, honey?"

"No Mom. As you said, I'll be thirty-eight next month. It's time I venture out on my own. If I can manage Chase Janice's finances, The Tenth Muse should be child's play."

"I'm holding your father accountable for this debacle. Buying the nightclub for you was his idea."

I hear my dad yelling in the background, "It was Pineapple's idea. She mentioned the concept during the seance we had to contact your friend, Tippy, remember?"

My mom's voice rises with a shrill. "Oh, Tippy isn't dead, dear. Pineapple was channeling Avalon, a distant cousin of Tippy's grandmother. Goddesses of mercy, your father never pays attention, but yes, Joleen, Pineapple suggested a party atmosphere could cure your shyness."

"Mom, shyness is not a disease, and I'm not shy. I simply don't like people. Now, I need to figure out the best prices for our spring collection, and I can't crunch numbers while on the phone."

"Fine. Pineapple and I are knitting willy warmers all week. What color would you like?"

"I don't have a penis, Mother, and I don't plan on getting one anytime soon."

～～～～

After several hours of doing the books for Chase Janice, I slip on sweatpants and a polo shirt and jog to Writerly to visit the green-haired woman again. Her flirting gave me a much-needed boost, and I enjoyed her company. I wish I would have gotten her name. I'll make certain to ask for it today.

Scanning my phone, I search for the "Pussy Is God" song. There it is! *"Pussy Is God" by King Princess, published in 2018.*

Under the Rainbow   D.A. Hartman

As I listen to the music, I think of the masked woman. I have never felt comfortable holding someone in my arms. The way she melted into me was pleasant, which is baffling. I don't normally enjoy hugs. Perhaps the barista and I are meant to become friends. My only friend, Virginia hasn't been available lately.

~~~~~~

New to Amboadia, this is only the second time I've visited Writerly. It's spacious, with a gallery slash sitting area in the front and a small library off to the side. There's a teenager working today. He's taking an order from two elderly customers. I walk up to the young man and introduce myself. "Hello, I wonder if you know what time the green-haired woman comes in?"

The boy who can't be much taller than five feet isn't a boy at all. He's an adult with a scruffy face, and wearing worn jeans, a black T-shirt and cowboy boots. The man winks at me. "Hello, beautiful. I've never met this green-haired woman you're talking about, but I'm here for all your needs."

I give the forward man a nervous smile, then ask the customers at the table, "Do either of you know the name of the woman who worked here yesterday?"

"No. Sorry, this is our first time here."

"Right. Right. Well, thank you."

I sit at a nearby table and reluctantly text my troubled friend to inquire about her barista with green hair. She responds within seconds.

Virginia Hudson: 11:16 a.m. *I'm not sure who you're referring to. I've had an influx of temporary baristas as of late. My apologies.*

I press my head into the palms of my hands. There's no one to converse with. I might as well head home.

"Hey, Brown Eyes. Things can't be that bad." The handsome short man fiddles with his earlobe and raises an eyebrow. "What will elevate your spirits, sexy lady?"

This guy is a bit much, but I could use a cup of coffee. "A cappuccino, please."

When he returns with my drink, he sits next to me. "I'm Cain." The man bends his wrist.

"Got a lot on your mind, cutie? Care to share your woes with this pretty boy? I may be small, but I've got big ears, love."

I point to the phone sticking out of his apron. "Search for The Tenth Muse and click on anything having to do with the grand opening last night."

He takes out his phone and does as I ask. His expression is not one of amusement but of sympathy. "People can be such assholes. Lucky for you. I'm a master at creating appearances." He glares at my sweatpants and says, "We'll work on your clothing and hair first. Then we'll give you a personality that will rock this city of angels."

I shake my head. "Uh, no. I don't want another personality, thank you very much."

Cain and I talk for hours while he tries to convince me to give him a trial run as the manager of The Tenth Muse. "Give me two months. If I don't have your club booming with success by then you won't owe me a penny, but if I do, you'll pay me what I'm worth."

It's not as if he doesn't fit the bill. He's charismatic, motivated, and has business savvy.

We stay behind after he closes Writerly to discuss things further. He must be trustworthy or Virginia wouldn't have hired him to work at her precious coffee shop. The man has numerous ideas to shape public opinion about me and make The Tenth Muse the top nightclub in Los Angeles.

I never planned to prove to my parents that their delicate princess could live on her own without tutors, PAs, household staff, personal trainers, and security. I'll admit, I never wanted to move out of my parents' sixty-million-dollar penthouse in New York. It's not like I could afford anything remotely as spacious or luxurious and I'm not interested in romance, so why would I leave such comfort?

It wasn't my idea. My parents got it into their head, that since I'm almost thirty-eight, which means I'm almost forty, that it's time for me to become independent. There were no discussions. It was like one day I was living in comfortable luxury and the next day my parents bought me a nightclub and pushed me out of the house for fear I would become a decrepit old maid.

Now, I need to make enough money from The Tenth Muse to reimburse them for the cost of the club and show them I can be independent and *still* not want to date. With this in mind, I'll take my mom's advice and hire someone to run The Tenth Muse.

After we eat a delivered pizza, I'm about to say yes to Cain's proposal when he touches my thigh.

I brush his hand from my leg. "Excuse my frankness, but I not interested in anything other than a business relationship with you. To be honest, I thought you were gay."

He removes his hand and holds it up to his face. "I'm touchy-feely for an auto. Sometimes I forget to rein myself in, but if you're going to label me like some damn food product, make sure the first ingredient is a spicey one."

Unfamiliar with sexual terms, I ask, "What is auto?"

Cain slaps his hand as if punishing it for misbehaving. "Auto-sexual. In other words, I prefer to please myself rather than be with someone. I like dirty talk and being flogged, but I'm not into having my junk touched, so we're good, love."

Relieved, I let out a soft sigh. "We have something in common. I'm not sexually attracted to people either. I've never met anyone like me. It's good to know I'm not the only oddball in the world."

"No, you're not alone or an oddball, Joel." He chuckles. "I mean, who knows more about what we like sexually than we do?"

By the time I print out contracts for Cain to sign and hire him to manage The Tenth Muse, it's after midnight. To get an early start on brainstorming more ideas for the club, I offer him my guest room for the night. The faster we make The Tenth Muse the hippest club in Los Angeles, the better.

The next morning over coffee, Cain shocks me with a new idea of his. "No one is hotter than a dominatrix. I'm talking whips and leather, love. We'll create a dungeon and practice all the moves, without the sex part of course."

Once I manage to close my opened mouth I say, "That's a little extreme, don't you think?"

"Yes, and that's why we're going to do it. The Tenth Muse has to be extreme to beat out the competition. Where's your laptop?"

I bring him my laptop, and we shop online for hours to create the stage for rehearsals, which in our case is a dungeon.

One night turns into weeks of Cain staying on and off at my house. I miss the company of my parents and their staff, and he takes the edge off of me living alone. From the moment Cain wakes, until he goes to the club at night, he teaches me how to talk, walk, dress, and behave in every social situation. Thanks to his knowledge, my ability to handle people grows stronger every day.

He set up the dungeon in the guest room where he often sleeps so we can experiment with role-playing. He even bought black wigs, purple lipstick, and dark eye makeup for me to wear.

It's fun for the most part, but talking dirty and flogging him doesn't arouse me in the slightest. Cain appreciates my attempts and amuses me with his charm while this nerdy bookworm camouflages under leather and simulated grace.

~~~~~

Virginia hasn't answered my texts in a few weeks so I'm at her penthouse to check on her, and I'll admit, to ask about the green-haired woman again.

She opens the door, and I'm stunned at her appearance. Her long brown hair is greasy and disheveled, with strands sticking to her forehead and cheeks. Her skin is pale and her eye bloodshot. Her stench and wrinkled clothes concern me.

"For fuck's sake, Virginia, what's going on?"

"Not to be rude, but I don't appreciate you coming to my house unannounced, Joleen."

"I've been texting you to ask about Cain, the man who covered for Christine one day at Writerly a few weeks ago."

"I don't know of anyone by the name of Cain. Christine is managing Writerly while I work through my issues with a life coach. So, if you'll excuse me, I need to catch up on my sleep." Without a goodbye, she closes the door in my face.

Rude! As much as this both baffles and saddens me, if Virginia doesn't want me to bother her, I must respect her wishes.

Back at my condo, Cain has lofty ideas of becoming a popular online influencer. Of what, I don't know, but unlike Virginia, at least he's sticking around. The man is such a lively character. Yesterday we went to a salon and had our hair done. I got the sides of my head shaved and a wavy mullet, and Cain had his hair straightened. Today we're going shopping for a sporty new BMW. Then we'll hit Rodeo Drive for some trendy attire and jewelry for both of us.

The new me should include a new Cain. Together, we are a remarkable business team. He opens and closes the club, does inventory and marketing, and books the shows. Cain is doing all the work, and business is flourishing! He deserves extra compensation.

With Cain's help, I've honed a new personality and after weeks of staying home, I'm ready to visit my nightclub as a powerful—and yes, if I say so myself—sexy dominatrix. I don't trust anyone fully, but his enthusiasm for me to thrive demonstrates dedication.

Before I head out, he suggests I wear one of the black custom-made leather tuxedos I bought on our shopping spree and garnish it with nipple clamps. White gloves and a pair of combat boots complete the look.

"Here, babe, toss this around your sexy-as-fuck neck." He hands me a red Dior scarf. "That's it, love. Show them how bad you are. I'll be there shortly."

It's a relief not to be alone in this endeavor.

"Please arrive before nine o'clock, Cain. The media will be present today for Diva Bi Night's drag show and I prefer not to face them alone."

He smiles. "No worries. I've got your back, Brown Eyes."

~~~~~

The club is packed. Everyone is here for Diva Bi Night's drag show. Cain has worked his magic. Ten times the people are here compared to our grand opening and nobody recognizes me as I elbow my way to the office.

I have little time to pull myself together when Cain texts me. He wants me to meet him at the DJ booth. Once again, I push my way through the crowd.

Before I reach the stage area, a petite woman bounces up on her tiptoes and kisses me on my mouth. I want to shove her off, but the media is here to snap photos of the infamous Diva Bi Night. As the experienced Dom Cain taught me to be, instead of making a scene, I wink at her. I'm the cool owner of The Tenth Muse. A strange woman kissing my lips doesn't startle the fabulous new me.

Someone is standing next to the Lip Kisser. The stunning woman has bewitching grayish-blue eyes and pitch-black hair, and her cheekbones are strikingly pronounced. The beautiful woman looks familiar. How strange. Her shoulder-length hair with bangs is the same style as the wigs I wear when role-playing with Cain in the dungeon.

I'm certain I've seen her face on magazine covers. She's as tall as I am and without a doubt, model material. The beauty has a glamorous twenties goth vibe with her purple lipstick and dark eye makeup. She's a modern-day vampire.

The mysterious woman reaches her hand out to me and I want to take it, but Lip Kisser steps between us. She wraps her hand around my neck, pulls me down, and screams over the loud music, "It's me, Cain."

I'm in shock. Cain is clean shaven, wearing a red dress, sparkling high heels, and pink lipstick. The type of girly attire he said he would only wear in the privacy of our dungeon. To my dismay, he tugs me away from the pretty woman and over to the DJ booth.

"For fuck's sake, what is going on, Cain?" I yell as he pulls me up the steps to the recording area.

Cain taps the microphone and in a higher pitch than I'm used to, he yells, "People, can I have your attention? Listen up." The music stops and the crowd quiets. Cain slings his arm through mine. "I have an announcement." He gazes into my eyes with fondness. "My name is Candice Delight. You can find me online, and this sexy as fuck woman is the owner of The Tenth Muse."

A few light claps scatter about, but mostly, the crowd remains silent. Have they realized I'm the woman in the degrading viral photo from the grand opening?

No. They can't recognize me in my leather disguise and new hairstyle.

A very confident Cain smirks at their silence. "For those of you who don't know, Joel Hunt is a lesbian dominatrix. And I'm proud to say she's also my girlfriend." He steps on a wooden box, a prop for dramatic effect, no doubt, and kisses my lips. The short man in a dress turns and winks at the audience, then hands me a flogger.

Outraged at his inappropriate statement, which is a monstrous lie, he is not my girlfriend—I react by whipping him. Only I miss the hand I'm aiming for and hit his crotch.

The crowd roars their approval and I'm surprised at how much applause we receive. Many who were sitting are standing and screaming for more.

I'm going to kill this little prick once I get him out of here. I seize Cain's arm and drag him to the office. He's such a ham he waves to everyone as we go. People are clapping and screaming things such as, "Whip her naughty ass," and "Candice is a bad girl." If my heart wasn't pounding an abnormal number of beats per second, I might be able to enjoy the positive attention and applause. How could Cain do this without consulting me first?

Once inside the office, Cain hurries to lock the door and close the blinds. "They think we're in here getting kinky. Have a seat. We can't go back out for a while."

Ignoring his request, I scream, "What have you done, Cain? We aren't together, I'm not a lesbian, and you're not a woman. Unless—are you trans?"

He hangs an expensive Giorgio Armani leather jacket I've never seen before on the back of my captain's chair. "No. I'm a man who wants to explore his femininity."

"So, you outright lied about both of us to over fifteen hundred people, and the media?"

"Yes, even Entertainment Tonight is here. Make sure you use she/her pronouns in public and we'll be golden, babe."

I step closer to my bold nightclub manager and glare into his dilated pupils. "She/her *are* my pronouns, Cain. Are you high on something?"

"I'm high on life, and from now on, my name is Candice Delight." He jumps on my desk and screams, "You acted the role of a badass Dom perfectly tonight. Believe me, the trolls can't bash you now. Lesbians don't need a self-help book on how to trap men. We did it! Goodbye, creepy nerd. Hello, androgynous stud-master of kinky sex."

"Get off my desk." I pull the hem of his dress. "I'm serious. Get the fuck off my desk."

An agile Cain hops to the floor and raises his hands. "I don't understand why you're angry. This is what we've been practicing in the dungeon for, and we pulled it off without a hitch."

"I'm upset because you told everyone, you're my girlfriend! Now, we're stuck having to act out this farce of a relationship."

Cain kisses my temple. "I used to model girls' clothing. Imitating a woman isn't much of a stretch. Come on. If you go along with this, I promise your club will soar to the fucking moon with success. Trust me, love."

Playing along with Cain's scheme might deter people from bashing me and, yes, he and the publicity are great for business, but my parents will never believe I've changed from a virgin recluse into a kinky lesbian Dom.

Cain twirls in excitement. "From this day forth, my name is Candice, and I'm your girlfriend. They adore us. The people and the media can't get enough. Hell, the flashes of their cameras almost blinded my ass." He guffaws and blabbers on, "Even when Diva Bi Night walked in, they kept their cameras on the hottest couple in the club!"

"I agreed to act like a Dom and sport a new style. I did not consent to being a lesbian or involved in a fake relationship with a man who is lying about being a woman."

He places a hand on his chest and winks. "I'm a man who is falling in love with you."

This man is full of crap, but I'll admit, I've never felt so alive as I have tonight.

I sit on top of the office desk. "I can't do this. I'm sorry."

"You've already done it. Your job's complete. You don't have to come to your club anymore, love. You can stay at home and read your books. I'll run the joint and you can enjoy life. Leave it all to me. I swear, nobody will diss your precious ass again." Cain kisses me on the cheek. "Your reputation is gold. You got what you wanted. Now go home and relax."

There's a bang on the office window and Cain opens the blinds. The face of the stunning woman with him earlier comes into view. She's smiling, but I can tell she's upset. Cain mocks slashing his throat with his fingers, then mouths, *"Not now."*

"Who is that pretty woman?" I ask.

"Her name is Deviant Wallace. She's just a whore, but her cocaine and meth connections are to die for, which makes her an asset to your business."

"Cain, I don't care if she's a prostitute, but I don't want a drug dealer in The Tenth Muse."

"No worries. She doesn't bring the goods inside. She's too smart. Devi is fucking toxic, but she's my roommate, and I'll handle her."

"Well, I want nothing to do with your roommate or her drugs."

Cain closes the blinds on the beautiful woman and turns to me. "I'll tell her if she says one word to you, we'll toss her out of The Tenth Muse. You have my word, babe. She'll never come within ten feet of you." The man who wants me to call him Candice winks at me. "Forget about Deviant. Leave her to me, Brown Eyes!"

My phone rings. It's my mom. "You're a hit! Sweetheart, you're going viral on social media, and in a good way! Why didn't you tell us you're a lesbian? And oh my gosh, your dominatrix act was hysterical, and your girlfriend is a total bombshell. Your father and I are thrilled you're dating. You'll have to bring her to Manhattan so we can meet her."

To hear the relief in my mother's voice delights me, but I'm too upset to talk to her. "I'm glad you're both happy, Mom, but I need to go. I'll call you later."

"Yes, of course. Talk soon, my voguish baby girl. We're so proud of you."

My parents, who normally give me solace, are cheering with pride. Their love is strong and they don't understand how single people can live happy lives. Having Cain live with me solves the problem of having to explain to people why I don't go out on dates. Pretending to have a girlfriend will reduce Mom and Dad's worries and ensure this virgin-owned nightclub remains the trendiest spot in LA.

Through the window blinds, I smile at the booming success on the dance floor. The many bodies moving under flashes of light confirms my independence is secured and with growing success comes increased confidence.

A loud thump comes from behind me and I turn around.

Cain is back on top of my desk. "You're the king and I'm the queen of the mountain. Only those with status and hefty credit cards need to apply to the most exclusive club in the city. Move over MainRo, Poppy, and Bootsy Bellows. There's a hot new place in town!"

3 - Devi

Two years and a ton of bullshit later

Once I enter the password, the wrought-iron gate of Amboadia seems to question my worthiness as it jiggles and jerks slowly to the north. I inhale the sultry summer air, preparing to throw an imposing growl at the judgmental barrier, but what emerges is a squeaky plea. "It's Deviant Wallace. Remember me? Please don't make me beg."

 Two years ago, I was on top of my game, raking in the big bucks with the ultimate modeling contract and lucrative proposals from several big sponsors. To my horror, only a couple of months in, I was terminated and my long-held dream was sliced and diced to death by Chase Janice.

My contract stated Chase Janice reserved the right to let me go at any time. They never explained the reason they fired me, nor did I find out why I was blacklisted by other fashion agencies. Hell, even my agent blocked me. To make things worse, I came home to an empty apartment.

Cain moved out while I was in Manhattan to live with Joel and now after two years of falling behind on bills, I have to swallow my pride and ask a friend for help.

The obnoxious metal gate slides wide enough for me to move my old gas-slurping motorcycle past its evil clutches and I drive inside. Sunlight is shimmering between evenly spaced palm trees in front of Amboadia-West. As I drive by, the reflection of my bike ricochets off the apartment windows, pricking my eyes with doubt.

When I pull up to the front of Nicole's place, she's standing on the curb with her chest puffed out, helmet in hand, and lips pursed.

Under the Rainbow   D.A. Hartman

Nicole doesn't own the multimillion-dollar unit on the second floor of Condo Building One. She rents at an extreme discount from the owners of Amboadia, Goth Hudson, the very first woman I ever slept with, and the woman she married, Virginia Hudson. Goth and Nicole are my teeny, yet vital circle of friends.

Nicole bitches at me as I pull up in front of her. "You're late, Devi. Did you forget how to find Amboadia or what?"

I hadn't been to Amboadia for several months because I live over an hour away by Union Station and was working two jobs until both of my employers closed shop. If I was a paranoid person, I might believe Chase Janice had something to do with it, but why would they? It's been two years since they fired me for no reason. It doesn't make sense.

"Um—traffic was bad." I blurt out the worst excuse for being late in Los Angeles.

Nicole hops on the back of my bike and squeezes the tops of my shoulders. "Don't bother. I don't have time for your excuses."

I drive toward the electronic bully at the exit. The fragrant scent of coffee from Writerly has my head turning in time to see Goth running out toward us. She motions for me to stop. Her turquoise eyes are gleaming and her arms wave in excitement. I squeeze the brakes and lift the visor from my helmet.

Nicole grunts her disapproval as Goth sprints toward us.

"Hey, it's been a long time, Devi. You better give me your hand."

Goth inspects each of my fingers with diligence. The artist was socially inept and shy when we met two years ago. Since then, I've learned she suffers from mental illness, but it doesn't affect our relationship. I love her as she is.

With Nicole in a rush, I sniff the aroma of Goth's mint shampoo and whisper, "You already know I'm not an android. You just miss me. Admit it."

This handsome woman and I formed a solid friendship after our one-night stand two years ago. From the moment we kissed, the realization that I'm a lesbian hit like the beginning of a Pride parade. *Dykes on Bikes* revving their engines and honking their horns vibrated throughout every facet of my being. The rush was exhilarating and I can't think of a finer person to have consummated the new and authentic me with. I will forever be grateful to Goth for being exactly who she is.

The determined blond reaches inside my helmet, takes hold of a strand of hair, and yanks it from my head.

"Ouch." I punch Goth's muscular arm in retaliation.

She glances down at my hand, still in a fist, and smirks. "You'll need more protection than that scrawny thing to save you. Devitron abduction happens in a flash and goes undetected by mere mortals."

I adore Goth, but she could have asked before stealing my DNA even if she believes I'm the last living Devitron on earth. Devitrons are creatures she conjured up in her mind. They're not even real.

Letting out a sigh, I lift my helmet and rub my skull. "That fucking hurt."

"Sorry, but we lesbians are a precious rarity and in great demand. We can't be too safe, Devitron." Goth stuffs the single hair into the pocket of her white T-shirt. "I'll have this analyzed later."

Virginia ambles out of Writerly with a thermos in one hand and a Diva Bi Night lunchbox in the other. Diva Bi Night is the hottest drag queen in Los Angeles. I have a coffee mug with her on it.

"Honey, you forgot your snacks." Virginia gives her wife the food and drink.

Goth's captivating eyes sparkle and her smile grows wide. "I'm working at Double Ds today. Bats are edible but jam-packed with neurotoxins and my insane ass can't eat them." She pecks Virginia on the lips in gratitude.

Double Ds is a colossal art installation Goth created behind Amboadia-West apartments. The vast two-acre structure contains two gigantic snow globes connected by a glass pipe large enough for people to walk through.

In short, Detronia is a rainforest, and Devitron is a desert, and apparently, bats live in these opposite but connected globes.

Goth drops my hand and moves toward Nicole.

Virginia pulls her back. "Sweetheart, Nicole isn't a robot. I'm sure of it."

Goth's trust in her wife is solid, and she removes her gaze from Nicole's fingers.

Virginia greets me. "Hello, Deviant."

Deviant is what my high-on-opium mom named me before she sold me to some dude for a bottle of booze. I don't mind the name but most of my friends call me Devi.

"Hi. Sorry, but we're late and need to get going." I smile and wave goodbye to Goth and her wife.

Nicole yells, "No more delays, dammit."

Pressing my helmet on, I rev the engine and release the clutch just as a sports car pulls in front of me from the parking lot. My bike rams into the bumper of the BMW with a jarring thud.

I check behind me to make sure Nicole isn't hurt. "You, okay?"

She yanks off her helmet and looks over my shoulder. "What the hell happened?"

A familiar woman wearing a tailored suit with silk boxers peeking out of pinstripe slacks steps out of the silver convertible and narrows her deep brown eyes. As she comes our way, her mouth remains as stiff as her hair. "Imbecile. Are you blind?"

"Oh, hell—it's Joel Hunt." I turn to Nicole, who is unaware of the terror I'm about to be hammered with.

I met Joel two years ago in front of Writerly. That is when her face replaced the faceless woman in my recurring dreams. I've tried taking a bunch of Benadryl before going to bed. I've tried sleeping in a chair, playing loud music, and listening to meditation audiobooks. Nothing works. I can't push Joel out of my dreams.

Every night while I walk the runway, I see her face as she hands me a bouquet of yellow tulips

Every night when our fingers touch, I topple over and fall off the stage.

Every night Joel tells me she loves me.

Every morning when I open my eyes, she fades away.

But this is reality, I'm awake, I'm not a model anymore, and Joel doesn't love me. She fucking loathes me.

The sunglasses perched above her forehead press her short hickory-colored hair with blond highlights back against her scalp and her expressive golden eyes broaden as she nears us.

"Deviant Wallace, the drug dealer who spreads her legs for all my customers. Of course, who else would be inconsiderate enough to drive recklessly on peaceful Amboadia Boulevard?"

Her insult doesn't land. This patronizing prude, whom I thought I had a connection with, was my ex-roommate's girlfriend. Hell, I'm stunned the eccentric woman is out of hiding. Rumor has it the hermit hasn't left her condo in a year.

Joel steps behind her vehicle and rubs the bumper with her index finger. "Why are you whoring around Amboadia so early in the morning? Are you still drunk?"

"Screw you, Joleen." I immediately regret calling the owner of The Tenth Muse by her birth name. Joel dislikes being called Joleen, and getting kicked out of the most popular nightclub in Los Angeles will eliminate my greatest source of happiness, gyrating on the largest dancefloor in California.

Inclining my head, I check for any damage my hitting her bumper may have caused.

She interrupts my assessment by shouting, "Trust me, you'll pay for any harm my baby has suffered."

Joel doesn't recognize me from when we initially met. I appear very different without green hair, a mask, and sunglasses. She believes she met me through Cain at her club. She doesn't know we met a few weeks earlier at Writerly. She doesn't know she was the comforting and nerdy woman who hugged me years ago.

These days the pseudo-big-shot does nothing more than associate with the elite and buy pricy things. She even ditched her SUV for this sports car she refers to as her *baby*. I can't believe how wrong I was about her.

I step closer to the rear of her BMW Roadster. "Joel, there isn't a scratch and my friend is late for work."

Joel's eyes intensify. "There could be internal impairment to the battery or computer system. The poor baby suffered quite a jolt."

Shit, she's out for blood, but I won't let her screw me over. "You pulled in front of me with no warning."

Joel's body straightens. "You gunned your engine purposely hitting me. With. No. Warning."

Being the same height, I stare dead into her eyes. "I don't have time for your bullshit."

"You fucking bastard." Joel lunges forward and fists the sleeve of my blouse.

Virginia grabs her wrist. "Joel, what has possessed you? Leave Deviant alone." She tries to pull the BMW driver off of me, but she isn't strong enough. I'm so scared I'm about to piss my pants.

Goth snakes her powerful arms around my waist and tugs me back, causing Joel to lose her grip on me.

My buddy is two inches shorter than Joel and me, but she's much stronger than us. This has me less fearful of the angry club owner.

"Fuck off, Joleen. Yes, I'm a bastard. Unlike you, I don't lie about who I am."

Nicole glares at me. "Stop antagonizing her. We'll handle this."

Nicole, Virginia, and the nightclub owner step in front of Joel's car out of hearing range.

Goth grips the top of my shoulders and massages her thumbs into my back. "Hopefully, they can smooth things out and everyone can be friends again," she says.

My artist friend is optimistic. Maybe because she's mega-wealthy and married to a woman who devotes her life to Goth's wellbeing. The relationship between the two seems centuries old. They not only finish one another's sentences; they are also aware of each other's needs and are quick to be there for one another. What I wouldn't give to have what they have.

The only thing I get excited about is moving my ass on the best dance floor in Los Angeles at the nightclub I'm on the verge of being banned from by an enraged lunatic.

There's laughter at the front of the sports car. My friends must be working their magic. I wrap my arms around Goth's neck. "Sorry, I'm such a pain in the ass. I've had a rough week."

Goth bops me on the head. "The oxygen on this planet has become too toxic for the delicate figments of my imagination. You and the Detronians will need cleaner air to thrive. We'll have an exhibit of your homeland this Sunday from noon to five exclusively for Amboadians." Knowing me well, Goth adds, "Don't be late. Virginia and I have to take off for Palo Alto that evening."

"Thank you, buddy. I'll be there." And I will be. There's nothing I wouldn't do for my bestie.

Virginia returns to the back of the BMW and catches my eye by running her finger down my arm. "Are you available to work at Writerly for a few days? Christine volunteered to run the place while Goth and I visit the bay area, but that's not until Sunday, and with summer on our doorstep, I have a lot of shopping to do."

Without hesitation, I whisper, "Yes, thank you."

We watch the club owner enter her shiny car, slam the door, and spin out as she speeds through the exit gate.

Nicole punches my arm. "Your pretty face doesn't work with Joleen. She's livid."

"Joleen prefers to be called Joel," I mutter before putting on my helmet.

"Whatever. This Joel person doesn't like you, so stay out of her way." Nicole slides on her helmet too.

When we mount my motorcycle, I twist around to face my friend, "Hey, this probably isn't the best time to ask, but I got evicted from my apartment. Can I stay with you for a while?"

Under the Rainbow

D.A. Hartman

4 - Joel

"Damn you, Deviant." Banging my fist on the steering wheel, I curse her for making me late for my appointment.

Twice a week, I drive to the Wilshire district to visit my life coach, Ms. Nedra Lane. Many Amboadia residents use her services. My friends and owners of East-Amboadia, Virginia, and Goth suggested I contact the growth strategist after my companion died. With Nedra's assistance, I have made significant progress. Deviant is pretty, and she knows it. Candice was beautiful too. Both are why I pay Nedra an exorbitant sum of money to assist me in regaining my sanity.

Once I strut into Lane's office, a squeaky-voiced receptionist, whose name I fail to remember, sits with her spine straightened. "Go right in, Joel. She's waiting for you."

I swing open the door and Nedra smiles. "You made it. You had me worried."

"Yes, barely. Why do you make me come to Wilshire for our visits? You're my next-door neighbor, for fuck's sake."

"I appreciate your willingness to make an effort. There are no rules or ethical guidelines regarding friendships with clients for life coaches, but until this office closes next week for good, I'd like to keep our talks on a professional level."

I drop on a small couch opposite the oversized chair where Nedra is sitting. "Sorry, I'm so salty—a wannabe cat-walker bumped into my new car on my way here."

One side of Nedra's mouth elevates. "A fashion model, or was someone walking a cat when they battered your vehicle? You didn't run over anyone, did you?"

"No, sadly. Anyway, I'd rather not talk about the absurd twit. She has shortened my time with you as is."

Ms. Nedra Lane, a woman in her early fifties with graying hair and the body of a marathon runner sits tall in her navy-blue pantsuit. "Other than the incident with the cat-walker, how are you today, Joel?"

"Fine, now that I'm safely away from the treacherous woman. On the plus side, my strained relationship with Virginia Hudson might be on the mend. We reconnected this morning. I've missed her."

Nedra pulls her phone from her front pocket. "True friends never leave us completely. Now, as you know, today is the day you selected to talk about the night Candice died."

My breath catches and I squeeze the arm of the love sofa. "Yes, and I'm mentally prepared to do so."

"Why don't you start with when you opened The Tenth Muse that evening?" Nedra scoots back into her chair and crosses one leg over the other in one swift motion. My life coach has no doubt listened to many horrifying stories before. This will merely be one more.

I rise from my seat, ready to wear out her carpet with my pacing. "Alright, well, at four o'clock, I drove Candice to the club. Like most days, she was too intoxicated to drive herself. Two of my three bartenders were in front of The Tenth Muse waiting for us to let them in. My bouncers hadn't arrived yet. Their shift begins at six."

Nedra waves her hand to attract my attention. "The tissues are on the bookshelf."

She's never seen me cry, but constantly roots for me to weep. Well, she can shake her cheerleading pompoms until her arms give out. I'll never shed a tear in defeat.

I nod in understanding and swallow the lump in my throat, then continue with the details of that dreadful night. "Candice and I began arguing the moment we entered the office. She wanted money. She always wanted money. I told her I'd give her some cash if she promised not to sit with Deviant Wallace. I was apprehensive about her excessive drug use, but her clinging onto

Deviant in front of everyone when we were supposed to be a couple was extremely embarrassing."

I rub my hands, hoping the friction will ignite my will to finish the story. "Candice said she wouldn't flirt with Deviant if I gave her money. I declined. She knew I kept money inside my desk and grabbed several bills—"

"Were you two still sexually active?" Nedra asks.

Not wanting to talk about my humiliating sexuality—I pinch the bridge of my nose. "Is what we did behind closed doors important?"

Lane rests her index finger on her chin. "As an ace woman, I don't think a lack of sexual attraction needs resolving, but during our initial meeting, you said you missed having orgasms. So, tell me, how did Candice pleasure you?"

"She didn't. Candice never touched me. Our encounters were always for her benefit, never for mine. At this point, we hadn't even kissed on the cheek for over ten months."

Nedra taps a pen to her chin. "Ten months? Weren't you and Candice only together for a year?"

"Yes, but several weeks after we met, I realized she was using me and our relationship faltered."

"Did you ever ask Candice to reciprocate?"

Throwing up my hands, I turn to Nedra. "Manipulation is one hell of a libido killer. I might have been more motivated to be touched if she cared about me—she never did." I want to tell Nedra I'm auto and that Candice lied to me about being auto as well, but talking about her death is the most I can handle in one session. "Being with Candice is the reason I can no longer have orgasms even though we had never touched each other. We didn't have sex, but because of what I did in the dungeon, I'm unable to masturbate, which was my only form of relaxation, and goddamnit, Nedra, yes, I miss orgasms."

"Do you miss being intimate with others?" Nedra appears to have a revelation. Although she isn't saying what it is.

"Not one person has ever felt the slightest depth of tenderness toward me. This includes Candice. I can't miss something I've never had." I'm ashamed to admit I'm a thirty-nine-year-old auto who has never experienced sex with someone else, nor have I ever loved anyone.

"As I was saying, the bouncers arrived and my girlfriend left the office to chat with them. I stayed at my desk to read a novel. At about nine p.m. I realized I had forgotten to pull down the shade on one of the office windows and people were peeking inside. While lowering the blinds, I spot Candice giving Deviant a lap dance and salivating like a love-starved puppy. I was tired of the two making a spectacle of themselves and rendering me a fool. So, I rushed to confront them."

Nedra holds up her hand. "Deviant, as in Deviant Wallace? You've mentioned this name earlier. What is your relationship with Wallace?"

"We don't have a relationship. She's the imbecile who smashed into my car with her motorbike today. Deviant was Candice's drinking partner."

"The cat-walker was Deviant?"

"Yes, she's also the woman my girlfriend had the hots for. Anyway, when I got to their table, I asked Candice if we could have a private conversation." Pressing my palm against my curdling belly, I try to push down the degrading memory.

Lane leans forward, but before she can speak, I say, "Candice rolled her fucking eyes at me and turned away. To make things worse, Deviant suggested she be more kind. As if giving *my* girlfriend permission to talk to me. Without dispute, Candice obeyed her and followed me to the office, where I promptly closed the blinds, lost control, and broke up with her. My heart couldn't take her abuse anymore. I was done."

An expressionless Ms. Nedra Lane asks, "How did Candice respond to the breakup?"

"She laughed at me and left my office to sit with Deviant again. That's how she responded." My hands are shaking because being humiliated again wasn't the worst part of the evening. I'm not sure I have the strength to describe the rest of what happened that night.

Lane shoves a bottle of water toward me with her slim arms.

Determined to finish, I refuse her offer and continue with the events of that tragic night. "I was livid and snatched a quart of Scotch from the bar to bring back to my office. Candice was oblivious to my pain. She was too busy pleasing Deviant to think about me."

With my stomach in knots, I plop onto the couch. Images of my drunk customers roaring in laughter and jabbing their fingers at me in disgust shoot through my mind, but I'm determined to proceed with the story.

"It was about one-thirty when I sat at the bar and ordered a cup of coffee. All I wanted was to close the club, take Candice home, and try to figure out how we could separate without too much drama or hardship."

Nedra lifts her hand. "What happened after you got coffee?"

"Right as the bartenders shouted 'last call,' a commotion stirred outside the restrooms. I searched for the bouncers, but they must have already gone inside. People were screaming near the bathrooms. Several women came out crying and covering their mouths in horror. When I entered the restroom, my bouncers were yanking Candice out of a stall. She only had her gaff panties and bra on. She had several hickeys on her neck and I became livid. Deviant was sitting on the commode in the cubicle they dragged Candice out of. I told her I'd fucking kill her. It was obvious my staff busted the two having sex."

"Please go on." Nedra urges.

"Candice's body was motionless. I kneeled next to her to check if she was alright. Her eyes were cold and blank—her wrist was without a pulse. Candice was dead.

Nedra leans toward me. "Was Deviant unclothed as well?"

"She was dressed, but her messy hair was telling."

Nedra searches through her candy bowl, finds my favorite, a watermelon lollipop, and tosses it my way. Out of the blue, she says, "I'd like to suggest visiting The Tenth Muse once a week."

I shake my head in defiance. "I'm not ready to go anywhere near my club."

"You could at least attempt a walkthrough? The sooner you return to managing your nightclub, the sooner you'll get your life back."

Running the club was supposed to be Candice's job, but I got stuck managing the place because she was always too high. I don't want the life I had at The Tenth Muse. I wish I could sell the place and return to Manhattan, but if I admit defeat, what will I go home to? What will be my legacy other than being a miserable failure?

I give Nedra a curious glare. "Are you trying to dump me?"

"Getting rid of you will be difficult, seeing how we share a common wall in Condo Building Three. It's just that—" Nedra wipes her face, but can't hide her concerned eyes. She walks to a built-in shelf and rubs her finger along several books. "I'm not sure if I'm missing something crucial, or if you're concealing information, but we've hit a lull in our advancement."

Squeezing the arms of the sofa, I ask, "What are you talking about, Nedra? I just told you about the night Candice died—is this because I won't cry?"

Nedra does something she's never done before. She sits on the couch next to me. This is why I refuse to take public transportation unless it's on a first-class flight. Her proximity is too intimate. I can feel the warmth of her thigh and it has me anxious.

Nedra catches me staring at her leg and scoots over a few inches. "This isn't a power play, Joel. You need to work with someone you can be vulnerable with."

Not wanting to lose her, I mumble, "I promise to make more of an endeavor. You have my word."

Nedra presses her palms into her thighs. "The reality of the matter is we've become friends, Joel. Our sessions are the equivalent of chums having afternoon tea. Not that I mind, but you need a professional, someone you're willing to do intricate work with and reveal your cemented repressions to."

She's right. My sessions with Nedra are all I have in the way of a social life, and I've become too close to her. Now my next-door neighbor wants me to pull up my socks before she hands me over to a licensed therapist.

My popularity as the lesbian dominatrix remains extensive, and managing The Tenth Muse is the only way I can claim victory over the last two horrific years. I can still win this fight.

I nod and give Nedra an understanding smile, then rise to leave. "I'll open the club this Wednesday."

If I could go back in time, I'd choose honesty over compliments and praise. I'd choose integrity over ego and popularity. I'd choose to be myself over the person I'm pretending to be.

I often wish I could return to the day I met the woman with green hair before Candice and Deviant came into my life, and before this nightmare began.

5 - Devi

Upon entering Writerly for the first time in months, my nostrils broaden with glee from the smell of coffee and fragrant teas. Familiar paintings by locals come into light as I pull open white velvet curtains draped in front of deep bay windows. I've missed this welcoming sanctuary.

My platform heels clink on the polished stone floor as I wander behind the bookshelves that divide the gallery from the library. In the center of wall-to-wall books are two sizable tables surrounded by chairs. There's also a comfortable beige sectional in the farthest corner.

The nonchalant French atmosphere of Writerly is cozy and inviting. Nicole and I have helped Virginia take care of this creatives' hangout before. There isn't much work to it. The house coffee and black teas at the Self-Help counter are free. Specialty teas, non-house coffees, and croissants from the French bakery next door are the only items sold here. Amboadia residents make up the majority of customers. I doubt this small, wealthy community has more than a few hundred residents, many of whom rarely, if ever, visit.

A jingle from the bells hanging on the front door draws my attention. Virginia's dimples deepen on her chubby cheeks as she walks in with a bag in each hand. "Other than stopping at the bakery in the mornings to purchase croissants, you remember all your other duties, correct?"

I return the smile. "Yes, I remember dusting and wiping tables was the hardest part."

"Christine is assisting me here with gritted teeth. Thus, you can stay on at Writerly if you like."

A rush of gratitude fills me, and I'm quick to react. "Yes, I'd love to work here again. Thank you. Thanks so much." I kiss her on the cheek, leaving a smudge of purple lipstick behind.

"Christine will be thrilled with the news!" Virginia hands me the two brown bags and sits at the bar. "I used to write when I worked here. You'll have to find something to do to help pass the time when it's slow, which as you know, is most of the time. A customer donated several sapphic-themed paperbacks yesterday you might enjoy."

"Thanks, I'll check them out. What are you and Goth up to today?"

Virginia giggles in delight. "I'm taking my wife to get fitted in a custom bathing suit and to purchase sunglasses. Warm weather is coming and we enjoy sitting on Writerly's roof. I'll need a floppy hat, a few boho dresses, and colorful yoga pants. Can you tell I like to shop?"

"Yeah," I admit, trying to keep the envy out of my voice. I miss the fancy attire I wore during modeling gigs and understand her excitement about getting new clothes. "What will you two do in Palo Alto?"

"We're interested in an experimental drug being researched at a Courtenay medical facility there. In case you aren't aware, Stephanie Courtenay is Goth's mother."

"Yes, she talks about her famous mom a lot. Is Goth going on meds?" I ask, knowing she doesn't like to take anything, not even aspirin.

"It's something she wants to try. The new drug uses a different molecular pathway than present-day antipsychotic medicines. This one targets the receptor to dopamine." Confusion must cover my face and she clarifies, "A neurotransmitter that contributes to schizophrenia."

"But Goth can't create when she's of sound mind," I protest. "What will happen to her art project if this new drug works?"

Virginia's adorable dimples deepen. "Goth only needed to come up with the concept. It's up to the architects and construction workers we hire to figure out the logistics and make her ideas tangible. Goth's job is complete and the construction of the Double Ds is almost finished. Being a natural environment, any further growth relies solely on the individual globes. The objective was to create a safe home for her brainbugs. Goth was concerned the treatment she'll receive might kill them."

Some rich people are, at a minimum, outlandish, but I bob my head, agreeing that giving imaginary insects a safe place to live is important.

Virginia and I turn toward the door when the antique bells jingle. My ears pound with anxiety when she walks in. The snobbish driver of the BMW Roadster eyes me. She stops for a moment as if contemplating whether to stay or leave. Then she glides past me to greet her friend. Her enthralling eyes become welcoming beacons of light, but not for me.

"Morning, sweetheart." She gives Virginia an air kiss. "My espresso maker is on the fritz."

"Take a seat, Joel." Virginia gestures to the nearest table and glances at me.

I pretend to hold a pen and paper. "What's your pleasure?"

Joel blows out a loud sigh. "If you didn't have the attention span of a squirrel, you'd already know."

Wrong, I'm not a fucking mind reader I growl internally, then politely ask, "A cappuccino?"

Candice once told me Joel likes cream in her espressos.

"Yes." She flaps her hand, dismissing me.

I was too irritated to notice Joel's appearance yesterday when she drove her sports car in front of my motorcycle. So, while brewing coffee, I sneak peeks at her. Okay, I'm eye-stalking her, but I'm curious. Candice told me her girlfriend had gender affirming surgery and is now a man, but when I met Joel, she had a baseball cap with she/her pronouns embroidered on the bill so I didn't believe Candice. Now, I'm not sure.

Joel appears taller, although most people do next to Virginia's five-foot-one frame. Her brows are still thick above her sublime light brown eyes. She's more androgynous than I remember when I saw her a year ago at The Tenth Muse. She has shorter hair a smaller chest.

Maybe Candice didn't lie. It doesn't matter, Joel hates me. Screw the handsome penis-toting bully.

I place Joel's cappuccino on the table. "Would you like something else? We have croissants."

"No, what I need is quiet time. Thank you." Again, Joel's obnoxious ass dismisses me.

Virginia curls her fingers around my wrist when I return to the bar and pulls me into the storeroom. "Joel and I were friends. We were close until she moved here and bought The Tenth Muse. I was mentally unstable at the time and we mutually pushed each other away. At present, we're opening our hearts to one another. I hope you'll do the same."

It's not as if my heart hasn't remained open, but nothing will change how Joel feels about me.

I smile at Virginia. "I guess you know Candice was my roommate when we lived in Chinatown."

She sighs. "Goth told me. I wasn't a big fan of Candice. Her treatment of Joel was abusive. However, I look forward to a deeper understanding of my wife's best friend."

This makes me smile. I usually hang out with Goth at her gallery downtown, but I'm staying at Amboadia now so I'll have the opportunity to get to know Virginia better.

"Sounds good. I'll be here for a while."

Virginia grins. "Wonderful. Goth was saying only last week that it had been too long since she'd seen you."

"Yeah, life got in the way, sadly." I squirm at the thought of how many overdue bills I have.

Virginia takes in a deep breath. "Can you show Joel a little patience? She has a loving heart. We'll have evidence of its existence again soon."

She says this matter-of-factly as if she knows something I don't. "I'll try, but it won't make a difference. Your friend hates me."

Virginia wanders into the library and I grab a towel to dust the furniture in the dining and gallery section of Writerly. As I near Joel, the irate club owner slaps a hand on the table. "Stop drooling over me. You're making me uncomfortable."

What the actual fuck? I want to throw the wet rag I'm holding at Joel's face, instead I say, "For your information, I'm only into vaginas and tits. In fact, I fucking love vaginas and tits." I twirl my finger in the air. "I'm not into dicks and balls."

Joel springs from her table. Frightened, I bump into a chair behind me. "What the hell?"

"You think I have a penis? You absurd little twit."

Okay so I was wrong. She doesn't need to lose her cool. The woman is visibly chewing the inside of her cheek and her anger is glaring down my throat.

Scared of losing yet another job and with my adrenaline pumping, I spout off the only excuse I have. "Candice told me—"

Joel's intense brown eyes stifle what I'm about to say. It's not like I can babble on about how I'm not interested in her new penis, since apparently, she doesn't have one. Why am I such a moron when I'm around her?

Joel's eyes narrow as she takes a long sip from her cup. She sets her cappuccino down, lets out an audible breath, and makes a beeline for the exit. At the door, she pivots on one of her Tory Burch laced-up boots and glares at me. "Right. You're only into vaginas and tits." She tilts her head as if in disbelief. "What a despicable liar. And for your information, the largest sex organ is the brain, an organ you seriously lack." She leaves in a huff and slams the door.

Screw her. Hopefully, she'll stay away from Writerly now that she knows I work here.

Virginia comes from behind a bookshelf with wide eyes. "Deviant, what happened between you two?"

There's a tightness in my chest, a strain behind my eyes, a throbbing pain in my head. A pain everywhere. I glance at Virginia. "Have you ever met someone you knew you had a connection with, but couldn't get close to? I swear the push and pull, tug-of-war I feel when near her wears me out."

"Poor Deviant." Virginia stuffs a book into the shelf. "It took almost a year to understand why Goth and I were characters in the same novel, why we interacted in the same chapters and breathed on the same pages. Not until the last scene did, I become aware of where the narrative wanted to take us. We couldn't have been more different, but can you imagine a world in which Goth and I aren't together?"

"No. You two are a perfect unit," I admit. "But in our story," I point to the door Joel just left from— "I'm the only one who feels anything because she invades my dreams. It sucks that I have a bond with her when she isn't even aware we have one."

Virginia brushes the bangs out of my eyes. "Some characters only have access to one side of the story. There's a reason *Novel Magic* insists we seek the truth, especially when writing a romance. No happy ending exists without it."

I seldom understand what Virginia is talking about. The author speaks as if we are all characters in one of her novels. Whatever *Novel Magic* is doesn't matter because Joel doesn't want the truth. She wants me dead.

6 - Joel

"A penis. Deviant Wallace thought I had a penis. She's exasperating and provoking, and she sucks me into her stupidity. Every. Single. Time."

Ms. Nedra Lane tosses me a watermelon lollipop from the candy bowl in her office. "Another day of living vicariously through the lives of lesbians. How exciting."

I let out a weak grunt. If Nedra finds out I've been holding back the truth for months, she won't want to be my friend. My father taught me the value of being quiet. Waiting until there's a reason to speak so that my words have more meaning, but Wallace galls me to no end and I'm paying Nedra for this last official session of ours to listen to me rant.

"I hate her." This sentence escapes my mouth in such a rush, I can't stop it. I have said these words dozens of times in the privacy of my home, but never to anyone else.

Nedra furrows her brows ever so slightly. "What irks you about Deviant?"

Welcoming the opportunity to vent, I divulge more about Candice's love interest.

"She endangered my business with her drug dealings, made a mockery out of me, and was responsible for Candice's death. Deviant supplied Candice with what she cherished most: cocaine." I'm rubbing my thighs with such vigor they burn. "They were made of the same avaricious cloth and both made a living off their attractiveness. Neither were concerned about the welfare of others. Deviant still scams women."

"Do you know Deviant well? Or are these assumptions?" Nedra asks.

Upset at her insinuation, I pace the floor. "Candice told me who her drug supplier was. I wanted to kick her out of my club, but Candice threatened to expose our dungeon videos to everyone if I did. Fortunately, the Deviant only came in once or twice a month and Candice kept her away from me."

"Dungeon videos?" Nedra types something into her iPad.

"Don't you understand? She lives at Amboadia now." I stand in front of Nedra hoping to get through to her. "A drug pusher at Amboadia. Think about it. Deviant got evicted from where she lived. Hence, a gullible woman invited the lowlife to stay with her."

Nedra rubs her temple. "When I met Nicole yesterday on my run, she mentioned Deviant Wallace. She said they were once co-workers and have been friends for years. So, I don't understand your concern."

"I'm not close with Nicole, but she must be a sucker for a pretty face. Now, Deviant resides in Condo Building One. This means she lives a mere two buildings from ours. Hell, she won't even inconvenience herself enough to park her filthy motorcycle inside the garage. She prefers to park on the street to taint our community."

Nedra laughs. "Taint our community?"

What kind of life coach mocks their clients? I suppose one who is on the verge of becoming a friend.

"Deviant has the brain of an earthworm. She insists she's not into men. The liar."

"Can you prove she's lying?" Nedra asks.

I'm not ready to reveal that Candice was a man, and with a defensive breath, I say, "No, I'm not a voyeur. But she and her bike are clearly a danger to Amboadia residents."

Vertigo throws off my equilibrium and I place my hand on the edge of the sofa. "Deviant Wallace reminds me of my failures and I want to put my horrific past behind me." Closing my eyes, I sag onto the couch and fold my arms in front of me.

Nedra twirls her iPad pencil and lets out a sigh. "What else is going on in your life? Anything positive?"

I lean forward and rest my elbows on my knees. "I'm thrilled to say that after two years of not speaking with Virginia, we're becoming friends again."

Nedra smiles. "How did you and Virginia meet?"

I'm sure Nedra already knows the answer to her question. She's Virginia's life coach as well, but talking about my friend and me reuniting might elevate my mood.

"Virginia and I went to the same university. We were both older students in our thirties. We shared many of the same business classes. Virginia is a genius. Her ambitions were with real estate, and mine, with finance. We both achieved our goals with graduate-level degrees the same year."

"I'm glad you two found your way back to each other. Do you enjoy accounting?" Nedra asks.

"Yes, I love working with my parents and numbers."

"May I ask what your parents do?"

I scoot deeper into the couch. My parents often warned me not to reveal who we are. They said if people knew we were wealthy they'd take advantage of us, perhaps kidnap me, and yet, I need to be honest with Nedra.

"We're in the fashion business."

"Ah, I wasn't expecting that. Sounds exciting. Why did you and Virginia grow apart?"

Happy Nedra isn't inquiring more about my parents and their company, I answer her question. "I moved to Amboadia two years ago when my parents bought me The Tenth Muse and was excited about living close to my only friend. I had a sheltered life. Never went out. Never dated. Then bam, at thirty-seven, my parents not only set me free, they shoved me into the limelight. Where, as you know, I've made terrible choices. Virginia didn't understand why I was with Candice, and I got tired of lying to her. She was going through a rough bout of depression and my life was shattering to pieces. Anyway, after Candice died, Virginia reached out to me, but I didn't feel deserving of her compassion or friendship."

Nedra glances at her watch. "Remorse, regret, shame—guilt. They serve a purpose, but these feelings were never meant for us to dwell in." Her smile reaches her eyes in full force and she sets down her pencil. "Have you visited The Tenth Muse?"

"Not yet. I'll go tonight. I've already texted the staff to warn them."

Her eye furrows. "Warn them?"

"A courtesy call of sorts. They've had the luxury of working without the presence of their boss for a year. The last thing I need is to walk in and catch them in an act of deception. Going to the club will be strenuous enough. I don't need extra drama to contend with."

"Do you believe everyone is out to deceive or take advantage of you?" Nedra checks her smartwatch.

Our time is up, but she doesn't rise from her chair as I make my way to the door.

Before leaving, I turn to her.

"Of course, everyone is out to screw me, Nedra. We live in a carnivorous world where all living creatures, no matter how strong, if careless or wounded, become prey."

7 - Devi

I'm at Writerly searching online for a second job. Nicole won't accept money from me. So, I buy our food and clean the house, but I can't depend on Nicole's kindness forever.

It's Friday and freedom is about to ring with fantastic music pulsing through my body, bright lights penetrating my brain, and an abundance of sapphics to dance with. And, let's not forget the best mojitos I've ever tasted. Nope, nothing shoots dopamine into my brain faster than the thought of hanging out at The Tenth Muse after five days of catering to others.

Christine Jordan, my sexy, six-foot-two friend, prances into the coffee shop with her little dog Laurengo. "Sweet Rita Mae Brown, I can't believe you're here. Dah'ling, I haven't seen you in almost a year."

"I was doing overtime, trying to catch up on my bills, but the chemical plant closed last month and the owner of the diner sold the place." Shaking my head in irritation, I pet Laurengo. The cute mutt nudges his face into the palm of my hand, making me smile.

I have missed Christine so much. We became friends just after her bottom surgery over a year ago. I made a pass at the sexy pan woman one night while dancing with her at The Tenth Muse. She said she already found the man of her dreams, Javier, Virginia's brother. So instead of dating, we became buddies, although I rarely have a chance to hang out with her because she and her boyfriend travel so often.

"Well, it's great to see you again, hot stuff. I've missed your gorgeous face." Christine bends to give me a loose hug and air-kisses my cheeks. "So pretty lady, a little birdie told me you're going to be a permanent fixture at Writerly?"

I nod. "I'm staying with Nicole for a while."

"How wonderful, sweet pea." Christine adjusts her bra through the cloth of her dress. "These lovelies are getting so big." She glances upstairs. "Have you seen Goth?"

Trying not to drool over her large boobs, I stare at my hands, "Not today."

She pecks her dog on the nose. "I promised to help my girl with her art exhibit this Sunday, but I'll have to leave early to pick up Javi at the airport. He was in Spain for a week." Christine tosses her head and long burgundy locks whip behind her broad shoulders as she walks away. "Ta-ta, Dah-ling." Her strong thighs and a sliver of pink underwear show under her shorter-than-short yellow dress as she sprints up the stairs. She's still sexy as fuck.

Christine bangs on the door at the top of the stairway. "Open up, babies. It's Momma."

Goth pokes her head out and pulls Christine inside.

It's time to close Writerly. My life is my own again, if only for the weekend. Deviant Wallace is free, and freedom is glorious.

With my credit card tapped out, I text Virginia before going to the club.

Deviant Wallace: 3:01 p.m. *Hey, can I get a small advance?*

Virginia Hudson: 3:02 p.m. *Certainly. Take what you need after you count the till and be sure to enter your withdrawal into the system.*

~~~~~

The Tenth Muse doesn't have a dress code, but most everyone here wears upscale casual. I have on a gray body-hugging mini skirt and a snug-fitting black Cami top to cover what little cleavage I have.

The door person is new, and the line is moving slowly. The cover at The Tenth Muse starts at $100 and goes higher depending on the DJ, the drag king or queen show, or other entertainment. A fundraiser thrown by a VIP can be hundreds or thousands more. Luckily, I've been a member since it opened, thanks to Candice Delight. I show the gatekeeper my ID card.

She points to a card machine. "You're not on the list. It's a hundred and sixty dollars for non-members. The infamous Sapphic Cream is spinning."

"Infamous? I've never heard of Sapphic Cream and I've been a member since the grand opening. Check the list again."

I should go home. I haven't been here in a while. They've probably raised the prices of drinks, and I only drew twenty dollars from my pay.

Luckily, one of the bartenders comes to my rescue and ushers me inside. I kiss her on the cheek, then stick my tongue out at the gatekeeper. Acknowledging a few regulars on the way, I gradually make my way to the dance floor, where women are flailing their arms to Fletcher's latest song.

Although she's been gone for over a year, I still envision Candice running my way, kissing my cheek, and dragging me to our special table. The same one she saved for us whenever I had a night off and could come out to party, which was seldom. Shaking the conflicting memory from my mind, I make my way closer to the beat of the music.

A rainbow of colors sprays my face as I enter the party zone, and bright white lights sweep across the dancers. Monitors spread throughout the club, showing a brunette with bright blue and yellow bangs bopping their head below a neon sign with the words, *Sapphic Cream*. The masc woman's fiery orange lips are blazing under a backward baseball cap. A huge X-shaped earring dangles in the DJ's right ear and Sapphic Cream's body language screams *whip me into submission, please.*

Most women consider me a femme because of my shoulder-length black hair, signature purple lipstick, or the short skirts and slinky dresses I wear to The Tenth Muse. I'm fine with their assumptions. As for who I'm attracted to, the answer is any woman who wants to dance.

Even with the weight I've gained, I'm not bad-looking, but the challenge of seduction and the need to be admired faded along with my aspirations of being a supermodel. Still, a brief sexual encounter once in a while is better than being alone.

Chase Janice will never welcome me back, nor will my name ever be taken off the fashion industry's shitlist. My one chance to succeed financially crashed and burned. This makes dancing at The Tenth Muse vital to my mental stability. Even so, guilt for being here rolls over me like a fallen boulder. I'm already bumming off my friends. It's not like I have money to blow on a night out.

If only Chase Janice hadn't fired me, I wouldn't need two jobs. Hell, I would have had time to take Business Management classes and maybe acquired enough money for a down payment on a small house.

Quit thinking of what could have been and stay in the moment, I remind myself. *You're at The Incredible Tenth Muse!* I'm surrounded by various body shapes and sizes, and the not-so-infamous Sapphic Cream is spinning for us. Life is glorious—if only for tonight.

The bass penetrates my chest, making my heart thrum to its rhythm. The beat energizes my body and invites me to dance. My endorphins are firing on all cylinders. Music thumps through my body and I move to its command. All thoughts are gone. No worries about my bleak future, nothing but the sway of contentment as sound drowns my thoughts.

There's a butch eyeing me from across the floor. She's dancing alone, wearing jeans, a pressed white shirt with the top three buttons undone, and a loose black tie. The butch can't be a day over the legal drinking age. Her messy thick black hair bounces with her every movement. A Mercury dime dangles from a piercing in her chin and a tattoo of a small Dara knot rests on her left cheek. Her dark eyes never leave me as I make my way to her. She's bold, I'll give her that, but sex isn't what I'm seeking.

My strongest craving is to dance, flirt, and forget the complications of my life for a few hours. The song, "Not Strong Enough" by boygenius, blares from the speakers with a slow beat as I make my way closer to the butch with hair the color of tar. When I reach her, I snuggle into her warmth and guide her hands to my hips.

My lips touch her earlobe as I make a suggestion. "Relax, it's not as if I'm asking you to make me come. It's only a dance."

She lifts her chin and presses it to my shoulder while we move to Sapphic Cream's distortion of an otherwise great song. "Your hair is as black as mine and you look like a young Gal Gadot. Are you Korean, too?" she asks.

Small talk is my least favorite thing to do, and Gal Gadot is not Korean, she's Israeli. My mother is a dark-haired Scottish woman who had many men in her life. I could be part Korean, but I won't discuss my unknown heritage with this butch.

My gyrating partner squeezes and pushes her hips into mine and asks another question I don't plan on answering. "Do you live in here in LA?"

I guide her hand over one of my breasts and ask, "Can you feel my hard nipple?"

She nods.

"Good. Now, if you say another word, I'll remove your hand from my tit."

The butch smiles in understanding. Intermittently, throughout the song, I press her palm against me, reminding her to enjoy this dance. When the music ends and she lets go of my boob, she awkwardly stares at my firm nipple poking through my shirt.

Smirking, I leave her and make my way to the bar. I want a mojito, but a bartender I've never met says they cost twenty-two dollars, which I don't have. This is how Joel Hunt can afford to buy a condo at Amboadia. She charges an outrageous amount for drinks.

A redhead cuts in front of me and plants a rough, sloppy kiss on my mouth. Then she sticks her hand up my skirt.

"What the fuck?" I try to push her away, but she's too strong and won't budge.

"Hello bea-u-tiful." She's tipsy and slumps against me.

With another glance, I realize she's someone I hooked up with several months ago. She's trying for seconds. The once sexy and intelligent woman has turned into a blustering mess.

Moving back, I give her a wink. "Sorry, I'm with someone tonight."

She wobbles closer. "Get rid of her. I'll make you come good, sweetheart. You know I can." The redhead squeezes the inside of my thigh hard enough to make me yelp.

Not liking to be handled roughly, I shove her with all my might, but she captures my arm and pulls me down as she falls to the ground. When I try to stand, she yanks my Cami top, exposing my tiny breasts. When I slap her hand away, she balls it into a fist.

"Fight. Fight. Fight," the crowd yells.

"No, we aren't fighting." Refusing to get in trouble, I rise to my feet and smile.

The redhead rolls onto all fours and struggles to stand on her feet. Without warning, she shoves me so hard my back hits the edge of the bar. The butch I was dancing with jumps in and tackles her into a booth at a table behind us. The next thing I know, a familiar bouncer clasps my upper arm and grabs the back of the young butch's shirt, allowing the drunk redhead to stumble out of the club unquestioned.

"Sure, let the instigator go," I complain as I try to pull my top over my boobs with my free hand, with no luck.

The crowd disperses when the pissed-off owner of The Tenth Muse struts toward us. Candice discouraged Joel from tossing me out, but nobody can stop her now. I'm screwed.

Joel scowls at my exposed breasts, then barks orders at the buff bouncer. "Get this slut and her boi-toy out of my club, and make sure they never return."

With a husky voice, the brute holding me answers, "Yes, boss."

"Wait a damn minute." I try to reason with Joel, but the bouncer tugs me with such force my arm might pop out of its socket. Seconds later, I'm tossed onto the sidewalk with my Korean protector. No. This isn't embarrassing at all.

I pull my top over my boobs and bend over to cup my knees. "Shit. This fucking sucks."

The butch taps the back of my head. "Do you need a ride?"

My motorcycle is parked a short way up the street, but I contemplate inviting *'my boi-toy'* to have her way with me. It might take the edge off of what happened tonight, but I decide against it. "No thanks, but hey, I'm sorry you got kicked out too. Be safe getting home."

The longest lashes I've ever seen lay flat against unblemished skin when she closes her eyes and as she opens them again, they become dark with want. "Do you want me to make you feel good before you go?"

Oh hell, she's too hot to say no to. I take her hand and guide her into the alley. She presses me against the building and kisses me clumsily.

I lift my top over my breasts and order her to suck my nipples.

She does as I ask, but much too slowly for my irate mood.

I take her hand and guide it under my skirt and into my panties. "Keep sucking my tits. Harder."

She finds her way inside me. It's obvious she's fingered a woman before, but again, she is moving at a turtle's pace. After the stunt Joel pulled this evening, I need something to release my built-up tension.

I pull the back of the butch's hair with enough strength; her mouth loses its grip on my tit.

"Fuck me like you mean it," I say through gritted teeth.

Tears well in her eyes, but her mouth regains its position over my breast and she sucks with more hunger this time.

With my fist still in her hair, I whisper, "Am I hurting you?"

"No, I like it," she whimpers.

"Good. Now bite my nipples."

She clamps down with her teeth and pulls a little too hard.

"Don't draw fucking blood." All I want is to forget about Joel tossing me out of her nightclub like I was a piece of trash. Kissing the woman's dark hair, I attempt to convey that I'm not upset with her.

She nibbles softer and mumbles over my boob, "I'm sorry."

Obedience must be this sexy butch's middle name. With every light tug, she becomes more vocal, groaning with each suck of my breasts. She's easily slipping in and out of me now.

Wanting more, I whisper, "Stick another finger inside and press your knee against the back of the hand you're fucking me with to add pressure to my clit."

"Mm, like this?" She's unskilled but obedient and does exactly as I instruct. I reward her by shoving my hand into her damp boxers to toy with her wet entrance. To my surprise, she's unable to wait. I feel a gush of liquid as the excited butch wails her relief.

Wow, what just happened?

The baby dyke's fingers slip out of me and she slumps her head. I pull out of her pants and press my hand against her back.

"Don't stop fucking me." I grind myself against her hand. The compliant butch recovers and pushes her fingers inside me. Shoving them deeper with each thrust. "That's it, handsome, make me come."

Someone is walking by shining a gigantic light. The wide-angle flashlight is so bright I have to shut my eyes.

My "boi-toy" doesn't mind the onlooker and continues to fuck me until I orgasm with a groan almost as loud as the one she gave earlier.

She pulls out of me and leans in for a kiss, but I pat the cute baby dyke's chest in refusal. "No, we're done, but you're quite the stud."

I pull my tank top over my breasts, adjust my panties and skirt, and then return to the front of The Tenth Muse. Feeling less tense, I turn back to check if the person who wandered by us in the alley is still around, but there's no sign of anyone.

The butch shadows me as I walk to my bike. "Do you want my name and number?"

A vision of Joel holding me and confessing her love for me storms through my mind. I shake my head to refuse the butch's offer. Not even this hot stud can stop me from dreaming of Joel.

I slide on my helmet and hop on my trusty Honda. The crisp night breeze on Santa Monica Boulevard sweeps under my skirt and cools me, but nothing can relieve the burning in my gut. Joel Cunt finally got her wish and banned me from The Tenth Muse. Fuck my life.

8 - Joel

I'm pacing the marble-tiled floor in Nedra's kitchen as I explain why I needed an emergency session today. Troubled with what happened at the club last night, I'm grateful she agreed to meet me at her home on a Saturday.

"Deviant got into a fight at the club with one of her past conquests. I ordered one of my bouncers to toss the little minx out. The audacity of that woman." My fingernails dig into my palms and oddly, I take comfort in the pain. "And that's not all. As I walked to my car, I passed her in the alleyway. She was getting fingered by her latest boi-toy in public for all to see." Relaxing my clenched fists, I add, "The exhibitionist is into public indecency."

Nedra picks up her laptop from the side table and places it on her lap.

Still pacing, I say, "I need to come up with a way to get her out of Amboadia. Better yet, out of Los Angeles."

Nedra rubs her eyes and squints at me. "I'm baffled by your animosity toward Deviant. She was cleared of any wrongdoing in Candice's case. The authorities must have informed you of this."

I flop onto her red and gold antique couch. "You researched the case? Why?"

"There wasn't much to research. Your parents and the authorities did a great job of keeping the story quiet, but it seems I know more about Deviant Wallace's participation in Candice's death, or lack thereof, than you do?" She turns her laptop so it faces me.

I raise my hand to cover my eyes. "Just tell me what you've learned."

Nedra turns her laptop back to where the screen faces her again. "I have notes somewhere. Ah… here they are. The police didn't find any drugs on Devi, aka Deviant Wallace, and she willingly submitted a urine sample to verify she wasn't on drugs, nor was she intoxicated. She also insisted she never had sex with her friend Candice. The bouncers fled the scene before the cops arrived. They were suspected of supplying your girlfriend with drugs and sexually assaulting her, but there wasn't enough evidence to convict them."

"That's what they said, but it's inaccurate. Candice told me Deviant gave her drugs. Everyone becomes smitten with Deviant. This includes the authorities. Being clean proves nothing. Not all drug dealers use. They're in the business of getting *other* people addicted."

Nedra stares at her laptop. "Deviant wasn't intoxicated or high, unlike you, who was at double the legal limit. The surveillance video proves she went into the bathroom much later than the bouncers, and only when a distraught customer pulled her off the dance floor."

Pacing again, I grab a lemon drop from the candy bowl. "Are you trying to make me believe Candice took a fatal shot of cocaine on purpose?"

"According to police reports, Candice died from a mix of cocaine and heroin. Speedballs are deadly. The coroner declared her death an accidental overdose."

I let out a long breath. "True, but I still feel culpable."

"Why?" Nedra asks.

There's an array of reasons I feel guilty about the death of my fake girlfriend, but a prime reason comes to mind and I go with it. "I wanted her out of my life. Her death was a relief."

Nedra rubs her chin with the tip of a finger and smiles. "Desires don't wield power over others, and guilt only destroys the people who embrace it. Your wish to rid yourself of her didn't make it so, nor is it something to be ashamed of."

Anger is a more comfortable reaction, but using a timid voice, I ask, "Then why do you want me to cry over her death?"

"The tissues I offer are for tears you might shed for yourself. Letting go of your traumatic experiences is worthy of tears. Don't you think?"

Shaking my head, I confess, "Sobbing like a fragile child may be cathartic, but I've never been much of a crier."

"Allowing yourself to be vulnerable can catapult you forward in your recovery. It takes strength to expose one's self. Tears are often a result of empowerment, not a sign of weakness." She rises from her chair and stands next to me. "May I suggest—"

"No more homework," I interject. "I'm at The Tenth Muse every night to make certain Deviant doesn't return. That's already more than I agreed to."

Her eyes broaden. "You're going to the club five days a week? Perhaps I should give Deviant these lollipops for doing my job for me."

I let out a low groan, "I doubt the woman eats carbs. Now what is it you want me to do?"

"It's a suggestion, not a request, but you might want to practice forgiveness." Nedra stands with her arms across her chest.

"You want me to forgive Candice?" Anxious, I leap out of my seat, knowing I'll never forgive her.

Nedra drops her arms to her sides. "You don't ever have to forgive someone who has harmed you, Joel. Despite popular belief, forgiveness isn't always healing. Being coaxed into forgiving the unforgivable is abusive. Something I would never do, but you could go easier on yourself."

I edge toward the exit. I'll never forgive myself for my gullibility. Never. I leave my neighbor's condo, hitting the door frame with my funny bone and scream, "Fuck."

Nedra pops her head out of her unit right as my phone chimes. I wave her off and open the door to my condo. It's a text from my mother.

Janice Hunt: 10:42 a.m. *Your father and I are out front, buzz us in.*

With my anxiety flaring from Nedra's suggestion and with my parents on their way up, my heart is thumping in my chest. A clanking of footsteps and my mother's voice complaining to my father amplifies.

"Why are we using these stairs when there's an elevator, Chase?" Mom yells.

"The best way to stay in shape is to walk everywhere, Janice. You know this," Dad retorts.

In under a minute, they're in my home, standing next to me. My father is sporting a tie-dye T-shirt, a fake beard, and a long blond wig. My mother is wearing a teal beret, a flowery sundress, a red wig, and rose-framed sunglasses. Several bead necklaces hanging around her neck swish side-to-side as she walks to the kitchen with me. Dad takes a seat on the living room sofa.

The boho attire they don has done well in masking who they are over the years. I doubt their fans or anyone in the fashion industry would recognize them in these clothes, and they enjoy dressing like old-school hippies. Seeing them reminds me of the woman in green hair. Damn, I really wish I got her name and number. Her embrace was warm. She made me feel something, although I can't figure out what, and I think of her often.

Both parents resemble me in appearance with their dark hair and boxy shoulders. Only my mother has blue eyes, and my father has the same brown eyes as I do. They're in fabulous shape for being in their sixties, and unlike me, they're gregarious people.

I open the refrigerator to get them some iced tea and speak inside the cold box. "Were you in the neighborhood, or is there a reason for your visit?"

"Can't we spend time with our daughter without an inquisition?" my mother snarls at me.

Crap. If she's this defensive over a simple question, they must have dismal news to share at best. "I'm merely curious, Mother."

"Your mother and I believe it's time to sell the bar," Daddy jumps right in.

My brain scrambles for what to say. They think I failed goddamned it. I'm not the one who wanted The Tenth Muse. My doting parents pushed the business on me hoping I'd turn into, at the very least, a social moth.

"We thought purchasing The Tenth Muse would get you out of your shell, but you haven't been invested in the business in over a year. The joint has lost its purpose." He swipes his hand as if chopping the problem away. "Sell the nightclub and move to New York. CJ needs their CFO closer to home."

Mom chimes in, "Yes, the bar was a crappy idea. You're busy enough counting numbers for your real job. You don't need the extra burden." She gives me a forced smile, but only pity shows in her eyes.

Wonderful. They don't believe I can handle my club, and perhaps I can't. What utter fucking cow poop. I slam a pitcher of tea on the counter. "I take care of Chase Janice's finances perfectly from here. Yes, you bought The Tenth Muse for me, and I have paid you back in full, with interest. Hence, I will decide what happens to *my* club." I'm not ready to admit defeat, not to them, and not yet.

Mother gets out of her chair and presses her hand on my back. "We bought the bar for you—"

"You bought The Tenth Muse hoping your geeky introvert of a daughter might magically become as cool as her parents."

"Yes," she concedes. "We were off base. We threw you to the wolves, dear. We should have asked what you wanted. Your father and I regret our mistake. Don't we, Chase?" She glares at her husband, who is staring at his phone, oblivious to our conversation. Mom places her attention back on me. "Sell the dance club and move back to New York. I miss you."

I miss her too, but I'm not giving up. I'm not a child.

"Janice." my father says, still not looking up from his phone, "there's an opening at La Prairie Spa, but we must hurry." He moves toward the door, ready to leave. "You tried to live on your own and we helped you in your endeavor. You gave it your best shot, now it's time for you to come home, Joleen."

"You have nothing to prove to us, dear. Take the time to think about what you want to do with the bar." Mother pecks at my mouth and digs into her purse. "Here, I made one for you," she giggles, "in case you get lucky."

I pull out something that resembles a rainbow knitted—a knitted something. "What is this, a sock?"

My mother leans closer and whispers, "It's a willy warmer. I sell them online."

I toss the penis warmer onto the counter alongside the pitcher of tea. "Why does everyone think I suddenly have a dick?"

My father pulls on my mother's upper arm and urges her toward the door.

Mom yells over her shoulder, "Of course, we know you don't have a willy, honey." She adjusts her hat. "It'll keep whatever phallic items you have warm, sweetheart."

I want to scream, 'Dildos aren't sentient beings, so they aren't in danger of freezing to death in sunny California,' but keep these thoughts to myself.

9 - Devi

Nicole glances around her spotless condo after working at a special event at the LGBT Center. "Dang girl, thanks for cleaning the place." She gives me one of the two beers in her hands. "I got these free from Goth's art opening. Drink up."

I take the beer and flop on the couch. "It's the least I can do for you letting me stay here. It's strange. Back when I dreamed of being a supermodel, I used to think it would someday be me with the home and you'd come live with me. Now, I'll never have a home or the time to go to school."

Nicole rubs her short dirty-blond hair. "I'm moving back to North Hollywood when my lease is up in ten months. You can stay here until then or you're welcome to come with me when I go. Shit, we may have started as co-workers, but you're important to me, Devi."

"You and Goth are my best friends and I love you, but I shouldn't depend on you, so much."

"I'm not your mom or one of her boyfriends. I'm your friend and friends depend on each other." Nicole glances at her phone. "Hey, it's Sunday. If we hurry, we can make happy hour at the club."

I cross my legs at the ankles and press deeper into the couch. "I can't go to Happy Hour anymore. Joel kicked me out of The Tenth Muse."

"What a snake. We should all refuse to go to her club in protest."

"No, this is between Joel and me. Anyway, I promised Goth I'd check out Double Ds today." I chug the beer and head for the door.

"There's no need to walk over to Devitron—it's just a mound of rocks and dirt, but you'll enjoy the lush, Detronia." Nicole's eyes narrow. "It's like Goth's creative mind blew a fuse when she got to the second cup. Oh, and leave your phone here. No photos are allowed. Christine will take it before you enter and toss it in a large petri dish with all the others."

I place my phone on the coffee table and take off for the Double Ds exhibit. A stroll behind Amboadia-East condos, through the shops, and past the Amboadia-West apartments to the Double Ds doesn't take long.

Christine waves as I close in on the massive art structure. "I'm off to the airport to pick up my man, but Goth is still here programming the misting system." She bends her hand at the wrist. "Ta-ta, sweet cakes."

The awe-inspiring construction is humongous, larger than the Amboadia-West apartment building, and it's in the shape of a padded brassiere, hence the name Double Ds. One gigantic cup is encircled with clear laminated glass, creating an earthy terrarium with pine trees, grass, and a raging waterfall that dumps into a pond. The other cup is encompassed by perforated glass and contains a barren hill with a modest number of wild plants and cacti.

Goth is fiddling with a fob. She closes, then opens the gigantic glass door entrance, and abruptly slaps the side of her head. "Shut up, Dick—you too, Dotty. We'll go when I'm finished double-checking everything."

My friend is forever yelling at the voices in her head. Sure, Goth is quirky, but she's also unique and fun.

"Hey buddy, am I too late?" I give my artist friend a quick hug.

"No, but you'll need to hurry. Virginia wants us to be at my mom's place before ten tonight." She taps buttons on an electrical panel. "I've marked everything except this top one. Here goes nothing." She hits a switch. "Oops, that was the lights for Devitron, or was it?" She hands me a brochure. "This has all the information you'll need about Double Ds and if you find Droopy, please take the little stinker to Devitron, the next cup over." She points to the second globe of the two.

"Droopy?" I ask.

Goth rubs the back of her neck. "Droopy is the only Detronian I haven't found yet."

"Ah, okay, I'll keep a lookout." I roll the pamphlet, pocket it, and kiss Goth on the forehead.

As I enter the closest orb, mist falls from above. Dammit, Goth, now is not the time to test shit out. However, the smell of moss, damp soil, and wood is reminiscent of a veritable rainforest and I'm loving it. The thick green pine trees are five or six rows deep and encircle a pink pond. Yep, the water is pink. I imagine that's how Goth saw it in her mind. Blocking the view of the apartments on the east side is an enormous marble boulder with a beautiful waterfall flowing over the top. The pink liquid over dark rock gives off purple hues. If not for the fact I'm getting drenched from Goth's over-active misting system, this is paradise.

Despite Nicole's warnings about Devitron being dull, I trek up a short dirt path to the opening of a glass tube that connects the two globes. The bottom of the cylinder is filled with white sand. The same kind you'll find in an hourglass. It's dryer inside the tube, but I can feel some moisture entering from the terrarium.

Nicole was right about the other cup. There's nothing in Devitron but a hill of decomposed granite, a few boulders, and some rabbitbrush and cacti. At least it's dry and airy with the awesome smell of baked goods and oak leaves—the smell of Amboadia. I walk another hundred feet or so and am surprised the other side of the mound is bare. Without ground covering, there's only a massive thick glass shell. Gazing through the large bubble, I can see ladders and other equipment down inside. Whatever they are building below will be vast and colorful. I walk back to the other section covered with earth and find a hole in the hill's side. The opening of the cave is almost big enough to stand in—could be an animal's den.

I open the brochure Goth gave me and check for information. It says a dozen Detronians live in the forest area. Detronians resemble ladybugs, only they have much longer antennas, walk on their two hind legs, and have lavender shells and white spots on their black bellies. Not realizing they are in danger of being eaten by birds, bats, or reptiles, Goth has gathered all but one. Droopy, the Detronian with bent antennas, is still in danger.

With no mention of larger animals, I bend to check inside.

How disappointing. It's just a dark tunnel, nothing special. I'm about to leave when I hear a moan.

Going in deeper, I yell, "Is someone here?"

A weak voice begs, "Help me."

What fool would venture so far into a dark cave without a flashlight? This fool I suppose. Keeping my head bent, I reluctantly make my way further inside. "Where are you?" Whoever it is, doesn't answer. "Tell me where you are or I can't help you."

In what sounds like disdain, they mumble, "Crap, it's you, isn't it?"

I turn toward the sound, and in a blinding instant, a blue ray of light beams through a wide opening in the rock. Goth was flicking switches at the entrance to Double Ds. She must have turned back on these lights. Once my eyes adjust to the brightness, I peek through a slight opening between boulders to view a much wider, illuminated cave. I shimmy through the crack between the dark and light caves. The temperature drops several degrees and I'm hit with a magnificent sight. Clear blue ice glows from every angle in this glacier cave. Icicles cling to the ceiling, but when I touch one, I realize it's not cold or wet. It's glass!

I cross a small stream of rose-colored water and hop on a turquoise stepping stone that resembles my artist friend's eyes. Sprawled on their stomach behind a blueberry glass mound is an adult human.

"Are you okay?" I ask.

Joel flops onto her back and the top button of her business casual linen shirt pops open.

I can't help but stare at the tops of her smooth round breasts peeking out of a black bra.

"Don't just lust over my bare chest, Deviant. Help me up."

Hell, not her again. The only drawback about living at Amboadia is the frequency with which I bump into the meanest woman I've ever met. Her face is flushed, and her eyes are bloodshot. I want to feel sorry for her, but the woman makes my life miserable.

She coughs, and her voice is sandpaper rough. "The lights went off and I couldn't see a thing. I have no idea what game Goth is playing." She rises to her hands and knees, then falls flat again.

"You might have vertigo. Stay put, I'll get help." I hop over the pink stream and make my way to the exit.

"No. Don't leave me," Joel says sternly.

"Don't order me around. It's not like I can carry your sorry ass out of here by myself." Wanting to flee as far away from her as possible, I rush to the giant crack in the stone wall that leads to the smaller dark cave.

"Please, I have nyctophobia and the lights may go off again." Her voice is gentler this time. It's the same voice she had when we first met. The voice I hear when I dream about her.

I return to Joel's side. Her hair is wet either from the misting system in Detronia or she's sweating profusely. Most likely the latter. Wow, a nightclub owner who's afraid of the dark, how ironic. Blowing frustration from my lungs, I hold out my hands. "I'll help you if you promise to call me Devi from now on. The way you pronounce Deviant sounds evil."

She cringes but nods in agreement. Joel has to be scared shitless to give in so easily. She grabs my hands and together we struggle to get her up. Bracing myself against a small mound of glass, I put more effort into lifting her. We are of equal height, but she is bigger boned with more muscle, and though she lost weight, she's still heavier than I am. When Joel is on her feet, I freak out when looking into the same eyes I see every night in my dreams, and lose my grip on her.

She stumbles backward and presses her hand against the blue glass wall to steady herself. "Go if you want. I need to stand for a bit."

"Thanks for the permission, but we both need to leave. Goth is taking off for the bay area any minute now."

"I don't know Christine very well, but I doubt she'd abandon me," Joel insists.

"She's already left to pick her boyfriend up from the airport. So, we need to get going."

Only then does Joel concede. She swats me back and walks in front of me. Fuck, she's irritating. I watch her hand glow purple each time she presses against the luminous blue wall as we make our way to the dark den that leads to the outside. Bending over, she passes through the crack and wobbles like a frightened duck with outstretched arms flapping until she reaches the light at the opening.

"You're welcome," I yell at her. I turn to bid the beautiful gleaming indigo space farewell. Radiant and invigorating, I seriously don't want to leave Devitron and hope to return soon to find out what Goth is building behind the plywood blocking the back wall.

Once out of the cave, I observe Joel in the distance, walking through the tube toward the dome that cups the terrarium. Her body returns to its original stuck-up position as she struts away like she owns the world and everyone in it. The drastic change in the once sweet and caring woman saddens me.

After passing the pond and several rows of pine trees, I eye Joel standing at the entrance of Detronia. The glass exit is closed and Goth is nowhere in sight.

"Oh no. Is it locked?" I punch every button on the panel, but nothing happens. A boy is walking his dog to the west of us and I jump up and down, waving my hands.

Screaming won't work from inside this solid orb, but Joel bangs on the glass and shouts, "Hello? Hello? Can you hear me?"

I press my hands against my ears. "Hush. You're busting my eardrums."

Her voice lowers to a fragile growl. "I can't be stuck in here. I have a business to manage. I don't live off good looks as you do."

She thinks I look good! Sweet, but I'm too upset to tease her about it. I could get fired for not showing up to work and this pompous ass acts as if my losing a minimum wage job is no big deal when she can probably live the rest of her life on the money she already has.

"Well, Miss Significant as Fuck, I feel much better knowing you're here. No doubt the National Guard has already been alerted on your behalf. We just need to kick back and wait for them to rescue you."

Joel's eyes wander as if she's in thinking mode. I doubt she has any friends other than Virginia, who is on her way to the airport with Goth. However, now that she's managing The Tenth Muse again, her staff might become concerned about her absence, but this is Sunday, and the club won't open again until Wednesday.

Devitron has perforated glass, allowing sound to travel, so I follow the path back to the tube and make my way to the other D in Double Ds.

"Where are you going?" Joel fumes.

"There's too much foliage in Detronia. People can't see us, and again, no one can hear us from this solid globe."

She squints her eyes but says nothing.

Passing the pond, a mosquito bites me and I slap my cheek to kill it. "Asshole."

Once in the clear tube, I notice most of the window coverings of the apartments are closed. Hell, don't people watch sunsets anymore? I sit in the middle of the glass tube between the D cups on soft white sand to read the pamphlet Goth gave me.

Again, on page seven, she pleads for readers to search for Droopy. She asks if we find the little brainbug, to please take it to Devitron, where it'll be safe from predators. I doubt I'll see my buddy's little imaginary friend, but Goth is right, the cave is the best place for us to be.

"Damn pests." Joel staggers up the path, swatting her bare arms. "Did you smuggle in your phone?"

"No. I respect the wishes of my friends."

She thinks I'm an outlaw without scruples. If she demeans me one more time, I'm going to give her a piece of my mind.

I hold out the pamphlet. "This says the mosquitos mostly come out at dawn and dusk, and only on Detronia. We'll be fine inside Devitron."

"Why did Goth build a world exactly like our own? What is the fucking point? And if she did her research, she'd know blue attracts mosquitoes at twice the rate as any other color. It's only a matter of time before they migrate to Devitron."

Joel continues walking on behind the hill. I stay in the glass pipe, hoping someone will notice me. The day I met Joleen aka Joel Hunt at Writerly, she became the face of the unknown woman in my dreams. Now I'm awake and stuck alone with her in a living nightmare.

It'll be an hour or two before it gets dark. Having no luck spotting anyone outside, I go to the cave, which the brochure says stays above fifty-seven degrees, even during California's winter months. It also mentions a heated sleeping area.

In the blue section of the cave, I search the east wall for a switch and find one just a couple of inches in. When I flip it on, a dim red light reveals a cubbyhole. I crawl into the cutout in the wall and lay on a king-sized mattress made of what feels like soft polyester. The heat radiating from the bed motivates me to shed my clothes. As much as Joel hates me, she won't bother coming in until it gets dark.

Once naked, I bundle my skirt and T-shirt up to use as a pillow. Other than the serene sound of the bubbling stream, this incredible retreat is quiet and peaceful. Like most evenings after a stressful day, I place my hand between my legs and fantasize about—no, not Joel. Not Joel.

10 - Joel

As the sun sets, I walk to the only place inside Double Ds that will provide light. I'm the opposite of Devi, the modern-day vampire, and the last thing I want is to be in an enclosed area with her, but my nyctophobia and an ever-increasing dark sky give me no choice. Hopefully, she won't be in the mood to chat.

A bat flies out of the small dark cave, hitting my arm. I slap my chest and shriek. This place is ridiculous.

The entrance is low and narrow, much like a lion's den. I bend forward to avoid cracking my head on the rock ceiling above. It's dim inside, but a beam of light from the glacier cave shines through a large opening about ten feet in.

I slip through the boulders to the bright blue cavern. The rear of this cave is boarded off with several slabs of plywood. Written on the wood are the words *Goth's Brain Under Construction*.

I'm elated not to see Devi. Then small whimpers pull my eyes to a nook in the wall.

Upon closer observation, I detect Devi's legs jerking up and down on a flat surface cut into the blue glass. My eyes move along her bare skin as she convulses. Is she having a seizure? I can't watch her suffer but with nightfall imminent, extracting myself from this cave isn't an option.

Devi is groaning and clearly in pain. Crap, I can't stand here and do nothing. I grab her foot to keep it steady and remember reading something about victims of epilepsy biting their tongues. I need something I can jam inside her mouth.

She raises her head with mussed hair and a flushed face. "Joel?"

It's then I understand what I walked in on. "You have got to be fucking kidding me." I stumble back with such speed I fall across the stream and bump into a chilly pane of indigo.

"Sorry. I didn't know you were here." Devi withdraws the hand she was fingering herself with and nonchalantly tucks it behind her neck.

I cover my eyes with my hand, although not fast enough to avoid seeing her naked body. "What a crock. You knew I'd have to stay in here tonight. Please get dressed."

"I don't sleep well with clothes on."

"Get dressed right now," I demand.

Devi's trying to get a rise out of me, and I'm giving her exactly what she wants. Along with a deep sigh, is the rustling of fabric. I keep my eyes hidden from her indecent exposure for the second time this week. The cheekiness of this exhibitionist is beyond belief.

"Alright. Your virgin eyes are safe now. How very Dom of you," she mocks.

Easing my eyes open, I'm grateful she's wearing clothes. Her skinny jeans are tight around her legs and her T-shirt has the word *MindFucker* in large letters plastered across the front. Devi twists onto her stomach and pops her head out of the compartment. "Coming is how I relax. This shit has me stressed out. You should try it."

"This may come as a surprise to you, Devi, but most people have more consequential things on their minds than orgasms, and most are sophisticated enough not to strut about in front of others naked."

"I thought since we're both women and you're a skilled Dominatrix, you'd be less of a killjoy."

"Don't give me that nonsense. Candice must have told you my Dom performance was a farce." I sit on a smooth ball of glass across the stream from her. What I wouldn't pay to get out of here. I've never felt this powerless.

Deviant rolls onto her side and faces me. "All Candice said was you hated me and if I ever spoke to you, you'd have me thrown out of your club, which is no longer a factor. I can talk to you all I like."

Damn, she's right. I no longer have leverage over her. Devi lifts her hands, stretches out her arms, and with the clear purpose of changing the subject, says, "This place is awesome!"

"Perhaps you haven't noticed Double Ds lacks a pantry or refrigerator. What will you eat?"

Reaching into her front pocket, she pulls out a brochure and flips through it. "*Edibles*. Let's see, Double Ds has reptiles, amphibians, insects, and flying mammals—that has to be the bats. Detronia has fish, earthworms, frogs, newts, crustaceans such as crayfish, and for vegans—flowers, cacti, and mushrooms. We are not allowed to eat the Detronians. They're a protected species."

"Detronians? For fuck's sake, I'm trapped in a loony bin." Tossing up my arms, I yell, "Whoopee, I'm salivating with delight." I sag against the cavern wall and fold my arms across bent legs.

Devi clears her throat. "You can sleep up here if you want. This heated mattress is soft and comfy." She wipes her palm over the surface of the bed.

The glass I'm sitting on is hard and cold, but I incline my head to rest when replying to the ludicrous offer. "I'd rather sleep with the disease-carrying bats."

Devi rolls over and mumbles, "Whatever. More room for me."

Of all the people in the world, I have the misfortune of being stuck in an oversized brassiere with the vilest woman I've ever met. Having to plead for Devi's help when she found me in the dark was humiliating.

This awful woman, who had sex with Candice and is responsible for her death, is lying in the more comfortable bed. Deviant Wallace takes what she wants with no regard for others. Of course, she offered to share the bed with me, but I won't fool myself into believing her intentions were pure. Moisture fills my eyes. I tap my thick lashes to verify a rare phenomenon. I'm crying, and Ms. Nedra Lane isn't here to witness my tears.

11 - Devi

Without a phone and with the light in the cave constantly on, I can't tell what time it is, but there's a thumping along with a panting noise coming from the small den leading to the exit. So, I slip out of my cozy spot to investigate.

Just inside the dim rock cave, Joel is running in place. I guess to keep warm. She tilts her face toward me and she glares. "What do you want?"

My bare feet on the cold indigo flooring cause goosebumps to form on my arms. Joel can't stray far because there's no light at the end of this tunnel. Ignoring her question, I retreat to the blue alcove and snuggle with warmth again. She isn't my problem.

When I wake up and stroll outside, the sun is cresting atop the Amboadia-West apartment building. I'm hungry and could use a cup of coffee, but I fasted a lot when I was a model. My body is used to going days without food, but I have to pee and walk to Detronia to squat behind a tree.

After I relieve myself, I peruse the Double Ds pamphlet. The freshwater was brought from a nearby lake and contains small fish, amphibians, invertebrates, and larvae. The pinkish color of the pond is created by iron sediment and algae that produce carotenoids. Everything in Double Ds is as natural as Goth is.

The sun is directly above us when Joel stands next to me. The bottom of her shirt is sagging from holding a plethora of mushrooms.

"They're all the same except for the more bell-shaped ones. Do you know if any are toxic?" Joel stretches out her shirt to give me a better look at them.

After examining several mushrooms, I say, "These,"—I point to the more flowery-looking ones— "are chanterelles. They're easy to digest raw. I'm not sure what these other ones are, but

Goth's brochure says no mushrooms in Double Ds are poisonous."

Joel walks off. She got her precious information, and now she's discarding me like I'm trash.

Screw her. I walk behind the waterfall and shed my clothes, placing them on a filtration system disguised as a boulder. There's fresh water gurgling over rocks. I bend to take a drink, then wade to the front and duck under the splashing fountain. After washing, I reach for my clothes and spy Goth's thermos and Diva Bi Night lunchbox on top of a small pump house. The lid to the thermos spins off with the twist of my hand, and I take a sip, "Mm. Yes, so delish."

Joel didn't offer me any of her mushrooms, so I don't feel guilty about drinking all the coffee. Besides, caffeine will only make her more obnoxious. I'm elated to find the box contains a peanut butter sandwich, potato chips, and two chocolate cookies. Oh, happy day! I get dressed and sit to eat the peanut butter sandwich and save the chips and one cookie for Joel.

On my way through the tube, I encounter the pretentious snob. Her otherwise pressed clothes are now wrinkled and her always-perfect short hair is uncombed.

She frowns. "I washed the mushrooms, and left some for you inside the cave, but don't eat them all."

Damn, she's offering me mushrooms and I bogarted all the coffee. I thrust the lunchbox at her and open the lid. "I have a treat for you as well."

Her eyes narrow when she sees the cookie. "I don't eat sweets."

"Take the chips then." I grab the cookie for myself.

Joel noisily chomps on her salty snack. "With any luck, someone will set us free from Goth's creation soon." She snags the cookie from my hand and dashes down to Detronia. So much for not eating sweets.

The rest of the day, I hang out in the tube. Intermittently hopping and flapping my arms, wishing for someone to see me, but nobody comes. Once again, a moonless night encourages me to go to the cave's cubbyhole.

When I slip past the crack in the boulder, blueness greets me. And yes, compassionate gods exist because Joel is lying in the cubbyhole. Hmm, so today she doesn't mind sharing. How interesting.

I climb in next to her, and to be considerate, ask, "What side of the bed do you prefer?"

A groggy-looking Joel rolls over and shoves me out with ease. "Oh, no you don't. There's no way you're sleeping with me. You had this cozy nest last night. It's my turn."

"And last night, I was willing to share. We should sleep together. The concept of body heat might be foreign to you, but it actually works."

"If we were talking about any other body on earth, I'd agree to your offer, but sleeping in the same bed as you will cause me to regurgitate what little food I've consumed today."

I glare into Joel's beautiful, dark brown eyes. "Just because Candice treated you like shit, your uppity ass hates me too? Really? That's fucked up."

Joel leans out over the cubbyhole, grabs a handful of sand, and throws it at me. "You are just like her."

Luckily, she misses my eyes and most of the sand lands on my chest. "Don't presume to know me, you don't."

"I know more than I want about you." Joel throws herself onto her back and slams the mattress with her fists.

This is such nonsense. I'm tired of getting punished for Candice's indiscretions. "Look, I knew your precious arm candy was cheating on you with the bouncers. Everyone knew what she did in the bathroom with them. How is that my fault?"

There's a hurricane of anger on Joel's face, a category six, and she's coming right for me. She leaps out of the cubbyhole and knocks me into the small stream. Joel sits on me and presses the back of my head into the shallow water, then brandishes her fist and holds it midair. Her chest heaves in and out. The smell of raw mushrooms spews from her breath and she screams, "I hate you. I fucking hate you, Deviant Wallace."

Her fist, still frozen above me, is shaking. My chest is fluttering like crazy, and I shut my eyes to prepare for the heavy blow. Candice told me Joel doesn't have a violent bone in her body. So why does she want to hurt me?

When Joel lowers her fist to her side, I continue my rant. "You're an idiot. You still pay the bouncers who stuck their dicks in Candice every chance they got, but sure, go ahead and punch me."

I feel the burn of her slap on my cheek. Enraged, I grab onto her hair and pull with all my might.

She pushes my forehead with one of her hands. "Stop it—you're hurting me."

Not wanting to cause her pain, I let go. Joel leaps to her feet. The sight of glistening tears rolling down her cheeks rips at my heart.

She raises her leather boot and presses it against one of my tits. "You are the one who had sex with Candice, not my bouncers. Admit it."

I place my hands around her ankle and try to lift her shoe from my chest. "No—never."

Joel withdraws her foot and stands back. "I'm baffled as to why you two wanted to be with each other. You're both takers, not givers. Greedy bottoms." She takes a broad step over me.

I lean against the opposite wall of glass from where Joel sits on the edge of the cubbyhole. "What the hell, Joel? Do you just make these lies up in your head?"

She picks up a small pebble and throws it at my face. "You two had the hots for each other."

What's with the damn stone-throwing? Ducking to miss the pebble, I reiterate, "I didn't sleep with Candice."

The tough woman trembles with her chin pressed against her chest, making eye contact impossible. "Why would I believe a drug pusher like you? Candice was always all over you," she mumbles into her shirt.

"Drug pusher? Your bouncers are the ones who gave Candice drugs in exchange for sex. Not me." Candice must have told her this bullshit. I've never met a more misinformed person in my life.

Joel raises her chin and furrows her brows. "You pathetic liar. Nobody slept with her but you. That was our deal."

I splash water on my sore cheek. "One thing you can count on, I never lie when I'm face-to-face with someone."

"Of course not, you prefer to lie behind our backs. Lovely," Joel scoffs.

I make my way to the exit cave. Joel approaches me and I flinch when her hand touches my back.

My heart is trilling with such force I'm sure she can feel it. I duck inside the dark cave where Joel can't follow and lean against the cool boulder between us.

She sticks her head into the darkness, spooking me. "Explain this to me—dammit. Everyone wanted my Candice. Why not the filthiest slut of them all?"

I slap my hand on the gritty cave wall. "First off, slut shaming shows more about your character than mine. I love sex and I'm proudly going to have sex as often as I want." Then I say something I know I'll regret even before the words fly out of my mouth. "You have everyone convinced you're a tough lesbian stud, when in fact you're just a whiny mouse who doesn't know a damn thing about fucking a woman."

Joel steps back into the light of the blue cave. Her face shows signs of a battle going on and I wait for whatever mood will become victorious. Her dark brows, bold cheekbones, and thin quivering lips are entrancing.

When Joel shows constraint, I rant on. "And second, she was not *your* Candice. Far from it. She gave you tiny morsels of herself to chew on, and your possessive ass nibbled away. Candice understood your insecurities, and your need to own people and things. She gave you the illusion she was yours to manipulate, but she belonged to no one, especially not your pathetic ass."

The sound of Joel falling to the floor startles me. When I check if she's okay, she murmurs from the ground, "You will pay for making a mockery of me and for killing her."

Shame scorches through my veins and I'm not brave enough to admit Joel's assumption is correct. I am responsible for Candice's death. If I confess, who knows what she might do? She's already pushed me into the stream and slapped my face. I should abandon her. Leave her to dwell in her anger. But my feet are stuck to the ground and I remain in the dark cave listening to her sniffles from the other side of the boulder. We're alone, but not alone. Her in blue light and me in darkness.

After a considerable amount of time, her sobs turn into hiccups. I peek around the corner just in time to see her body jolt from a spasm. Taking several mushrooms from the lunchbox, I hand them to her. "Chew on these. It'll help."

Sympathy coming from the woman Joel thinks made a fool out of her by sleeping with her girlfriend must be unbearable. So, I silently endure more of her brooding as she finishes all the mushrooms. After an hour of peaceful silence, she rises to make her way outside, and I follow her through the tube as she mopes down the path to Detronia.

"Stop following me." She slaps a palm to her thigh.

Keeping my distance, but worried about what she might do to herself, I rummage along the trail and come across some wild asparagus and dandelions. Gathering a handful of each, I head back to the cave to store our food inside the lunchbox for later.

Before I reach the tube, I'm distracted by a noise behind me. Someone with a dramatic voice is singing. Someone must be in Detronia! I set my harvest on the ground and scurry to the waterfall.

"Hey, is someone here? Anyone?"

Nearing the pink pond, I see Joel. She's naked. Yep, completely nude and singing. I recognize the song as LP's "*Lost on You*." She lifts her arms, revealing round bare breasts above the water. I sniff the air and the smell of pine and wet dirt seeps into my nostrils. I'm awake. This isn't a dream.

Twirling in slow circles, Joel hums the lyrics. She spots me and dips her hand into the water, splashing water my way. "Sing with me, Devi."

I can't keep my eyes off her and stumble over something, toppling into a tree. "Ouch." I'm such a klutz.

Leaning on a branch, I watch her dance. Periodically, she hops out of the water, revealing her not-so-firm belly. Her breasts are small, although bigger than mine, and her mons is shaved clean. Her hips are held by thick quads. Damn, Joel is fucking hot. With her money, she could have had whatever and whomever she wanted. Too bad she's lost her mind over a flamboyant drug addict.

Joel's eyes are unexpressive, yet she smiles and reaches out to me. "Come here, and stick your fangs into my neck, vampire." With a curl of her finger, she beckons me to enter the water.

A twitch of arousal has me squeezing my legs together. Vampire? This sexy woman can't want me. What is going on?

Then it hits me. Joel isn't insane, she's high. I gave her bell-shaped mushrooms to eat. They must be magic mushrooms. It's the only logical explanation. They aren't poisonous, but shrooms are intoxicating. The respectable thing to do is to make sure she stays safe. Keep my eyes on her—no, I mean keep my slutty eyes off her for the next several hours until she comes down. Oh, but her body is enticing, and she wants me. Joel Hunt wants me.

My clit throbs with need and I shut my eyes and chant, "Watermelon, watermelon, watermelon." Or is it oranges, oranges? Fuck, calling out the name of fruit to kill my arousal isn't working, and when I open my eyes again, Hunt isn't in the pond anymore.

I jog up the path to check if she's in the tube, but it's empty. There's no way she made it to Devitron in such a short time. Could she have gone under the water?

With gasping speed, I shed my clothes, and dive into the deep end of the pond. The water is clear, but I don't see her. After coming up for air, I take another dive, this time making it to the bottom where I scan through the lush aquatic plants. Still, I can't find her and swim toward the waterfall as fast as I can.

"Joel, you irritating asshole. Where are you—Joel?"

She comes from behind the large boulder at the base of the gushing water feature and stands with her hands on her hips.

"Why are you making so much noise, you naughty slut?" She's in dominatrix mode.

And now I'm a naughty slut? Okay, I'll take that. At least she's not yelling at me for being naked this time.

Joel wades through the water to where I am and throws an arm around me. Her touch sends shivers through my arms and legs. She pulls me closer and her body warms me. We are skin against skin and I shudder with elation.

Fuck, my body aches for her, but I keep my arms at my sides.

She presses her hand between my thighs and my center heats with such voracity I might self-combust. Unable to deny her access, I spread my legs for her and silently beg for her to fuck me.

Joel is high. She wouldn't want this if she were clear-headed, but I crave her touch too much to care about morality.

My conscience isn't entirely lacking and when her fingers linger close to my pulsing clit, I mutter a weak protest, "We probably shouldn't—"

A moan escapes my mouth as she pushes a finger into my opening. Fuck, it feels euphoric.

"Ah, so wet. You're a thirsty girl, aren't you?" She watches herself stick her finger in and out of me in astonishment.

My face warms. This is embarrassing. Does she think I'm too wet? Why is she watching herself fuck me with such interest, or is that amusement on her face? Her actions are bordering on creepy. Does she want me or is she researching the female anatomy?

Shit. That's exactly what she is doing. She's examining my twat. I press my fingers into her soft hips. "I'm sorry Joel. We shouldn't do this. You're too high."

She stares out into the forest, and her eyes broaden. "Oh my gosh, there's Droopy!" Joel pushes me away and rushes to the shore, yelling, "Droopy, Droopy, don't go. Let's hang out, Droopy."

What the fuck. I step out of the water, mystified. I can't believe she's chasing after one of Goth's non-existent brainbugs.

Joel makes a sudden stop in front of me. "Crap. I lost the little twerp."

I follow her as she sneaks beneath trees in search of Droopy. Without warning, she turns and jabs the same finger she shoved inside me into my chest. "Lie down and open your legs so I can see what another woman looks like. Go on, lie down."

"What?" It's a strange request, even for someone buzzed off their ass. Still, I do what Joel wants.

On damp warm grass, I lie on my back and spread my legs wide. Joel stands in front of me and stares between my thighs. It's awkward and uncomfortable.

"Please," I beg her. "Either touch me or knock it off."

She rubs her chin but doesn't answer me.

My aching clit numbs. No, it doesn't just become numb, it fucking dies. I'm naked in front of the woman I've been dreaming about for two years, and the confusion—or is it disdain?—on her face proves she isn't the least bit attracted to me.

Ashamed, I rise to my knees and try to remember where I put my clothes.

"Sing with me, Devi." Joel spins and dances behind a tree, then peeks out. "Or should we dance? I know how much you like to show off your sexy moves."

She stumbles as she attempts to follow the path to Devitron. Fearful she might hurt herself; I wrap my arm around her waist and guide her to the cave where she curls up in the cubbyhole.

"Hurry, if you want to snuggle." She giggles and scoots over to give me room. I crawl in and Joel big spoons me. I melt against her, but why does she feel so soft? This woman is a fucking tyrant. Why does she feel so soft?

Still, I freeze, unable to move, unwilling to breathe for fear she'll retreat. I want her to remain against me more than I've ever wanted anything in my life.

Joel presses her breasts against my back and rests her palm on my stomach. Her naked body next to mine feels amazing and I can't sleep for fear of missing out on her touch. I barely breathe while her chest rises and falls peacefully against me.

This is a mental utopia. I'm lying next to the woman I can't push out of my dreams. No matter how much she hates me, she will never leave me. She won't abandon me like my mom or Candice did. She's an everlasting fantasy.

The trickling of contentment flowing through my veins is the same as when I dream of her, but this is real. I'm awake and she's touching me. I want to remain in her arms, inhale her scent, and feel the beat of her heart forever on my back.

~~~~~

I must have fallen asleep because Joel is gone. The new moon leaves us in darkness and she's not inside the light of the blue cave. Wherever she is, she must be frightened. I race to the crack in the boulders and check inside the dim exit tunnel. "Joel. Are you here? Joel?" It's quiet and I can't find her in this blackness.

I zig-zag, touching both sides of the cave, hoping to find her still inside and my head bumps into the ceiling and a stab of pain fills my brain as I make my way out into the night. "Joel? Joel, please answer me." Tripping over a rock, I fall on the gravel below and bite my tongue. There is a sweet metallic taste in my mouth. I'm bleeding, and I can't find her.

Getting up, I yell, "Joel, where are you?"

As my eyes adjust to the darkness, I gradually make it to Detronia. "Joel. Come on. Say something, please."

She's either too pissed off or too frightened to reveal her location. I took advantage of Joel and this torments me as I search Double Ds for her. I yell out her name, but she won't respond to my calls. I'm not giving up, and scream out her name through another sob. "Joel!"

~~~~~

Finally, the dawn gives enough light and I find her sitting behind a tree. Her face was much like when I found her in the blackened tunnel when Goth was playing with the light switches. Her night must have been harrowing.

"Are you okay, Joel? I'm so sorry. You can sleep alone in the blue cave tonight."

"How heroically kind of you," she sputters.

Behind Joel, a fishing knife is stuck in the tree. Above the blade are carved-out letters, which spell, *Goth & Virginia Forever*. I try to explain to Joel, "Look, um, last night, I uh—you wanted me to sleep next to you."

"Wanted you? A goddamned player who has no issue with exploiting women under the influence of a hallucinogenic? Right, of course." She grabs the knife, wiggles it loose from the tree, and points it between my eyes. "Don't come near me again or I will kill you." She peers down at her nude body, her voice cracking. "I can't find my clothes. I don't remember—"

It's true, what I did was wrong. "I'll search for your clothes. You're right. I'm fucked up, but—"

"No buts. You abused me." Trembling, she scans her naked body, perhaps for evidence or a memory, then crosses her arms over her breasts. "You sexually assaulted me." She scrambles to stand, only to fall back down onto her ass. "You're a greedy, self-absorbed manipulator. So, you see, I know exactly who you are."

Joel is uncomfortable in her nakedness and struggles to stand again. I can't say or do anything but stare at my feet, and give her privacy from my lustful glare for however long she needs to get away from me.

When the crunching of leaves stops and I think Joel has made it to the tube, I slap my arms around the sturdy trunk she was holding. The woman who loves me in my dreams, in real life, still wants me dead.

After an hour of searching, I find Joel's Prada wool jeans, a button-up shirt, Versace trunks, and a sports bra folded neatly behind the tree closest to the exit door in Detronia. I race up the path and through the tube to the cave. Closing my eyes, I leave her clothes just inside the entrance of the bright blue cave. It was wrong what I did to Joel last night.

Tonight, I stay outside in the cold and walk from one end of Devitron to the other numerous times to stay warm as I wait for daylight. For the first time since we arrived at Double Ds, I want nothing more than to be free from this torment. Tired from a lack of sleep, I stretch out on the white sand and watch the sun rise above the hillside.

There's a loud screeching noise, and I glance at the giant glass door. Christine enters Detronia, and she swabs her finger across the leaves of a fern, apparently checking if the misting system works properly before making her way to the tube.

I leap up and race to the den, yelling, "Joel! Joel! Christine is here!"

Within seconds, Joel exits the cave. Christine reaches the tube, and we both run toward her.

The larger-than-life woman plants her hands on her hips. "Sweet Melissa Etheridge, what are you two doing here?"

"Goth will get a piece of my mind for locking me in this monstrosity with this despicable human being." Joel snaps as she squeezes by us and sprints past the pond with such speed, Christine and I can do nothing but watch her with our mouths hanging open.

Christine furrows her brows and peers at me with concern. "This paradise a monstrosity? My Lord, I can't believe you survived being stuck here with the devil in Prada."

12 - Joel

Nedra sits on a folding chair across from me and taps her fingers on her thighs, "Not only were you not scheduled for today because as you can see, I'm nearly done moving out of my office, you are no longer a client of mine. So, you have fifteen minutes, Joel."

Rubbing my brows, I try to remember what happened inside Double Ds. "As I told you on the phone, I was trapped with Devi for two days, and only recollect bits and pieces of the second day. Devi gave me so many shrooms, hours are missing from my memory."

Nedra propels forward in her metal chair. "You call her Devi now? Do you believe she gave you magic mushrooms on purpose?"

"I wouldn't put it past her. Yes, I call her Devi, and she calls me Joel. The point is, the woman is a menace to society and to make matters worse, we might have had sex."

A normally stone-faced Nedra crinkles her brows. "You aren't sure?"

Sticking my fingers inside Devi might have been a hallucination, although I don't think so, and waking up naked next to her was very real. I press the palm of my hand against my thigh in angst only to be reminded of Devi's firm butt, probably from all the dancing she does, against me last night.

Returning my concentration to Nedra, I say, "When I accused her of sexually assaulting me, she didn't deny it."

Nedra rubs her forehead. "Did she force you to have sex or not?"

"She's thin, and has good dancing legs, but I'm much stronger. Still, I feel as if I was violated in some way." I let out a hysterical laugh. "It's like I'm living in a fantasy book and my character's role is to dive into bizarre situations with Devi."

"Is Virginia writing another manuscript?" Nedra asks.

I don't know why the change of subject, or the question about Virginia writing another novel, but I reply, "Not that I'm aware of."

Nedra leans back into her chair and flips one leg over the other. "If you believe Deviant had intentions to harm you by giving you an illegal substance, or if she hurt you in any way, you should report her."

"I can't substantiate anything, or I would."

Nedra peers at her watch. "I have painters arriving in a few minutes. We'll have to talk later."

I stand to shake her hand. "Thanks for your time. All I want to do now is go home to sleep."

"Speaking of home," Nedra says, "I'm transforming my guest room into an office. I'll be out of this building by tomorrow and will limit my clientele to Amboadia residents only."

"Wonderful. I won't have far to travel for my next visit," I tease.

Nedra becomes more serious. "You can visit me whenever you like, but this is our last official session."

"Right, right. I'll see you soon, my friend."

~~~~~

The next day, I stop at Amboadia's little store before going home to pick up milk and I see Virginia is searching for yogurt and I walk up to her.

"Virginia. Hello. How was your visit with Goth's mom?"

She smiles. "Lovely as always, and I fixed a plot hole in my latest novel while viewing seagulls play above the bay."

"I sometimes forget you're an author." Leaning closer to her, I whisper, "I miss you." This makes my face heat up but I'm determined to get my friend back and wave my hand between us. "I miss our friendship."

I've always been self-absorbed, and I enjoy my solitude, but because of Virginia, I know what it's like to have a friend, even though I never treated her as such. The mistake I made was not giving enough of myself to her and our friendship. I should have been more compassionate, and more of a participant in our relationship.

Virginia grabs a pint of blueberry yogurt and then turns to me. "So much has happened in the last two years. We have a lot of catching up to do."

"I should have listened to you. I have so many regrets. Losing you is at the top of the list." I wipe moisture from my eyes.

Virginia hugs me for the first time, and surprisingly, it doesn't feel awkward.

"The demise of our friendship was a dual effort. My depression was in full swing. I wish I could have been there for you," she says,

When she releases me, I reach for full-fat milk off the shelf and say with earnest, "I wish I would have been there for you too. Hopefully, we can get back to where we were."

She smiles. "I don't see why we can't. I miss you terribly."

A spark of glee fills my heart as I remember the hungry green-haired woman who hugged me.

I smile at Virginia. "I miss you too. I'll do better this time around."

13 - Devi

After showering and eating, I feel refreshed and ready for a new day.

Nicole rubs her hand on the arm of the sofa. "Being locked up with the ice queen of Amboadia must have been exhausting. By the way, Lovette is working at Writerly this week. Christine hired her when you were a no-show. She said you can either work with Lovette today, or kick back and relax until Saturday."

"Lovette? The bingo manager?"

"She's not a bingo manager. She's our event coordinator—a damn good one, and she did you a favor, so be nice."

Nicole and Lovette are employed at the LGBT Center. Lovette is about my age. I met her once when I volunteered to help Nicole during Drag Queen Bingo Night at The Tenth Muse.

As I walk to the bedroom, I say, "Tell Lovette I'm on my way.

I miss the blue glow of the glacier cave in Devitron. I didn't hate being stuck there, not like Joel did. It doesn't help me to be free of the Double Ds when I can't go to The Tenth Muse, thanks to the cruel woman who has mastered resting-bitch-face. A woman who still enters my dreams no matter what I do to detour her. Last night I set my alarm to go off every half an hour and Joel still snuck into my dream to tell me she loves me.

After brushing my teeth, I slip into white slacks, put on a lacy button-up blouse, and press my bare feet into glossy red sandals. I leave Nicole's condo for the short walk to the coffee shop. Once there, the brass hinges on Writerly's dense gothic door squeak, and bells rattle as I enter.

Lovette is dusting shelves in the library and peers over at me. "You're Deviant, right?"

"You can call me Devi. We met at the Tenth Muse last year."

"Oh, yes, I remember. I bought you a mojito." Her cheeks redden as she makes her way to the Self-Help counter. "Virginia mentioned someone was working with me today. I'm glad it's you." Lovette pours grounds into a coffeepot.

She's wearing a sleeveless orange dress covered with yellow roses. Her hair, dyed blue and red, almost reaches her shapely ass and sways with her every move.

Lovette stretches her back and her boobs bulge through her blouse. She closes the lid to the coffeepot and swings her curvy hips as she approaches me.

"Is there a nail salon in Amboadia? I need these polished." She shows me the chipped pink paint on her long fingernails.

Her claws can easily slice through skin and flesh by the looks of them. Does Joel have long fingernails? No, or I would have felt them when she fucked me. She needs to keep up her Dom lesbian appearance.

"Not that I'm aware of," I finally answer Lovette's question.

She nods, then winks at me. "You're prettier than I remember."

I crave a relationship similar to what Virginia and Goth have, but I have yet to meet a woman who is attracted to more than my face. No one but Joel has ever asked me what my dreams are, but I was wrong about her. Candice repeatedly told me Joel was incapable of love and only cared about the ownership of people and things. Screw that. I slap my thigh with enough force, the sound ricochets off the walls of Writerly.

Lovette shouts, "Oh shucks! What's that about?"

Not caring what she thinks about me, I say, "Sorry. I was thinking of someone, someone I can't have."

"You're silly." She giggles while dropping various tea bags inside empty jars. She must think I'm talking about her.

Seldom do I flirt with a coworker, but I miss dancing and the touch of women. Christine and Javier are attending a social gathering at The Tenth Muse tonight. When they invited me, I gave the excuse of having other plans, although they'll find out I was kicked out of Joel's place eventually. She'll tell them, along with accusing me of sexually assaulting her.

I enter the library section of Writerly and inhale the woodsy and dusty smell of books before plopping onto the couch. Lovette tiptoes in and whispers, "There's nobody here. We're alone."

She fists her dress at both hips, lifts, and mounts my leg. Raising my blouse and tank top, she takes one of my breasts into her mouth and rubs her warm wet center against me.

I dig my fingers into the cheeks of the short redhead's ass and guide her back and forth over my thigh.

"Oh, god, Deviant."

~~~~~

After a shower and a change of clothes, I drive to The Tenth Muse. It's 3:51 p.m. and I'm sitting on my motorcycle with my foot on the curb of the sidewalk. If I apologize for taking advantage of Joel when she was high and explain to her what happened with the redhead last Friday, she might give me another chance. Through the rearview mirror, I see a silver BMW Roadster pull in behind my bike and try to ignore the pounding in my chest as Joel exits her car and walks toward me.

She's carrying a humongous flashlight. Is she going to bash my head in with that thing?

"What are you doing here?" Oddly, it's not hatred I hear in her voice, only minor frustration mixed with curiosity. She's checking out my bike. Does she recognize it from when we first met? If so, she doesn't say anything.

"I came to say I'm sorry. I feel awful about, well, you know."

Looming anger doesn't come as I expect. Instead, her shadow slides across the sidewalk to the entrance of The Tenth Muse. The sound of a lock clicks and she swings open the mammoth steel door of her club. Running in behind her, I follow Joel to her office.

Once she places the gigantic flashlight on her desk, she spins around. "We might as well get this over with."

"Get what over with?" I ask.

"Didn't you come to apologize?"

Shit, I'm such an idiot. I walk closer to her and she rushes to the other side of her desk.

"I can hear you fine from where you're at, Devi."

"Okay, well, um, the woman I was fighting with on Friday punched me. I've never hit anyone in my life. She was drunk off her ass and I, uh—"

Joel's face becomes one of puzzlement. "I thought you were here to apologize for drugging and taking advantage of me in Double Ds, but naturally, you're here to weasel your way back into The Tenth Muse. I should have known."

Rubbing my chest to encourage my heart to beat again, I mutter, "I'm nervous. You make me stupid, and I didn't intentionally give you shrooms. I'm not a mushroom expert." I can't bend my head enough to hide the unruly blinking of my eyes when I say, "I'm sorry I didn't stop you from sticking your finger in me."

Her expression again is one of confusion. "What's with all the eye-twitching?" She lowers herself into a chair and places her feet on the desk. "You do many things you say you're sorry for, but you aren't here to make amends. You're here for your own selfish reasons."

She's right, which makes me feel like shit. I should walk out, but my feet won't move. "Dammit, Joel." There's a crack in my voice and my eyes water. The silence between us lingers for several minutes as I stare at the door until Joel's cell rings and I turn around to face her.

"Virginia, you're on speakerphone. And before you say anything, Goth's mischievous friend is trespassing in my office."

"You're with Deviant?" Virginia asks.

"You receive no extra points for stating the obvious. How is Goth?"

Virginia laughs. "Fabulous, she says Devi is incapable of telling a fib and you and her should talk. Personally, I'm thrilled you haven't killed the woman. She's growing on me."

"Like a fungus no doubt." Joel scowls. "Let me get rid of her. I'll call you back."

Joel places her phone on the desk and glares at me.

I point to a door behind her. "Is that a bathroom? I have to pee."

"It is, but you'll need to hurry. My staff will be here soon and they don't take kindly to stalkers."

I ignore the dig and enter an enormous bathroom. In the corner is a mini-refrigerator with several liquor bottles sitting on top. I take a drink of Casa Dragones Joven tequila. The combo of sweet and earthy entertains my tongue and burns in my stomach. Mm, yes, liquid bravery, as Virginia calls it.

Joel yells from the other side of the door, "Do not drink my booze!"

When I finish relieving my bladder, I exit the bathroom and explain to the Liquor Police, "It was just a sip."

She flips her palms into the air. "A sip of something that doesn't belong to you."

"I wanted to give you a bona fide reason to have your asshole security guards evict me from the premises."

Joel steps in front of her desk. "Perhaps you can talk one of them into fucking you, but please don't have sex on The Tenth Muse property ever again."

Stepping in front of Joel, I feel my face heat with rage. "Your slimy bouncers have never touched me other than to throw me out of here at your command."

She backs up a step. "Are you telling me you've never slept with any of my customers?"

I pounce with a verbal attack. "I'm not in a committed relationship. I can have sex with as many women as I want. Don't you dare attempt to make me feel ashamed for enjoying the company of women. I don't answer to you." I poke my finger into her chest. "Because I'm often the fuckee, the bottom, the submissive. I'm a slut, right? Why have you *never* called your penis-flinging bouncers who fuck more people in this club than I do, sluts? Why? Because they're the fuckers. I'm guessing when you shoved your finger inside me, you considered yourself a proud stud and me a dirty slut, and still you insist I sexually assaulted you—what bullshit."

Joel broadens her shoulders. "You know I despise you, and yet, after you fed me shrooms, you pressed your naked body into mine in the cubbyhole. You're a goddamned pervert."

The memory of Joel hiding blindly in the darkness after she discovered herself nude and cuddling me enters my mind. I knew she would be upset when she woke up naked and pressed against my body. Even so, I did all I could to keep her next to me. The one thing my mom got right is my name. I am a deviant.

Joel remains mute for a while as I ponder my indiscretion, then leans over the desk avoiding eye contact. "If you must know, I'm ashamed of what happened between us. I'm not proud of what I did to you."

She's ashamed of fucking me. Great. I adjust my blouse, which is bunching up around my waist, and mumble, "Wanting pleasure isn't abnormal, and orgasms are, well, euphoric. You should try having one sometime."

Joel grips the edge of her desk, then puffs air as if trying to blow negative thoughts out. "What I'm trying to say is slapping you was wrong, and fingering you was disgusting of me. I don't like who I am when I'm around you. Hence, I'd like to call a truce."

Fingering me was disgusting? Shit. She doesn't understand my slutty ass, and I don't understand why she has a stick so far up hers.

"A truce?" I rub the cheek she slapped when we were stuck inside Double Ds, and stare into Joel's beautiful brown eyes.

"We stay away from each other with the same rules of a restraining order. I'll have my lawyers draw—"

I step in front of her. "When I realized how badly Candice treated you, I was livid."

She walks to a window and glances out at the empty dance floor. "No need to lie. I have no intention of letting you back into my club."

"If you knew me, you'd know if I'm asked a question face-to-face, I can't lie. My eyes twitch. It's a dead giveaway."

Joel spins around and gazes at me with fresh interest. "So, when you said you were sorry for not stopping me from fingering you, you lied?"

"Yes. Feeling you inside me was euphoric." I admit without a bat of an eyelash.

Her glare pierces my eyes. "So, you didn't sleep with Candice?"

Without a blink, I answer. "No."

"Why didn't you?"

"I told Cain I was a lesbian. He didn't believe me at first because I had slept with a handful of men years ago, but once Cain realized I was indeed a lesbian, he changed his strategy and became Candice. He thought he'd have a better chance at being with me as a woman. But again, I'm not into dick and balls and Cain enjoyed his penis too much to get rid of it."

Joel lifts my chin and pins me with her stare. "The night she died, what was she doing in the bathroom stall with you?"

I don't want to answer this question, but Joel's touch lowers all my defenses. "When some woman dragged me into the bathroom, I saw Candice's head sticking out at the bottom of the stall door. Once I knew she was dead, I checked the stall for cocaine. I was going to flush it down the toilet so you and the club wouldn't face drug charges, but there wasn't any to flush. The bouncers must have taken their dope and the paraphernalia they used to shoot her up with and ran. So, I put her panties and bra on to cover her up. I didn't want you or anyone else to see the bruises the bouncers left on her breasts and groin area."

With a trembling hand, Joel keeps her hold on my chin. "Do you sell drugs? Did you supply Candice with the speedball that killed her?"

"My mom was a junkie. I want nothing to do with drugs."

Joel loses her grip on me and slowly crouches to the ground. "You never had sex with Candice, and you never gave her drugs." She says this as a statement, not a question, and for some uncanny reason, she's in severe agony over this realization.

I shake my head. "No. Drugs took Mom and my roommate from me. I tried to help Candice, but her addiction was too strong."

Joel wraps her arms around her knees, lets out a primal wail, and slaps the side of her desk. "What have I done?" She covers her eyes and her bottom lip trembles. "Oh fuck. I am such a fool."

What is happening? I try to remove her hand from her face to check if she's okay, but she flinches. I want to touch her, comfort her, but I'm the last person Joel wants consoling her.

"Hey, you didn't do anything to Candice. She ruined her own life."

Joel groans and weeps uncontrollably.

To give her alone time, I head to the restroom. When I twist the doorknob, I hear her rise and stand behind me.

"I'm sorry for calling you a slut, Devi."

Keeping my eyes on the door, I reply, "*Slut* isn't a dirty word. Call me slut all you want. It's not my problem if my being me makes you uncomfortable. That's on you."

"Fair enough. I'll admit I don't understand the joys of having sex with one person, let alone many people. I also don't understand why, after all I've done to you, you still wanted to protect me."

Still facing the bathroom door, I feign a laugh. "You threatened to kick me out of your club if I talked to you. So what?"

She grabs my arm and spins me around. "I've done nothing but berate you, yet you don't want to hurt me. Why?" Her eyes penetrate mine as if needing to understand me.

"I don't know." My eyes twitch furiously.

"Evidently, you do know." Joel's brows furrow. The wrinkles between her eyes deepen. "Is it possible you have feelings for me?"

I break loose from her grasp, and my back hits the bathroom doorframe. "What an egotistical piece of shit you are."

Joel's eyes are questioning. "I don't understand, Devi."

Maybe I should tell her how we met—about our hug, and how we made each other laugh. What is the worst that can happen? If she scorns the most precious day we ever spent together, I can move on. Maybe she'll stop invading my dreams.

I look at her lips. They're puffy and pink. I fight with myself not to lean in, not to press my mouth to hers, but my heart won't listen to my mind and my face moves closer and closer to Joel's. Then it happens. My pulse accelerates as I press my lips against hers.

Joel's mouth opens slightly as if she wants to say something, but she isn't pulling away. So, I fist her hair and pull her closer. On weak legs, I dip my tongue inside her mouth, searching for a reaction. There is none. She doesn't move. Is she in shock or completely appalled?

"Is this, okay?" I ask.

"Uh," Joel utters. Her mouth remains still. Her eyes are closed and her entire body becomes rigid in my arms.

Oh fuck, my kiss repulses Joel. When will I learn? What is the matter with me? Backing away, I release her hair and race out of The Tenth Muse.

14 - Joel

Devi didn't supply Candice with drugs, nor did she have sex with her. Everything my manipulative fake girlfriend told me was a lie. Everything I did to harm Devi in defense of Chase Janice, The Tenth Muse, and my family, was malicious and unwarranted.

My stomach twists in regretful knots. I have done everything within my power to destroy Devi because I believed she brought drugs into my club and sold them to Candice. I thought Devi was disrespecting me by sleeping with the person the public thought was my girlfriend. All this time my number one enemy, the drug dealing murderer, the person I vowed to eradicate from my life, was merely a woman who has a crush on me.

The sudden jolt of this new knowledge has my mind spinning. Everything I believed about her is inaccurate. The only foe I've ever had is myself. None of this would have happened if not for my greed and a need to fit in. I would have never listened to Candice—never experienced unnecessary hate—never consented to lying and I would never have shattered an innocent person's life.

Dwelling on these uncomfortable truths won't help. It's time for action. Deviant Wallace has to be at the forefront of my mind. This disastrous situation will take a while to analyze. I must rectify my actions and I will not make mistakes this time.

Devi could have had a stellar life if not for my interference. Instead, she has barely survived the last two years. Her hardships have been detrimental and extreme. The proud and independent woman had to stoop to asking her friends for help. A degradation I'm responsible for.

The remorse I feel for harming this blameless woman has my throat closing up. Leaning forward, I rest my hands on the desk and try to catch enough air to breathe. I must make amends to Devi. What I've done to her is criminal.

Still panting, I rush to my office bathroom, strip off my clothes, and step into the shower in a futile attempt to wash the guilt and filth that has seeped too deep to scrub off my skin. Placing my fingers to my lips, I remember Devi's mouth pressed against mine.

Why didn't I push Devi away? Perhaps shame for ruining her career paralyzed me or I was dazed with ignorance. It was too much—too many emotions. I froze, not knowing how to feel and yet knowing I've never felt so much before, but for fuck's sake, I can't think about the kiss, not now.

My hatred for Devi has morphed into disdain for myself. I've done appalling things because of my stupidity. The ire I feel toward my bouncers is equally overwhelming. Nothing I've done in the last two years has been honorable. Who I am is not who I want to be. Pretending to be someone I'm not, ends today.

First things first. I step out of my office shower and slip into an old pair of sweatpants and a purple T-shirt I had stashed in the bathroom for emergencies. Then I go in search of the gauche security guards who bruised and killed Candice.

The bartenders and a few early-bird customers watch as I stomp my way to where my bouncers are standing by the restrooms.

I jab my finger in their direction. "You two, follow me."

Once we're back inside my office, I close the door behind us.

"What's up, boss?" the taller bouncer asks.

Squeezing my eyes shut, I gather my strength and make eye contact with one of them, then the other.

"You're both fired. You will gather your things from your lockers, leave my property, and never step foot in my club again. Understood?"

The shorter bouncer whips his head in the direction of the more impetuous one, who steps forward. "Candice had a cock and I've never met a lesbian who likes to suck dick, so you might wanna think twice about letting us go if you don't want the media to find out you're a fucking liar."

Even though the bold man is bigger than me, I reach for his collar, which is sticking up, and I fold it neatly into place.

"Yes, the majority of lesbians prefer to date cis women, a small minority of us will date trans women who pass, and this lesbian doesn't care what's between the legs of the women I date. I'm not opposed to built-in-straps and a teeny amount of testosterone. Who are you to say what women lesbians can or cannot be attracted to?"

The brute stays muted.

I step back and smile. "It would behoove you to believe when I say I no longer care what people say or think about me. You can tell he media whatever you want, but you might want to keep your mouth shut, seeing as how I have footage of both of you in the bathroom dealing drugs to my customers."

Hoping they'll fall for my bluff. I glare at the short one, then back at the man who threatened me with slander.

The tall bully puffs his chest out and growls, "Cain told us he only acted like a woman to make Deviant Wallace fall in love with him. How would you like that embarrassing bit of info to get out?"

I roll my eyes and grin. "Everyone knew Candice was obsessed with Devi, that's not news, but you two not only disrespected and abused Candice, you provided her with the lethal drugs that killed her. I have the proof on video."

Both bouncers become rigid, their breathing grows heavy, and they won't look at me or each other. They're scared.

I point to the exit. "If you don't want to go to prison for manslaughter, you'll leave my club and stay as far away from me as possible."

The shorter one shuffles to the door, twists the knob and runs out of the office. The tall bouncer ambles and mopes toward the locker room. This is one of those times I wish I owned a handgun because I'm sure he does and he looks like he's about to blow up. My heart is pounding as I lock the office door and sit at my desk, hoping he leaves without a confrontation.

A couple of minutes later, he walks by my office window carrying a garbage bag. And my heart slows with relief as he leaves my establishment along with the trash he brought in.

Though I'm livid with them, I'm angriest at myself. Devi has been my foe for over two years. I despised everything about her. I blamed her for getting '*my girlfriend*' hooked, and for being the reason my home life was hell.

My assumptions about Deviant Wallace were incorrect, which renders my brutal retaliation against her a barbaric act of sabotage. I destroyed the life of a blameless woman, a woman who has feelings for me, a woman who kissed me.

I must clean up the quagmire I created. I'm tired of blaming others for what was—and still is—my fault. I have to do everything possible to rectify my mistakes and put someone else ahead of me for a change.

On my way home, I turn onto Amboadia East Boulevard. Devi's old motorcycle is parked in front of Condo Building One. I recall her hitting my bumper and am ashamed for yelling at her.

When I reach Condo Building Three and step into the elevator, Christine Jordan pushes through the doors with her scroungy little dog.

"Oh honey, Laurengo had to pee something fierce tonight. I thought he'd flood Hudson Drive."

"Do you and Javier live in this building now?" I ask.

"Heavens no, we'll never leave our ritzy Amboadia-West apartment. I'm helping my spiritual guide move office furniture into her place."

"Are you talking about the life coach, Ms. Nedra Lane?"

"Who else dah-ling? Now that she's opening shop here, all us silly bitches won't have to travel so far for a chit-chat. I'm gayer than ever, now baby!"

"I would have helped, but she didn't ask," I mutter.

"You're too much of a prickly Dom to be of help." Christine chuckles. "I'm teasing sweet pea. If Ms. Nedra Lane will listen to my whiny patootie, she can deal with your studly behind. Anywho, we're blessed she's here at Amboadia."

The elevator door opens and the assertive woman walks out into the hallway and waves to me. "Ta-ta, Ms. Grumpy."

I flank Christine down the hall. "Grumpy? Well, alright, but I'm only a door away from Nedra's if you need help."

Christine turns and gives me a questioning look.

"I'm Nedra's next-door neighbor." I point to the door of my unit. "I've been a hermit, but you'll see more of me in the future."

Christine picks up her little dog. "Stick me with a fork, Sarah Waters! For a minute, I thought you were stalking me." She scratches her dog behind the ears. "Laurengo, sweetie, be a nice boy and say goodbye to Ms. Not-so-grumpy-after all."

15 - Devi

I kissed Joel. If you can call what I did kissing, and she gawked at me in a stupor the entire time. I slap myself several times on the head with both hands. If Joel wasn't aware of my crush on her, she is now. And hello ignoramus, the reason you can't find love is because you're stuck in a dream. Dreams mean nothing. Dreams don't come true, they aren't reality. It's time to move on.

Seeing as how the get-under-one-woman-to-forget-another-method doesn't work for me, there's only one solution. I'll just fuck myself. Today is International Women's Day and there's a thirty percent off sale at the adult store in Silver Lake.

~~~~~~

This neighborhood isn't as luxurious as Amboadia, but it's all the rage and my second favorite area of Los Angeles to visit. I plan to take a beautiful walk along the reservoir after purchasing some new toys.

The humming between my legs soothes me as my motorcycle takes me down Santa Monica Boulevard. Joel's naked body flashes in my mind as I veer right onto Sunset Boulevard. Her soft skin, perfect breasts, and those deep piercing—Oh! Shit.

I miss the turn into the parking lot of the sex shop and slam on the brakes. My front tire skids into the curb and the back of my bike pops up like a rearing bronco, throwing me out of the saddle. I raise my arm to protect my face as I fly over the handlebars into a bus bench.

Metal scraping against cement screeches as my motorcycle flips and skids to a stop just inches from my right foot.

"Ouch, ouch, shit!" I let out a guttural scream as I crawl on the sidewalk.

Ugh, my poor bike. When I attempt to pick it up, I cry out in pain. Great, anywhere other than in front of the adult store would have been a better place to crash.

Once again, I try to bring my bike upright, but my shoulder is killing me and I have to surrender. An older woman rushes to me, shopping bags bouncing in both hands as she nears. "Did you get hurt? Do you need help with your bike?"

"No, I'm fine. Thank you." I realize other people are gathering and staring, so I wave my hand and smile.

"Are you sure?" the petite older woman asks.

"Yeah, I'll call my friend. She'll pick me up, thanks." I manage a smile that feels more like a wince, and the amiable woman walks off.

I call Nicole. "Hey, I had an accident and can't drive my Honda home. I'm not sure what to do."

"Oh hell! Do you need to go to the hospital?" Nicole sounds concerned.

"Nah, I'm not going to die or anything." Although, I feel like I might faint.

"Who here has a truck?" I can hear Nicole yell. "Where are you, Devi? she asks.

I give her the location. She says someone at Writerly has volunteered to help me. Calmer, knowing help is on the way, I give picking up my bike another go. On the third attempt, I'm victorious and engage the kickstand. Tired and currently in excruciating pain, I lower my head to shun passersby while I wait for help.

Almost twenty minutes pass when a blue two-ton truck pulls up next to me. A massive person wearing overalls lowers the tailgate to the pickup, slides out a ramp, and pushes my bike into the bed with ease.

"You alright, little one?"

I nod, but I feel dizzy.

A much smaller person with long orange hair jumps out of the front passenger side and opens the rear door for me. "Pleasure to meet you," they say in a high-pitched voice.

Peeking in the truck, I see Joel sitting inside, and my heart jumps into my throat. Why is she here?

She glances at my face, then at my hand, which is clutching my elbow. "Are you sure you have a license to drive that contraption?" To my surprise, she has a smile on her face when she asks this question.

Dumbfounded, I stare at my rescuer.

Joel pats the seat beside her. "Do you need help to get in?"

I guess Nicole couldn't find anyone else to come this early on a Sunday. Still, I'm shocked Joel is willing to help.

My eyes twitch like crazy as I assure her, "My shoulder hurts, but I'm good." I place a hand on the door handle and jump inside the truck, banging my shoulder against the seat. Pain jets from my arm to my neck and I stifle a scream.

The person who put my bike in the bed hops into the driver's seat. Joel points to the couple in front. "This is Danni and her wife Linda. Danni is one of my new bouncers."

New bouncers! Joel must believe what I said about the two assholes who shot up Candice with drugs.

"Thanks for the ride. I appreciate it." I can't wait to be home and down a bottle of vodka. My shoulder hurts like a bitch.

Joel glances at the sex shop, shakes her head, then taps the back of Danni's seat. "Do you know where the nearest hospital is?"

"There's one on Fountain," she says.

"Get us there, like yesterday." Joel turns to me. "We'll have your arm x-rayed."

With no health insurance, I can't afford an x-ray. Leaning close to Joel, I whisper, "Just take me home. I don't need a doctor."

She turns her head away from me. "The hospital will take you. I'll make sure of it." She continues to face the window as if not wanting to hear a protest.

This control freak is pissing me off. "Fuck," I growl. "Will you make sure to pay for my care too big shot because I'm asking you to take me home?"

Joel's chest expands as she faces me. I assume she's about to verbally attack but doesn't. Her eyes are sympathetic and she slowly leans closer to me. Her hand is quivering as she pushes my hair behind my ear with her warm fingers.

"Don't cry," she whispers.

Don't cry? Am I crying? I wipe my uninjured arm across my eyes and feel the moisture on my face. Ah, shit. I am crying. The pain in my shoulder is worsening and with her tender touch, my resolve disintegrates.

Joel places her hand in mine. "Everything will be alright, Devi."

Her hand is the most precious thing I've ever held. She's comforting me, just like she did two years ago inside of Writerly. Her touch feels the same, temperate and loving. Why is Joel being kind to me? Am I dying? I try to keep my eyes open, but they close and everything fades to black.

~~~~~

I'm lying on the floor of the runway wearing a metallic mini-dress with a satin scarf around my neck. The yellow tulips Joel gives me fall from my hands when she tells me she loves me.

Tan-colored walls of a hospital room come into view, but instead of a scarf and a metallic mini-dress, I have a sling around my neck, and I'm in a metallic Thermo-gown. This is close enough to my nightly dreams, I guess, but where is the audience? Where's Joel?

Then I see her. Joel is sitting in a chair to my left and I almost leap out of bed when I see her holding a vase of yellow tulips.

"Easy tiger! You dislocated your shoulder. The space suit is courtesy of the nurses. Even with all their doting, they couldn't make you warm enough." She grins.

Glancing at the sling on my arm, I grin. "Good, it's not broken."

She stands and sets the bouquet on a portable table in front of me. "Did you know teeth are the only part of the human body that can't heal?"

I try to sit up, but I'm too groggy, or too high. Has it clicked in Joel's head that I'm the green-haired woman she met at Writerly? Is this why she brought me yellow tulips?

Joel pushes a button and raises the bed. "I could hear you screaming clear down the corridor when they pulled your shoulder into place."

I wiggle my toes and fingers to make sure my digits still work. "So, I'm definitely more of a bottom than a top, huh?"

Joel laughs a deep-throated laugh and what a fantastic sound it is.

"You're as bottom as they get, Devi."

I gaze at her and ask, "How's my bike?"

"Fortunately, Danni, is also a motorcycle enthusiast. She had the parts to fix your bike right up. Anyway, I have things to do, but the Hudsons are on their way to take you home."

Joel stares at me with curiosity and her eyes water when she says, "Did you know Jimmy Carter was the first president to be born in a hospital?"

Then it dawns on me. Joel utters these tidbits of knowledge when she's nervous or emotional. I smile, hoping to calm her. "No, but it's a cool bit of info. And hey, thank you for everything. I mean it, Thanks, Joel."

I lean closer to her and inhale her new scent of oranges and cedar into my nostrils.

"Are you sniffing me, weirdo?"

"No." My eyes flutter at the lie.

She smirks and peers through the small window of the door. "Virginia and Goth are here."

When they walk in, Joel rushes out, and I grunt in pain.

Virginia pecks me on the mouth. "I'll let someone know we're here to take you home." She walks back out.

Goth rubs her neck. "This place gives me the creeps, and that metal gown you're wearing makes you look like a robot." She stands and scans the area. "Where are your clothes?"

I motion to the arm of the chair Joel was sitting in. "There."

She hands them to me. "Need help to the restroom?"

Goth is different somehow. More present, more aware. A lot like when we met. A lot like she was when we slept together—clearly, her meds are working. This is a sweet déjà vu.

She helps me to the restroom, and although I'd be fine with changing in front of her, out of respect for Virginia, I don't.

"Do you need help to put them on?" Goth asks.

"I can manage. Thanks." I smile at my bestie.

Pain shoots through my shoulder as I slip into my shirt. I can't get my sling back on either.

When I walk out of the bathroom, Virginia lectures me about trying to dress myself and hurries to put on the rest of my blouse and adjust my sling.

"You have to wear this for a few days. A dislocated shoulder is nothing to sneeze at, Devi." Once she gets the sling on correctly, she walks to my other side and loops her arm in mine. "The nurse is here with the wheelchair."

Once I'm in the chair, the nurse gives me instructions on how to care for my shoulder.

"What about the bill? How much will it be? I ask.

Virginia helps me out of the wheelchair at the exit of the hospital and thanks the nurse. "Goth, honey, can you pull up the car for us?"

Goth takes off for the parking lot.

"What about the bill?" I ask Virginia sternly, frustrated at being ignored.

"Don't worry about the cost of your stay. It's taken care of."

"How much was it? I want to pay you back."

Goth pulls up and Virginia helps me into her Beemer. "We didn't pay for your medical treatment. When I inquired about the charges, the clerk said a charity program is footing your bill."

"Wow, that's fantastic. I was stressed about it."

My friends drop me off in front of Condo Building One and Nicole runs out. "Oh my gosh, I've been a nervous wreck."

She waves to Virginia and Goth. "I've got her. Thanks, you, guys."

Once inside, I let out a groan as I lower myself on the couch. "Fuck, what a day."

"I was shocked when Joel volunteered to pick your butt up. Nobody else could—wait. Oh hell. Did you sleep with her?"

"No. That will never happen." My tummy churns at this dismal truth.

Nicole hands me a pill and a glass of water. "Thank goodness. Sleeping with a famous Hollywood Dom is just asking for trouble."

16 - Joel

Wearing a short black cotton robe, Nedra reveals lean and muscular legs when she opens the door. "Hi, Joel, let me put some clothes on. I'll be right with you." She takes off down the hall and enters a door I assume is her bedroom.

"I can come back later. I shouldn't have bothered you this early in the day."

"No bother, the carpenters are coming in fifteen minutes to build shelves in my office, anyway." Nedra returns to the living room buttoning her shirt. "What are you up to today?" She stares at me and crinkles her nose. "Have you been crying?"

"Yes, all last night."

"Sit down. You're as pale as a porcelain doll. A *dying* porcelain doll."

My friend is trying to humor me, but my eyes burn with despair.

Nedra gestures to her couch. "Please Joel, take a seat." She sits in a recliner across from me.

Once on the sofa, I rub my hands together and blow air out from my lungs. "I've made horrible mistakes I need to correct, but I'm not sure how to go about it."

"Mistakes?" she asks.

I cradle my face in shame. "Ruthless transgressions. I fucked up, Nedra."

"Go on," she encourages me.

"I need to repair the damage I've caused Devi. Then I'll move back to Manhattan and try to forget what I have done."

"Hold on. What? Move? I don't understand."

"I've hurt Deviant Wallace in ways she'll never come back from, and I have to apologize to you as well." I rub the chill from my arms. "I haven't been honest. I've made such a mess of things."

"Don't be rash. Devi is doing well and she's safe here with her friends." Nedra stands. "Please take a step back and let's observe the situation first. You can act later. Deviant Wallace isn't in danger, is she?"

I avert my eyes in profuse humiliation and shake my head.

In a soft voice, Nedra says, "Joel, running off alone is the last thing you should do. You need to work on yourself further before you put a major plan into action. The stronger you are, the more helpful you'll be to others. This includes Devi."

I scratch my neck with such force I'm sure I've drawn blood. "I must help her."

"And you will. We need to attend to your needs first." Nedra takes hold of my wrist. "Promise me you won't leave Amboadia until we can work this through. Promise me, Joel."

I nod in agreement. There's a knock on the door.

"That must be the carpenters. How about I meet you at your place in twenty minutes?"

"My house cleaner is there. How about we meet at Writerly's? Maybe seeing Devi will help me think of ideas on how to help her."

"Yes, sounds good." Nedra opens the door and the workers step aside to let me pass.

I arrive at Writerly before Nedra and sit by a bay window. Devi rushes to my table and I'm surprised at how happy I am to see her. She's wearing her sling incorrectly. It appears as if it might fall off. I glance at her lips and remember her mouth on mine. The shock of how marvelous it felt paralyzed me. I can't believe I once had such disdain for her and now I'm gazing at her mouth, wondering what it would be like to kiss her again.

"Hey Joel, what's your pleasure?" Devi has on a cream-colored skirt and it bounces against her tan legs with her every step.

"I'm waiting for a friend." I glare at her arm. "The way you have your sling on doesn't do you any good." I stand next to her and rearrange the cloth, so it covers her elbow as well as the rest of her arm.

She leans into me and my heart flutters. Her hair smells good, like sour apple.

"Are you sure you put it on correctly?" She smiles and winks.

I tighten the strap, then reprimand Devi. "Don't flirt with me. I'm not interested."

"Sorry." Her smile fades. "Let me know when your friend or uh—when you're ready to order." She walks away with her head lowered. Crap, did I need to snap at her? Yes, she shouldn't be flirting with the woman whose primary goal of the last two years was to take her down.

Nedra waves through the window and jogs to my table. Devi is staring at my friend with narrowed eyes. Does she think Nedra is my date?

"Excuse me for being late. The carpenters had questions," Nedra says, panting.

I pull out a chair for her. "Do you know what you want to drink?"

She sits and wipes bangs from her forehead. "I've been craving gunpowder green tea with a twist of lime."

Out of her business suit, and wearing sweats, Nedra looks like a different person. Not every strand of her grayish-brown hair is perfectly in place. She looks as if she ran here. She probably did.

Devi stands at our table and eyes me. "What would you beautiful people like? We have a special on raspberry tea today?"

"No, thank you. We'll have a couple of gunpowder green teas with lime and—" I glance at Nedra. "Do you want a croissant?"

"No, just the tea is fine." Nedra smiles at our server.

"My name is Devi." She questions Nedra with hawkish eyes. "Is this your first time at Writerly?"

"I've been here a few times before. It has a great vibe. I like that it's quiet, which gives customers plenty of privacy to chat."

"Okay, well, I'll let you get to it then," Devi says and then darts off to fetch our teas.

Nedra presses her elbow to the table and rests her chin on her palm. "She's exquisite. Tell me what's going on between you two. By the way Deviant scowled at me when I walked in, it's easy to tell her green monster is incensed."

We watch Devi pour hot water, drop tea bags, and shove a wedge of lemon on the rim of our cups. She returns and sets the teas in front of us. Her T-shirt has the words *Self-Induced Orgasms Rule* plastered across the front and she catches me staring at them.

"That's right. I'm off women. I can satisfy myself just fine without all the drama." The shirt explains why she was at the sex shop the day of her motorcycle accident.

Trying not to seem affected by her shirt, I smile with mirth. "Good for you." I sip hot tea into my mouth and it burns. I want to spit the scorching liquid out but hold it in my mouth until Devi turns to walk away. About to gag, I swallow.

Nedra notices my face contort in pain. She places her hand on top of mine. "Are you alright? Do you need water?"

"No." I clear my throat. "I mean, yes, I'm alright."

Nedra squeezes lime into her tea. "Deviant Wallace is spunky and rather blunt, isn't she?"

I wait until Devi is out of hearing range, then whisper, "She's not the drug-dealing murderer I thought she was. Now I have to think of a way to help her anonymously."

Nedra leans in closer. "Why can't she know you're helping her?"

I glance around to make sure no one is within hearing range. "I'll tell you later. First, I need to come clean with you."

Nedra does her usual leaning back and crossing one leg over the other motion, signaling she's all ears.

"I needed the Tenth Muse to succeed for many reasons. So, when Candice came into my life, I hired her to manage my club and create a new persona for me as a confident dominatrix. But this was and still is an act. I've never slept with a woman in my life, nor do I want to."

Nedra rubs the rim of her cup and says, "Were you fake-dating a woman?"

"No, Candice was a man."

Devi is in the library and we are the only ones in the coffee shop's sitting area. Still, I scoot my chair closer to Nedra's. "This must remain strictly between us."

Nedra gives me a consenting nod.

Lowering my voice, I say, "The day after my club's grand opening, I came here in search of a green-haired woman I met the day before. The quirky barista and I bonded. At any rate, I never found her. Instead, I met a cis man named Cain who was working at Writerly. He said he volunteered to take over for Christine because she wanted to indulge in a spa day. Cain claimed to be autosexual. I was thrilled to have met someone exactly like me. To my dismay, he lied about being auto as well."

"So, are you still a virgin?" Nedra asks.

I take a sip of tea to wet my dry throat. "This depends on how you define virginity. Before meeting Cain, I had enjoyed self-pleasuring and penetration with various toys, but I've never been with anyone. Perhaps I'm a narcissist." I drop my chin into my palm, exhausted by my ignorance of who I am.

Nedra takes a sip of her tea, then says, "Gender fluidity is an actual phenomenon, as is fluid sexual orientation. Who you love or how you love doesn't have to be stationary. You don't need to etch your nature in stone."

"I understand my ideas, especially of who I am, are not the ultimate authority, but I'm confident I'll never fall in love. I'm an autosexual who has lost her desire to masturbate, and I'll never have another relationship, pretend or otherwise. So, I'm fine with people thinking I'm a lesbian Dom. It's better than them knowing I'm dull and frigid, but it's important to me that you know the truth."

"Your confident dominatrix act is attractive, but being ace, auto, or aro is equally as beautiful. Some of us are content with our quests, some of us follow an ever-changing labyrinth. Not one path is higher in quality than another." Nedra glances over at Devi. "Is the woman at the bar aware you're not sapphic?"

I catch Devi glaring at Nedra and roll my lips in an effort not to laugh. "Why she's fond of me is a mystery. I'm certain my fake girlfriend had nothing nice to tell her about me."

"Was Candice a trans woman?"

Placing my attention back on Nedra, I whisper, "No. Candice acted femme in public and when we performed in the dungeon. Otherwise, he was masc. He considered himself a man who wasn't afraid to embrace his femininity. At least that's the story I got from him, yet she insisted everyone use she/her pronouns when addressing her and everyone still does, myself included."

Nedra leans in. "What was Candice's relationship with Deviant?"

"Candice was obsessed with her and when this became clear to me, I wanted to kick her out of the house, but she threatened to expose my gullibility to the media. Candice said she had videos of me in compromising positions. Even though we never had sex, how easily I was deceived during roleplaying in the dungeon is something I can't bear for the world, or my parents to witness. Candice was heartless."

Nedra glances at Devi, then smiles at me. "So, the barista, who can't keep her eyes off of you, is barking up the wrong tree much like Cain was with her?"

"Exactly. I'm not interested in any gender. I'll never pine over someone as Candice did for Devi, or as Devi does for me."

"How long did this role-playing in the dungeon go on for?" Nedra's eyes turn sympathetic.

"Only for the first several weeks of our relationship, but let's talk about you now. How is your new office coming along?"

"Sorry, I've always been too inquisitive. Even as your friend I can't seem to stop myself from asking questions." She smiles. "I promise to tell you all about my office and myself another time, but I need to return to the house soon. Thanks for confiding in me." She nudges her head in the direction of the bar. "I feel sorry for Deviant Wallace. Please let her down gently."

"I prefer not to lose Devi's affection. She's fun and good-hearted. It's not as if she can lie to me. Her eyes twitch when she lies." I laugh. "Because of this, I can trust her enough to be friends with her as long as she never finds out what I did."

Nedra looks over at Devi. "Are you thinking of forming a relationship with her?"

"She is struggling financially. What if I pay Devi an exorbitant amount of money to be my companion? The proposal could benefit us both." I don't tell Nedra it's the least I could do after ruining Devi's modeling career.

"Repeating harmful behavior is detrimental to your health." Nedra becomes serious. "Despite the *Self-Induced Orgasms Rule* T-shirt she's wearing, if you think Devi will magically cease wanting you all while cherishing the ground you walk on, you're more disturbed than I thought."

Scooting back into my chair, I grin at my absurdity. "I suppose most people want sex. I haven't cleaned out Candice's old room yet, anyway. In addendum to a lack of space for Devi to sleep, you're right, acting on rash ideas is unhealthy. I'm merely lost on how to help her."

17 - Devi

Joel is busy drooling over a good-looking older woman wearing Nike high-tops. Her act of kindness by driving me to the hospital had nothing to do with me. She was doing Nicole a favor. But she bought me yellow tulips. The same flowers she gives me in my dreams every night. That can't be a coincidence.

The cowbells hanging on the door jingle and everyone turns to see who is entering Writerly. Goth and Virginia come in toting shopping bags.

When Goth gets to the bar, she says, "I heard about you and Joel getting locked inside Double Ds. Sorry, I didn't check to see if anyone was inside the cave before leaving. You didn't find Droopy, did you?"

It's not like Goth purposely locked me inside Double Ds with Joel, and it's impossible to be mad at my big-hearted bestie.

"It's all good. And no, I didn't find Droopy, sorry." I take one of her bags and peek inside at tubes of paint. "Is this for here?"

"No, the expansion of the glacier cave is almost completed! Good thing because I'm becoming so fucking sane right now my creativity level is about nil." Goth's face lights up. "The crew will finish the entry steps to my brain next week. When I paint them, we'll be officially done with your and the Detronians' homeland!"

Virginia waves to Joel and Nedra then makes her way to the bar. "Don't let my wife fool you. She's still brilliant and the newest addition to Double Ds is fabulous. The Rainbow Cavern is bedazzling. By the way, we're opening Goth's art installation to the public this weekend. I realize you might still be upset from being trapped in Double Ds, but Kurt, our security guard, has enough to do protecting Amboadia-West. We need someone to guard Devitron this weekend, especially while the stairway in the Rainbow Cavern is under construction."

"I'll keep people clear of Devitron," I hear myself saying.

"Perfect." Virginia pulls her shawl tighter around her torso. "I've given the contractor my plans to create living quarters in the Sky Viewing Cave, but they can't begin working until next week. However, there are many soft spots in Goth's brain. You will be comfortable if you decide to spend the night."

"I might just do that. It will be like camping. Thank you."

So, the Rainbow Cavern behind the plywood resembles Goth's mind and there's some sort of sky viewing. I can't wait to see it.

Joel glances my way, then says something I can't hear to her tea date. It's not like I blame her for wanting Amboadia's intelligent healer, or whatever she is. Nobody really knows, but everyone speaks highly of her. She's more mature than I am and closer to Joel's financial level.

Virginia hands me a fob key. "Take this so you won't get locked in again. I'm trusting you, Devi. You cannot allow anyone in the cavern. No hot dates while the crew is still working on Goth's brain. We don't want anyone getting hurt."

I point to my T-shirt. "Yo… I'm not wearing this for the fun of it."

Virginia tilts her head toward Joel, then back at me. "I'm glad you two haven't obliterated each other yet." She motions to the bag on the bar. "Can you take the paint to Double Ds after you close up this afternoon?"

I nod. "Sure. Rest up you two."

Goth grabs her wife's hand and pulls her up the stairs, then turns to me at the top. "Just put the bag in the blue cave. It's too dangerous for you to go inside the Rainbow Cavern right now. And please keep your eyes open for Droopy."

"Will do." I take a peripheral glance at Joel, who is still deep in conversation with her date.

The cowbells ring and Lovette strolls in beside me with a naughty grin on her face. She places a leg in between mine and pulls me close. "Is anyone in the library? I'm in the mood to have your hands all over me."

I point at my T-shirt. "Sorry, I'm celibate now, but thanks for the invite." I dash away and return to Joel's table to ask if the two women want more tea.

Lovette follows me. "For how long? A day? A week? A month?"

Distracted by Joel's inquisitive eyes, I stare at her while asking Lovette, "For how long what?"

In a soft voice, but by no means a whisper, she pokes her finger into my chest. "How long are you going to play with yourself instead of me?"

I don't respond to her question. Instead, I direct my attention to Joel's date. "More tea, uh... I'm sorry I forgot your name."

"Call me Nedra. I live in Condo Building Three right down from Nicole's place."

Lovette squeezes my arm and tugs, but I plant my feet firmly on the ground and smile at Nedra. "Nice to meet you. So, is it a no on more tea?"

Nedra stands. "I'd love to, but I have a lot of work to do at home."

Twisting out of Lovette's grasp, I point at my shirt and mouth, "*Stop it*."

She frowns yet stands her ground.

Joel exits her chair, takes Nedra's hand, and sneers at me before she exits Writerly with her tea date.

What was that look about? If anyone should give dirty looks, it's me. This said I'm pretty sure I glared at Nedra the entire time she was here. Screw this, I twirl and smack into—. "Dammit Lovette, what do you want?"

She presses the front of her dress down with a huff. "If this is how you act when you go without women, Devi, I suggest you get back to fucking someone other than yourself."

18 - Joel

It's Friday and I'm having drinks with Nedra at my club later. Tonight, I prefer to dress as I used to. I miss the old me. I'm not a stud or a dominatrix. I'm Joel Hunt, number-crunching-extraordinaire.

Upon examining my wardrobe, I realize most of what's in my walk-in closet consists of leather getups, power suits, several tuxedos, and dozens of silk shirts, all organized by tint and style. None of this is what I want to wear.

Digging through some of my older clothes, I find maroon corduroy pants and a yellow sweater. Perfect!

My phone buzzes. It's Nedra.

Ms. Nedra Lane: 3:22 p.m. *Do you want to come with me to the public exhibit of the Double Ds before we hit The Tenth Muse?*

Joel Hunt: 3:23 p.m. *Sure, meet you in fifteen*

When I arrive at Double Ds, Goth and Christine are waiting by the entrance of Detronia.

"Holy Radcliffe Hall, you fill out those corduroy pants just fine, honey." Christine places her hand on her chest, seemingly in shock.

I pat her on the forearm and nod at the art exhibit. "It's crowded this evening."

Goth swaggers our way, beaming with pride. "Right? Whew, good thing I'm sane—too many people make me anxious, otherwise."

Nedra steps by my side. "Sorry, I'm late." Her phone rings. "Toby? Yes, but please, start from the beginning. Are you home?" When we reach the door of Detronia, Christine throws her arm in front of Nedra's chest. "Sorry. No phones, Sweetie."

Nedra shrugs. "Go ahead, Joel. Looks like I'll have to skip the exhibit. This is an emergency."

I meander inside alone and when I approach the pond, a flash of a naked Devi with my fingers deep inside her enters my mind. Panting at the alarming vision, I push through hordes of people on the path and enter the tube. No wonder Devi thinks she has a chance with me. I did finger her in Detronia.

Virginia is standing by the den in Devitron, and when we make eye contact, she beckons me over.

With a hand pressed between her legs, she says, "This is the place to be if you want to escape Goth's fans."

"Is that why you're here, to enjoy the peacefulness of Devitron?" I stare at her quivering legs. "Are you alright?"

"I'm waiting for Deviant. I can't allow anyone to wander inside the Rainbow Cavern." Virginia crosses her legs. "She's supposed to take over guard duty in a few minutes, but the outhouse is located in Detronia, and if I don't relieve myself soon, I might have an accident."

"Just go." I swish both hands in the direction of the tube. "I'll wait here until Devi arrives."

Without hesitation, Virginia trots down the hill, yelling, "Thank you, Joel. I owe you one."

Bending to peek through the cave, I'm surprised the place doesn't evoke negative memories. Rather, I'm drawn to the muted light at the end of the tunnel shining in from the blue cave. I venture inside, then slide through the crack between boulders to a familiar space. The cubbyhole where I woke up holding Devi in my arms comes into view.

Beyond the cubbyhole is an enormous opening where once a solid plywood barricade blocked the entrance. With the wooden wall removed, a colorful structure on the other side is revealed. Its vastness is intimidating yet stunning, and I'm frozen in awe. This must be the Rainbow Cavern, aka Goth's Brain.

The walls and ceiling are glowing with a spectrum of every hue imaginable streaming through glass piping in the shape of a brain. I wander out to a platform and view the spectacular pool below me. Goth's team is in the process of making stairs. Currently, there isn't a way to reach the floor of the brain-shaped cavern.

Goth's latest creation is mammoth, and a metallic sheen reflects off the cylinders of her brain like mirrors. The high ceiling and walls have pipes filled with liquids of various colors flowing through them. The radiant art piece strikes at the negativity in my mind with a positive jolt of white light and exuberance. This is Goth's mind, Goth's brain, and it's magnificent! Energy pulls me to the edge and I marvel at my surroundings. The floor of the cavern has glittery white sand and the water in this Rainbow Cavern is pink as well.

I'm about to give up on exploring this new world when I hear a tumultuous snapping sound. The ground gives way beneath my feet, and I instinctively use the tuck and roll technique to land and end up on my back in the sand below.

I spit dirt out of my mouth and assess my injuries. There's a slight pain in my ankle. I try rotating it. Good, it's not broken. One of my arms hurts, but I can move it about with ease.

The platform is about six feet above my head. There's no way for me to get out of Goth's brain on my own.

I hear mumbling. It sounds like Christine and Devi chatting. If I can hear them, hopefully, they can hear me too.

"Hello, Christine, I'm trapped in here. Hello."

This time I stand and scream at the top of my lungs, "Devi? Are you there? Please help me. Devi."

The loudness of thumping and grinding of gravel increases as if someone is running at great speed. I raise my hand over my head when the few remaining boards on the scaffolding come crashing down on me along with—who? What? —oh crap, it's Devi, and she's falling. The weight of her body smacks me back down into the sand, and with her on top of me, I'm gasping for air.

Her eyes widen, and a smile forms on her face. She truly is beautiful. She has bright hazel eyes that alternate between grey and blue, a symmetrical nose, and perfectly sculpted cheekbones.

"Joel. Hey, are you okay?"

I want to yell at her for not thinking, but she's knocked the wind out of my lungs and I can't say a word.

She grabs my arm and pulls me up to pat my back. "Breathe. Come on, Joel, breathe."

"I'm fine." I cough out the words. "Quit hitting me."

Devi's arms circle my neck, holding me in a sitting position. Her embrace feels familiar and warm. She tightens her grip and winks. "Mm, damn right, you're fine."

"Stop it, Devi. This is serious. You pick the worst times to seduce me."

She smiles. "Do you want to tell me what times are best for you?"

I push her back far enough, her hands topple over my boobs, which gives me a tingle throughout my body and heat burns my cheeks. Surprised at my arousal, I push her off me and rise to my feet.

"Do you see any way out of here, Devi?" With hopes Christine hasn't left, I yell, "Christine, hello!"

Devi looks up at the destroyed platform and mutters, "She left before I ran in here. I'm sure someone will venture to Devitron soon enough. If you're scared, we can hug again." She smirks.

"No, now stop flirting with me. I'm not into women for the umpteenth time and none of Goth's fans will visit Devitron. In case you haven't heard, Goth and Christine are discouraging people from coming here. Not that people pay attention or are competent. Did you know in 2012 a woman in Iceland joined a search party to find herself? She, nor the group searching for her, knew she was the person who had been declared missing."

Uninterested in my minutiae, Devi hops to her feet and spreads her arms out. "But how fucking cool is this, huh? I knew there was a cavern underneath here, but I never imagined it was so incredible." She raises her hands over her head and winces, obviously still favoring her shoulder. Then she yells, "Gray fucking matter my ass! This is spectacular." Waiting for the echo, and then hearing it, she looks as if she'll burst with excitement.

Devi's dark, almost pitch-black hair sparkles in the colorful glow surrounding us, and her sometimes gray eyes are now the color of a summer sky. Her cheekbones are high like Virginia's. Her nose is dainty, and her lips are full. She seems taller under her lacy blouse and high-waisted ruffle skirt.

I take a seat on a round orb of glass and absorb our surroundings. It is spectacular.

Devi strolls from one end of the cavern to the next. She spots me rubbing my ankle and dashes my way. On one knee, she asks, "Did I hurt you?" She slips my foot out of my sneaker and examines it with gentle hands.

"It's fine. A little tweaked is all," I say, although her concern is heartwarming.

Devi's bottom lip droops. "Are you sure?"

"Yes." Her closeness creates feelings in me I can't comprehend and I pull my leg from her grip. The sadness on her face from my actions has me wondering why I'm such a bitch.

Devi hops a foot or two upwards in an attempt to reach the platform above us.

"You're only several feet shy of your goal." I laugh.

She grunts and gives more effort to her leap, only to jump the same small distance from the ground. Devi turns toward me. "Give me a leg up."

My first step produces a tiny limp and Devi quickly says, "No, never mind." She walks to the opposite end of the cavern. When she reaches the farthest side, she peeks into a small opening. "This looks like a passageway. I'll check it out."

I'm worried about her leaving me. What if the lights go out? What if she gets hurt? What if she doesn't come back? I want to say, *please be careful.* Instead, I dust off my pants and mumble, "Don't take too long."

19 - Devi

The narrow tunnel curves along the massive Rainbow Cavern. Its outer wall is glass and gives a clear view of the outside. The trees lining Amboadia are shadowing Double Ds, and the sun is dropping lower. What if there's no electricity in this cavern and nobody comes looking for us? What will happen to Joel if we're trapped here after the sun goes down?

At the very end of the tunnel, I come to a stop in an area about the same size as my last one-bedroom apartment. The entire outer glass wall has a fabulous view of the north side of Amboadia and on the ceiling is a luminous albeit fake full moon and stars. There's no place I'd rather be than gazing at this astonishing night sky, artificial or not. I've always thought the moon was most beautiful when seen in the daytime. The light pollution in Los Angeles prevents us from seeing stars here, but these stars are Goth made and solar-powered. I'm in such awe I don't want to move, but I want to show Joel this fabulous space.

As I turn to go, I spot an icebox and a water thermos in the corner of the room. This must be where the construction workers hang out. Ladders of all sizes lean against the back wall and I grab the tallest one—

Without warning, my biggest fear is realized. The tunnel lights go off. This place remains lit by the bright moon and the artificial stars above, not to mention the twilight coming in through the glass walls, but what if the cavern Joel is waiting in went completely dark? I drop the ladder and take off as fast as I can through the tunnel until I reach the blackened cavern. Unable to see, a jolt of fear for Joel strikes through my lungs and I scream, "Joel? Talk to me. Where are you?"

Her voice is weak and almost accusing. "I'm here, right where you left me."

I need to get to her as fast as I can. "Okay, stay put." I splash through the water, following her voice. When the ground turns dry, I feel her hand whack one of my tits, then another scrapes my collarbone.

"Stop flapping your hands, I'm not into getting boob slapped," I yell, but I'm happy to have found her.

"Sorry," Joel replies in resignation.

Wrapping my arm around her waist, I can feel her body tremble and her breathing is rapid and heavy.

"Hey, there's light from an artificial night sky in a small tunnel that wraps around this cavern. We need to get to the other side of this pond." I lead her into the shallow pool, and she jerks me back.

Pulling her into the water again, I beg her, "Trust me to take care of you. Please, Joel."

She moves in close to me and I place my hand on her back. There's light coming from a hole in the wall just in front of us, and I guide her forward.

Joel must see the light too, because she walks faster and says, "I do trust you."

We reach the tunnel, which is illuminated enough for us to make our way to the room with the manufactured night sky.

Once we reach the Sky Viewing Cave, Joel releases my hand. "Fabulous, Goth's full moon shines so brightly."

Smiling, I gaze into her gorgeous brown eyes. "The glow of this night sky is constant because of the many solar panels outlining the perforated dome of Devitron. You don't have to worry about this place going dark, ever."

She gazes at me with a smile on her face. "How extraordinary."

I motion to the icebox. "The workers left food, water, and plenty of ladders. I can guide you out now, or we can wait until the sun rises. It's up to you."

Joel drops onto the sand and sits with her legs crossed. She pulls out a pamphlet from her pants pocket. "The Devitron Galaxy was created with thousands of teeny solar-powered lights and eighty-eight different constellations set to a timer. Which one is this do you suppose?" She squints her eyes as if trying to find the answer to her question. She lets out an excited holler and motions upward. "It's Scorpius. See the tail?"

"You got a brochure? Hell, Christine didn't give me one." I slump on my back next to her with my hands behind my neck and we both watch the sparkling night sky. She seems comfortable and not in a hurry to leave. This gives me hope and I can't stop grinning.

Joel is lying on her side, a dull snoring coming from her nostrils and mouth. She's wearing a hideous neon yellow shirt that doesn't match the maroon pants she has on. The way she's dressed reminds me of the day we first met and I have to cover my mouth to prevent myself from laughing aloud.

Cold, I scoot against her back. She grunts but doesn't move.

I shouldn't take advantage of her warmth while she's sleeping, not again. I'm aware of how flawed I am, but I can't help myself. An eternity is how long I want to remain snuggled next to the woman of my dreams.

20 - Joel

Devi is wrapped around me like a cozy duvet. Normally uncomfortable when touched by other humans, I'm amazed at how soothing the warmth of her body feels. The newness of this intimate act is frightening, yet exceptionally pleasant. I'm also very aware of how she energizes my libido and has me wanting to touch myself.

To have someone as beguiling as her adore me feels unreal and glorious too. I'm certain Deviant Wallace will never choose to remain celibate for my sake. She'll crave sex with women again. She'll want more from me than I can give. We, as in her and I, are an impossible concept. This leaves me with no choice but to alienate myself from her.

I lift Devi's arm off of me and drop it behind my back.

"Hey, I'm freezing." She throws her arm over my stomach and grinds her pelvis against my ass.

Heat pings between my legs. *For fuck's sake, what is happening?* I haven't wanted to masturbate for almost two years. If Devi weren't here, I could give myself an orgasm. Ironically, it's only because Devi is here and pressing herself against me that I'm aroused.

Bewildered, I wonder what connects us. Her power over me is not only mystifying, it alarms me. I've been wrong about so many things. Can I be wrong about being auto? Wrong about being sapphic? No, I have no desire to touch Devi, but she spikes an ache between my legs like no other has.

It's clear she has more motive to fear me than I do her. Why am I debating this crap in my head? I'm here to help Devi, not to pretend we can be together.

I scoot from under her arm and roll over to face her.

"We should talk," I say.

"Huh?" Devi sits up, slinging both arms around her torso. Evidently, she is cold.

There's no way to sugarcoat what I'm about to tell her, so I just come out with it. "The only reason I helped you when you had your bike accident was to compensate for how unfairly I've treated you in the past two years. What I once believed about you was inaccurate. This said what happened between us when I was hallucinating on mushrooms will never happen again. I'm a curious person, but I'm not into women, not in the least." As I say this, my words ring hollow. Devi has moved me in ways no other has, but I must deny whatever these feelings are that I have for her. A relationship between us isn't feasible—at least not an honest one.

Devi stands and walks to the far side of the glass cave and stares out into the darkness. "Your eyes don't twitch when you lie."

"I'm not lying, Devi. I'm sorry if what I'm telling you causes you pain. I don't want to push you away."

"Yes, yes, you do." She pounds on the glass with her fist.

I take a step in her direction, then change my mind about getting too close and speak to her from several feet away. "No one has ever cared about me the way you do and I enjoy your company. I even tossed around the idea of having you become my paid companion. Fortunately, I came to my senses before I made you the offer, but the thought was there."

Devi presses her palms against the transparent wall of the cave. "Oh, I understand now. You need to secure your bogus Dom lesbian label. So, tell me, Joel, what's the going rate for companionship these days?"

If she's considering my proposal, living together would be a superb way for me to make sure she's safe and to stay aware of her financial needs. Once we know each other better, I'll understand what is best for her.

"Well, if we do this, you must agree not to have sex with anyone, and our relationship must remain strictly platonic. Since you're on a masturbation kick, I assume this won't be a problem."

Devi slaps the wall with such force I jerk back and straighten out my legs.

"You bitch. You wanted to become an ice queen and congratulations, you have fucking achieved your goal, but you're wrong if you think you can buy me."

Deviant Wallace genuinely can't be bought and my true colors just exploded all over the Sky Viewing Cave.

Devi releases her connection with the glass and turns my way. She stretches her arms out in front of herself and glares at me. "Candice said nothing about you comes from the heart. You buy things, places, and people. Money and power are all you care about and I'm beginning to believe, of this much, she was telling the truth."

I won't let Deviant Wallace push my buttons. "You want to bash me because I rejected you, fine, but I refuse to talk about Candice, who by the way, unlike you, had a goddamned penis."

Devi laughs. "A penis you didn't want. You're only passionate about living in the best places, having the finest cars, and owning the most expensive things—oh, and owning beautiful people. All to *compensate* for what, I wonder?"

I stomp over to the cooler, raise the lid, and take out a bottle of water. Twisting a reluctant cap off gives little relief to my irritation. "You're ridiculous. You know absolutely nothing." Now I sound like a petulant child or someone with the brain cells of a gecko.

Devi darts in front of me with her eyes steady on mine. "I know plenty. You never let Candice eat what she wanted. Instead, you *encouraged* her to try exotic foods. Exotic fucking foods—an acquired taste even for snobs. Boiled duck fetus? Really? And did you think if you forced her to drink Scotch enough times, she'd finally like it? She thought the crud tasted like Band-Aids, and guess what? It does."

Duck fetus? Is this woman insane? "What are you talking about? My favorite food is pizza. How exotic is that? I'm perplexed—my gods, Candice must have been wasted out of her mind to come up with such drivel."

Devi inches closer until our noses almost touch. "Yes, Candice was a habitual liar and probably fabricated most of what she told me about you, but you can't deny how materialistic and self-absorbed you've become."

Devi has never looked at me with such disdain. The indignation on her face pinches my heart.

She acts as if we've known each other for years. Other than our time in Double Ds, I've only seen her from a distance at The Tenth Muse, which isn't long enough to know someone. It breaks the three-month rule. And what does she understand about the many people out to exploit my family? Who will protect me from the Candices in the world if not me? Expensive things convey power and strength, and ice queens don't get screwed with.

She snarls, "What the fuck happened to you?"

"Stop talking, Wallace."

Devi jabs her fingers into my chest. "You don't own me. I'll talk whenever I want to talk. You might have bought Candice, but you failed to gain her pink slip. In the end—in the fucking end, Candice not only owned your pathetic ass, she took you down with her."

I shove Devi into the sand, sit on top of her, and push her hands above her head. "Look, I don't want to argue and I refuse to talk about Candice."

Devi's greyish-blue eyes are beautiful, distractingly so, and she manages to free one of her hands. Before I can move out of the way, she grabs my shirt and pulls me close to her face.

"Stop it, Devi."

"Nope, not happening." She grunts.

"Damn you." I try to pull away. "Let me go."

"If only I could," Devi whispers.

I regret slapping Devi when we fought before and won't do it a second time.

Her lips brush my neck as she speaks, and goddamned if it doesn't feel good. "Why should anyone care about you, Joel? You treat people who love you like shit."

Is she talking about herself? Why else would she say such a thing?

"Please stop talking." Warm tears roll from my eyes, wetting both our faces. I'm not sure if I'm crying because Devi is telling me she loves me or because she has a hold of my shirt and we're so close.

Devi lets go and rolls away with her back to me. "I wish I could hate you as much as you hate me."

"I don't hate you. Not anymore. I know I'm a difficult person to like. I apologize."

I watch her lungs expand and sink, expand and sink, as she curls onto her side. Devi isn't a liar, nor is she a whore. I'm the whore. I'm the one who sold myself to prevent people from knowing the real me. This beautiful woman lying in the sand doesn't have to hate me. I hate myself enough for both of us.

Defeated, my only course of action is to leave the woman who loves me alone.

The passageway out of the Sky Viewing Cave isn't bright, but it's not completely dark either. When I reach the pitch-black Rainbow Cavern, I stop with nowhere to go, and sit against a mound of cool glass to wait for daybreak.

A bright glare penetrates my eyelids, and when I open my eyes, the illumination blinds me. Through blurriness, a seemingly deranged bearded man holds a ladder. He pushes large pink sunglasses higher on his nose and asks, "Do you see me?"

"Barely." Which is true. The gaunt man is almost transparent. My eyes must be playing tricks on me.

I glance up at the busted platform, then back at him. "Please hold the ladder. I need to get out of here."

21 - Devi

The grinding of pebbles and sand becomes louder as Joel nears me in the Sky Viewing Cave. With it being dark, she has no way out of Goth's brain, without me helping her.

When she taps my shoulder, I turn to face her with a smile. "Alright, let me grab a ladder and we'll go."

The form of a gaunt man solidifies.

"Amboadia security. There's no loitering at Double Ds." The skinny dude is wearing pink shades and he stretches over me while tugging on his scraggly beard.

I gasp at the freaky-looking man. "Who the fuck are you, and where's the woman who was here?"

"The transmigration of her dead soul has begun."

"What? She better be okay, you crazy fucker."

"Hey, that's no way to talk to Kurt." Goth reaches for my hand and pulls me up. "Joel just left. Did you spend the night with her again?"

I remember now. This weird dude is Kurt Hartman. I give him an apologetic smile.

Goth leads me out of the caves to a folding table near the tube. "Have some caffeine, my friend."

I take a small paper cup and fill it with a dark brew.

Goth fills her mug. "Virginia and Christine left early this morning to attend a sapphic writer's convention in New York. One of them usually makes the coffee, but we're stuck with mine today."

Goth brews the worst cup of joe. It's terrible. How she gets coffee to smell like horse shit and taste like moldy alfalfa is beyond me. Still, I endure one baby sip while trying to keep my face from contorting in distress.

I scoot away from Kurt, who is way too close. "Your security guard needs a bath. He stinks worse than this coffee."

Goth's mouth broadens. "Ah ha! You *are* in love with Joel." She grins. "Nobody sees Kurt Hartman unless they're in love. And, if they can smell him, it's the never-ending kind of love."

"Great, that's just great. Hey, I've been meaning to ask—do you and Virginia want to jog the Getty Trail Sunday morning, say at seven-ish?"

"Virginia is more of a hiker than a jogger. If Nicole walks with her, she might go," Goth says.

"Okay, I'll ask Nicole too." I get up to leave, then ask, "One more thing. Do you mind if I put up fliers offering cleaning services to Amboadia residents?"

"You clean houses?" Goth gulps down the last of her coffee.

"I'm not a domestic god or anything, but I can clean a messy house."

Goth presses a finger on her chin. "Ms. Nedra Lane was asking about a house cleaner. She's in Condo Building Three. My sister could use help over at the Amboadia-West penthouse too."

"Thank you. We'll meet at Writerly for the hike. Don't forget, Sunday at seven a.m." I kiss my bestie on the nose and head over to Nicole's place.

On the way, I think about my predicament with Joel. My love for her will never fade as long as she's in my dreams. If I make enough money to move away from Los Angeles, maybe she'll stop visiting me in my sleep.

Jogging out of the French bakery is Nedra Lane, and I run to catch up with her.

"Hi, Ms. Lane, I don't know if you remember me."

She stops and pulls the waistband of her teal sweats tighter. "Yes, Deviant Wallace. How are you?"

"Good, thank you. Um, Goth said you might be interested in hiring someone to clean your condo, and well, I'm looking for extra work. I'd be happy to service you." *Oops*, that didn't come out right. "I mean be of service to you, cleaning your house."

She shakes her head. "I am, but because of the tension between you and Joel, I don't think hiring you is a good idea. Sorry." She keeps jogging.

I run alongside Nedra, and she gives me a look of irritation.

"I understand. You two are friends and she hates me, but I'll work my ass off and you can pay me whatever you think I'm worth when I'm done."

Nedra sighs. "Joel doesn't hate you."

"Please. I can work all day today and after I'm finished with my shift at Writerly tomorrow. I'll work all night if you want. I'm fast and—"

Nedra stops and lets out a sigh. "I'm in apartment eight, Condo Building Three. Meet me at my place in an hour?"

I throw my fist toward the sky and yell, "Yes, thank you, awesome gods of Amboadia!"

Again, Nedra shakes her head, but this time she smiles.

22 - Joel

Nedra is at my place. She says she has something to tell me, but instead of mentioning what, she stares at me with a puzzled look on her face. "Have you been crying again? What's going on with you?"

"A platform I was standing on in Devitron collapsed yesterday and I fell into a vast cave, aka Goth's brain."

"Fell? Were you hurt?" Nedra places her hand on my biceps and gives my body a once-over.

"I'm fine, but when I couldn't find a way out of the Rainbow Cavern, I screamed for help and Devi came speeding toward me and crashed down through the already broken platform and landed right on top of me."

Nedra slaps her thigh and laughs. "Hilarious."

I place a hot cup of green tea in front of my delirious friend. "The woman is infuriating."

"I'm seeing a very different you lately." Nedra sips her tea and winks in approval.

"Yes, very different. I'm weeping like a scared toddler."

"Letting go is a symptom of growth. Strength is measured by vulnerability. When you're concerned about someone other than yourself and honest about who you are even when it hurts this exposes your heart, leaving it unprotected. Expressing yourself via tears takes valor. It means you've gone beyond the walls of safety."

"Do you think Devi would accept a small van filled with fancy clothes from me? I can say I used to be her size and outgrew them?"

Nedra pushes her hands between her outstretched legs. "Why do you want to give Deviant clothes?"

"She loves clothes. If she had become a supermodel, she'd have several closets full of pricy garments."

"I didn't know she had aspirations of becoming a model." Nedra takes another sip of her tea and spits it out in laughter. "I can't believe Deviant fell on top of you."

"I can't believe you are making fun of my dilemma. Are you sure you have a therapy license?"

"A life coach doesn't require a professional license. We aren't therapists, although we can give advice much like mentors do. Besides, you and I are friends now, so please tell me why you've been crying?"

Pulling out a stool, I sit across the kitchen island from my friend. "We got into an argument, a bad one."

Nedra places both palms firmly on the table. "Maybe, you two should give each other some breathing room."

"If only we could. Amboadia isn't big enough." I get up and throw a clean dish towel in the sink.

Nedra crosses her arms in front of her chest and rests against the back of the barstool. The warmth in her eyes and the gratitude on her face tell me I don't have to feel shame for the myriad of conflicting emotions I'm feeling.

Eventually, I say, "Devi said I treat people who love me like shit, and I could tell she was talking about herself. She's upset because I put myself first. Isn't greed beneficial? Why not be self-absorbed? Who else is going to have an interest in my welfare? And don't say my parents. As much as I care about them, they don't have an inkling of what my needs are."

Nedra grins. "Such a dichotomy. You prefer detachment and Deviant's feelings are profound, deeper than a mere crush, which puzzles me."

I grip the edge of the table. "Thanks a lot. Am I so repulsive?"

"You yourself said you've been harsh in your treatment of her. Deviant's intense reactions have me worried."

"I slapped her so I can't claim she's any more intense than I am."

"You did what?" Nedra flaps her hands as if she wants to make my comment go away. "This behavior isn't healthy. You could go to jail for such an act. You need to stay away from Deviant. You have feelings for her—don't deny it. You pondered making her your companion."

I take my friend's cup and rinse it in the sink. "You're right, I should stay away from Devi. I'll have to help her from a distance. Now, what is it you came here to tell me?"

Nedra walks to the door grabs the knob and pauses. "Deviant will be in our building in a few minutes to clean my condo."

23 - Devi

It's a cool Sunday morning after an exhausting work week. I'm excited to walk outside and enjoy the fresh air after spending several hours working at Nedra's place yesterday. Nicole and I are wearing similar beige shorts as we enter Writerly. Goth, Virginia, Nedra, and Joel are sitting together and rise from their chairs when they spot us.

Goth, the fittest of our squad, leads us out of Writerly. "We'll leave through this gate and walk to the trail from here." She points to a dirt path on the north side of Amboadia.

Nedra runs alongside Goth, and Joel and Nicole take off behind them. So as not to leave Virginia alone, I stay with her.

"Are you okay with Joel hiking with us?" she asks.

"Sure. I won't be at Amboadia for much longer anyway. I'm working my ass off so I can pay first and last month's rent for another apartment in Chinatown."

"I don't understand. Why are you leaving?"

"It won't be for a while. I don't have the money yet."

"Goth will be saddened by your departure." Virginia grabs my wrist. "If a person believes in something strong enough, it becomes their reality no matter how fictitious the belief appears to others." She places her hand on my back. "We should never believe the negativity our minds spew."

"Are you saying my dreams about Joel won't come true?"

She reaches for my hand. "No, I believe it's possible for dreams to morph into reality. What I'm saying is a person can become blinded by ideas so dense they can't read the writing in front of them. This makes them lag and fall chapters behind. The most loving thing you can do is have patience until they land on the same leaf you're on."

Up ahead, Nicole and Joel have stopped, and my heart races.

Virginia releases my hand and gives me a sympathetic smile. I kiss her cheek and thank her for the advice.

I should tell Joel when and where we met. Maybe she'll remember our embrace. Or maybe I'm the only one who feels at home when we're in each other's arms. What if I tell her only to have her confirm she doesn't want to be on the same page I'm on?

When our group reaches the top of the hill, we perch on small boulders and watch traffic zoom by on the highway below.

Virginia asks, "How about we all head back to Writerly and have some raspberry tea?"

Joel smiles. "I'm up for it, my friend."

I shake my head. "Can't, I need to finish cleaning a unit over at Condo Building Three."

~~~~~

After grabbing a bite to eat at Nicole's, I head over to Nedra's place. In the garage of Condo Building Three, I see Joel making her way to the elevator. I slow my pace so as not to have to ride up with her. As soon as she nears the elevator, all the lights in the garage go out.

Joel yelps in panic. It sounds as if she's fallen to the floor. I run in her direction and hit my arm on something, most likely a mirror from one of the vehicles.

"Ou-eww. Fuck."

Joel shouts, "Devi. Is that you?"

When I reach Joel, I plop to the ground next to her. She's flat on her stomach, much like she was in the blue cave when the lights went out.

"We'll be alright. Some dumb-fuck probably hit a power pole. Same thing happened last week in Echo Park. But hey, you need to sit up."

"I can't," she whimpers.

"Come on. This pavement is filthy." I look for my phone, then remember I left it to charge at Nicole's when I changed clothes. "Where is your phone, Joel?"

In seconds, Joel has her phone turned on and mutters, "It's not enough light. What if someone is hiding behind a vehicle? This is ridiculous. Nobody gets stuck together as much as we do."

"It's more than enough light, and, just like when we were in the Sky Viewing Cave, I'm not stuck. You are. The dark traps you, not me."

The elevator behind us clanks and grinds, then whines into silence. Joel's arm rubs against mine as she sits up.

She's too close and I nudge her away from me.

Ignoring my attempt to separate us, she grips my lower arm. "I have responsibilities, places to be."

"Do you think you are the only one here who does?" I yank out of her hold. "I don't have rich parents to buy me a fucking nightclub. I'm supposed to be scrubbing your pricy life coach's toilets right now. Instead, I'm taking care of your privileged ass."

Joel's voice gentles. "Sorry. I've never worked as hard as you do. Not even for a day. Nor have I ever endured the hardships you have."

Still angry, I scoot another couple of inches away from her.

"Devi, I know how self-absorbed I am, but I don't considered self-obsession a flaw."

I sigh, "If you want to live the rest of your life alone, I guess caring about someone other than yourself is counterproductive."

Her fingers tighten around my arm and she surprises me by asking, "Are you close to your family?"

She reminds me of the old Joel, inquisitive and caring and once again I want to tell her everything about myself. "I don't have a family. I was raised in the system—never knew my biological dad and I haven't seen my mom since they arrested her for selling me to some guy when I was a kid."

"You deserve much more than life has given you, Devi." Joel points her phone directly in front of us. It's not very bright, although, bright enough to get us out of here. She scoots against me and slings her arm around my waist—squeezing tight. "Did you hear something?" She shines the phone behind us in a panic. "With the luck I've had lately, I should carry my flashlight with me during the daytime too."

No wonder she has muscular arms, the huge flashlight she carries at night must weigh a few pounds.

"Nobody else is here. We're safe." I point toward what I believe is the entrance. "Just beyond that corner and down the ramp to the left, is light. The sun shines into the garage at this time of day. It fills the entrance with a brilliant beam and the ray of light will remain for another hour or so. Afterward, it'll move to the west and brighten Writerly's rooftop. Have you ever been up there?"

"No," she whispers.

"There's a huge rainbow umbrella, lounge chairs, tables, some plants, and trees too. It can get hot on the roof in the summer, but it's a great place to sunbathe or people-watch."

"Thank you." Joel grips my arm again. "Why aren't you afraid of the dark?"

"I am. Not on the same level as you, but I think most people are. It's probably an evolutionary trait humans honed. Bad shit happens at night."

Joel sniffles. "Focusing on myself is when I feel the most comfortable. I couldn't hop from one bed to another like you do. It would give me angst. I'm too afraid to be a slut."

"I've lost my interest in bed-hopping, thanks to you," I mutter.

Joel's raspberry tea breath hits my cheek as she scoffs. "I bet your eyelashes are flapping at rapid speed."

"No. They aren't."

On instinct, I turn my head toward her to prove my eyes aren't twitching even though I'm sure it's too dark to tell. Our noses bump and my mouth grazes hers and I let out a low hum.

Joel presses her smile to my mouth. Her gentle kiss creates tingles throughout my body and makes my clit throb. My heartbeat quickens when Joel sucks on my upper lip. She's not a skilled kisser. She's trembling and her kiss is wet with sporadic licks and pecks, but I give her complete control.

Her breasts touch my arm and she quivers as she slings her hand around my neck and continues to kiss me. Joel isn't just exploring this time. She's kissing me tenderly and with yearning. She's breathing heavily and when I open my mouth, she dips her tongue in, then quickly drags it back out.

I whisper, "It's okay. Put your tongue inside my mouth if you want."

She slips her tongue back in and I move mine to her rhythm. As our tongues do a slow sensual dance to the beat of our hums, the vibrations rumble across my face, down my throat, and into my lungs. This is the sloppiest kiss I've ever had, yet, never in my life has a kiss felt so special or significant.

My entire body is burning with want, and my skin becomes sensitive to her touch. I want more, much more. Joel must feel the same way because she presses her mouth harder against mine. Her lengthy eyelashes tickle my skin as I lap at her eager tongue and taste raspberry tea.

I pull the back of her hair and lick her perfumed neck. She smells of roses today. This must make Joel hot because she releases me, and I can feel and hear her struggling with the top button of her pants, then comes the sound of a zipper lowering. Oh fuck, my heart is racing. I'm not ready to be with her, especially not in this grimy garage. But I have to take advantage of this opportunity—don't I?

When Joel guides my hand inside her pants, I nervously work my fingers under the elastic band of her underwear, making the wannabe ice queen whimper.

She spreads her legs for me, and as I feel her soaked panties, my eyes water. A miracle larger than all miracles, Joel is hot for me. Joel Hunt wants me to make her come. I'm shaking as I question my skills as a sex partner for the very first time. Never have I feared being physical with anyone before, but this is Joel. The woman who tells me she loves me every night in my dreams.

My fingers reach her slick warmth, and before dipping in, I ask, "Are you sure you want me?"

Joel grabs my wrist, pulls my hand out of her pants, and springs away in one drastic jump.

I hungrily reach out to nothingness. "What the fuck, Joel?"

"Devi, I apologize. My mind turns to mush when I'm scared and you know I'm not into—"

Heat rushes up my neck into my face as I finish her sentence. "Women. You're not into women."

Joel grabs my ankle. "I don't understand what happens to me when I'm with you. It's as if I possess someone else's body."

"No need to explain. You got horny. It happens to the best of us sluts." I stand to go, but as upset as I am, I can't leave her alone in the dark. "Turn your phone on as bright as it will go and butch the fuck up. I'm taking you out of here."

Joel is shuffling on the floor and the sound of her zipper being pulled up scrapes at my ears.

"Please, let me explain," she pleads as her phone is brightening.

Nothing she says will make me feel better and I'm about to tell her I don't want to talk about it when the electricity comes on and its brightness has us both covering our eyes from the glare.

Joel stands next to me and intertwines her fingers into mine. "I'm so sorry."

A touch that seemed natural yet exciting earlier now burns me with humiliation and I wiggle free of her hold. "Damn you, Joel."

I sprint out of the garage and when the California sun hits my face, I lift my fingers to my nostrils to inhale the sweet scent of the woman I love. Fuck, she smells so good. My heart sinks into my stomach. I need to stay away from her. She does nothing but hurt me.

24 -Joel

It's been seven days since I tried to seduce Devi in the garage. I can't comprehend why I wanted Devi to touch me. With the unpredictable onset of my libido, I suppose, my urges are misfiring or unbalanced somehow. I'm uncertain what to do with this attraction I have for Deviant Wallace.

I'm standing at the gate to the hilltop path, ready for our Sunday hike. If I had Devi's phone number, I would have called her to apologize. I miss her face, her smile, the way she makes me laugh, and while I'm still as naïve as I've always been when it comes to people, I miss her.

Everyone in our hiking group shows up except for Deviant Wallace, which creates a somber atmosphere. Christine and Goth walk ahead and I wait for Nicole and Virginia to catch up to me.

"How is Devi doing?" I ask, not caring how desperate I sound.

Nicole points toward Amboadia-West. "She works every waking hour. I'm taking her apartment hunting next week."

Virginia glares at Nicole. "Can't you convince her to stay?"

Nicole jams her hands into the front pockets of her shorts. "Trust me, I tried. She doesn't want to be at Amboadia anymore. She won't tell me why."

Virginia stops walking. "This is no good. She can't afford anything nearby. She'll be too far away for frequent visits and Goth will miss her terribly."

It's my fault Devi is moving away. If only I hadn't shoved her hand down my pants. What was I thinking? Why did I want her, a woman, to stick her fingers inside me?

"Devi will have to move to some unsavory place riddled with crime. Do you think it's wise to let her go?" I ask.

Nicole gives me a curious look. "Let her go? I'm not her mother. Besides, I thought you'd be happy she's leaving."

I want to tell Nicole that on the contrary, the moment my mouth touched Devi's in the garage, I wanted her to be mine, all mine, and I wanted to give myself to her. Then, like an absurd twit, I panicked when she asked me if I wanted her. Absolutely, I wanted her, but when she asked if I was sure, I panicked. We were in public, in a dirty garage, for fuck's sake.

"I'm sorry you're stressed, Nicole," is all I can think to say.

She sighs. "I've known Devi for years. Her mother was arrested for selling the kid for a bottle of gin—or was it some fancy Scotch? Yeah, it was Scotch. Anyway, I promised her that, unlike her mom, I'd always be here for her. So damn right her leaving stresses me out."

Virginia has her finger against the side of her nose. "If imploring Deviant to remain with us hasn't worked, I wonder if a more solid connection to Amboadia will."

"What's going on inside your clever mind?" Nicole asks.

"I can't voice my intentions. Sounding things out before writing it down could throw off the magic, but you'll learn of my plan soon enough."

Not being a believer in magic, I need to come up with a surer way to prevent Devi from moving. But, if her goal is to stay away from me, nothing will keep her in Amboadia.

When we return to Writerly, Nicole sits next to Sapphic Cream, a DJ who works at my club on the weekends.

Nicole wipes the dampness from her face on the sleeve of her shirt. "I'd hug you, Sapphic, but I'm sweaty from jogging."

The bouncy DJ gives Nicole a light squeeze. "It's all good, I brought the flyers I told you about."

Nicole glances at me. "These are the flyers for her gig at The Tenth Muse next weekend. I promised to take some to the Center. Have a seat, Joel." Nicole points to a chair across the table.

Sapphic Cream springs to her feet and pulls the chair out for me. "Yeah, have a seat boss."

"You don't have to call me boss," I tell Sapphic.

My adrenaline pumps as Devi takes quick strides out of the stockroom toward the bar. The way she makes me feel when I'm near her has me questioning my sexual orientation. The irony of me pretending to be a lesbian when I might actually *be* a lesbian is bizarre. Devi appears tired, yet her beauty takes my breath away. There's a rosy streak flowing like a river down the left side of her head. She's attractive, even to me, but I wince at the sight of her signature purple lipstick. Candice coaxed me into wearing the same purple lipstick when we were in the dungeon together.

"Sorry, I was stocking shelves," I hear Devi say. "I'll be right with you."

"Hot fucking damn. Who's the sexy chick?" Sapphic wipes imaginary drool from her chin.

Virginia and Goth wave goodbye as they ascend the stairs to Writerly House.

Devi arrives at our table and locks eyes with mine. Unable to form a coherent sentence, she sputters. "Um, what um?"

Sapphic stands. "Oh snap, you're hot. Please tell me you're into women and single." The bold DJ is almost purring with want. I should fire her ass. Wonderful. Now I'm jealous of the woman I'm too scared to be with. These feelings are new and puzzling.

Devi glances above her adoring fan and stays focused on me. "Do you know what you want? I mean—to drink?"

Sapphic Cream gawks at Devi. "Come to the club and watch me spin this Friday. I'll pay your cover and buy your drinks."

I glare at Devi, waiting to hear how the woman I eighty-sixed from my club replies to the smitten DJ.

She remains quiet with her eyes still locked on mine. I'm livid enough, or perhaps fearful enough to keep her gaze and dare her to disappoint me.

Sapphic Cream reaffirms her offer to Devi. "As many drinks as you want on me, and you can hang with me in the booth too."

Devi huffs as if blowing all her trepidations out onto the table and turns to the blatant DJ. "Well, cutie, I have already been to The Tenth Muse to listen to you spin, but my night was rudely interrupted by your judgmental—and might I add—oblivious, boss." Devi scowls, then stares at me. "Would you be okay with me visiting The Tenth Muse to watch this Sapphic Cream her pants?"

My face warms as I'm reminded Deviant Wallace can have anyone she wants. She's not mine.

Sapphic Cream leans over the table. "Say yes, boss. I'll work for free Friday. Hell, you won't have to pay me for the whole weekend. Please."

I'm flabbergasted at how unabashedly Sapphic Cream is pleading with me to allow Devi to be with her this weekend. Should I play Devi's silly game, pretend I don't give a crap about Sapphic Cream's infatuation with her? Or should I remind Devi she's permanently banned from my club and put a stop to this nonsense? It doesn't matter what I decide because I can't speak. No sound comes from my mouth. I think I'm having—what am I having? A heart attack?

"Are you okay?" Devi calls my name. "Joel? What's the matter?"

I stand and press my hand to my chest, trying to catch my breath, but I can't breathe. My heart is racing. Slightly embarrassed and a lot frightened, I run to the exit and stumble out onto the sidewalk, gasping for air.

Devi barges through the door behind me. "Joel. I'm sorry."

Leaning over I cough out the words, "Move, I'm going to throw up."

Devi ignores my warning and drops to her knees beside me. "I'm so sorry. I'm leaving Amboadia soon, but I'll leave right now if you want me to."

Under the Rainbow — D.A. Hartman

Once my heartbeat slows, I say, "I shouldn't have come here. Your friends don't want you to leave Amboadia, and I don't want to be the cause of everyone's sorrow."

I can tell Devi wants to say something, but her mouth is trembling, and she can't speak. So, I keep talking. "How about we have some rules, make it so you can remain here with your friends? Writerly is your place of employment. I won't come here or attend the Sunday group hikes anymore."

Devi wipes her runny nose. "And I won't enter Condo Building Three or The Tenth Muse? Is that your master plan?"

Sapphic Cream pushes through the door. "Are you two together?" She leans against the brick wall of Writerly and pouts to Devi. "I should have known a woman like you wouldn't date a DJ, not when you can have the owner of The Tenth Muse. But damn, you should have said something." She slams her body into the door and pushes her way back inside.

Devi lowers her head. "I'll apologize to your DJ in a minute, and I'm willing to give your plan a try." She buries her face in my neck and presses her body into mine. She fits perfectly in my arms as she whispers, "I'm going to miss getting stuck with you."

A familiar smell of apple shampoo has me feeling melancholy and I instinctively embrace her. I haven't hugged many people, but the warmth, the release of tension, her softness, and her chest tapping my heart with each intake of air is reminiscent to the green-haired woman I met over two years ago at Writerly. I squeeze her body closer to mine, and without fear, say, "I'm going to miss you so much. Perhaps, eventually, we can_"

Devi breaks away with a shove to my chest. "No, we need a clean break." The brittleness of her voice is a drastic indicator that a friendship between us can never happen.

She leaves me alone on the sidewalk and I stare through the window at her. My body becomes cold and I can feel myself breaking apart from her piece by piece. I'm alone again, only this time I don't want to be.

Under the Rainbow   D.A. Hartman

25 - Devi

After serving Nicole and Sapphic Cream lemonade, I apologize to Sapphic for using her the way I did.

Someone taps my shoulder and I turn to see Virginia standing next to me. Goth is on the other side of her.

I force out a weak smile to greet them. "Do you two want fresh lemonade? We have a little left.".

"No, but Goth and I have something to discuss with you." Virginia wiggles her finger, gesturing for me to follow them.

Hell, I'm probably getting fired. How else would this sucky day end? I follow them to a small table next to the bar.

Virginia kisses her wife on the lips. "Do you want to tell her? You're savvier about Devitron?"

Goth scratches her ear. "No, I'll join in if you need me."

So, this is about Devitron and not about me getting fired. More relaxed, I lean on the back of my chair. "What about Devitron?"

Virginia scoots closer to the table. "As you may have noticed when you were in the Sky Viewing Cave, it is spacious enough to live in."

I nod. "Oh yeah, and then some. The place is awesome!"

Virginia smiles at my excitement. "The Sky Viewing Cave has electricity and the crew installed plumbing for both a bathroom and a kitchen since you were last there. It won't take much to transform the place into a spacious studio apartment. To leave Double Ds vacant and unguarded is impractical, and who better to protect her homeland than the only Devitron in existence?"

"What are you suggesting?" I almost bristle in elation but manage to keep seated.

"We're offering you permanent residence at Amboadia. A forever home." Virginia gazes at her wife who is beaming with joy. "You are why Goth built Devitron and we both believe Double Ds is where you belong."

Goth smirks. "Devitron is your homeland and the rambunctious Detronians must have a guardian—especially Droopy, if we ever find the little stinker." She punches my upper arm. "So, what do you say? Are you ready to own a piece of Amboadia?"

My smile is wide and glued in place. If I talk, any words will become jumbled. Looking like the Cheshire Cat, I bob my head trying to convey a yes.

With Joel and me agreeing to keep clear of each other, there's no reason I can't stay in Amboadia, and after several seconds, I blurt out, "Um, hell yes. Who wouldn't want to live in the Rainbow Cavern?"

"Great." My bestie stands and rests her arm on my shoulder. "You'll receive a better filtration system to keep earth's toxic air from entering my external brain by the end of summer. I'm also going to create a magical walkway so you can roller-skate to the Double Ds entrance from Amboadia Boulevard."

"Create?" I ask. "Are your meds not working?"

She glances at Virginia. "Yes, they work, but I'm taking a low enough dose to allow my imagination to flow freely."

Virginia winks at her wife, then rubs her hands together. "We're trying to find a happy medium." She holds my hand. "You will need furniture, and the kitchen will take a few more days to complete, but you can move in at any time." She releases me and takes Goth's hand. "Let's go upstairs and get naked, honey."

As they stroll upstairs, Nedra and Christine enter Writerly and I quickly tell them the fantastic news about me being an Amboadia resident.

Still exhilarated about my new home, I can't seem to quit blabbering. "I don't have furniture or a bed to sleep in yet, but I'll hit some thrift stores after I get off work today."

Nedra raises sunglasses off her nose and pushes them onto her head. "I have a couch, reclining chair, coffee table, and enough chairs to put around a dining table. If you take them off my hands, I'll save on storage fees."

"I can't accept such lavish gifts, but thank you."

"Yes, you absolutely can," Nedra insists. "My reading room has become my office and I'm feeling cramped with all the extra furniture strewn about. You'd be doing me a favor to take it off my hands."

Christine stands. "Well, this queen will not be left out when it comes to giving Hot Stuff housewarming gifts. Get your tight behind over to our place and raid our kitchen, but you must promise to take the oversized toaster and every single plate, bowl, and cup with a cow on it. There are also cutleries under the stove. Javier won't let me use them. The handles are lavender. Don't ask dah-ling, but if I can't have lavender, he can't have cows." I make my way to the other side of the table and embrace Christine. She presses my head between her massive boobs. "Mamma don't mind having another child to worry about."

When I was a kid, I dreamed of owning a business. Modeling was my only means of obtaining one. With a mortgage-free home, my life has just opened up to a bunch of opportunities. I'll be able to save money and have plenty of time to take business classes. Granted, I didn't get the girl in the end, but I'm safe and wanted here at Amboadia with my friends.

26 - Joel

Nedra invited Nicole and me to her place for a game of dominoes. I'm shuffling bones when Nicole says, "Devi told me about your two's agreement. I love her, and you are not my favorite person, but I think you got the raw end of the deal."

"Yes, I miss having green tea with you at Writerly's," Nedra says.

"It's fine," I mumble.

Nicole scoops up eight bones. "I should find you a girlfriend, so Devi can stop drooling over your Dom ass." She yawns as she scoops dominos in front of her.

"Are you bored already?" Nedra frowns.

Nicole peeks at each of her dominoes. "Never bored with you, Nedra, but it drives me crazy when friends get the hots for each other, then become butt hurt when it doesn't work out. They're breaking the circle."

"Didn't Deviant apologize for flirting with Sapphic?" Nedra sits her eight dominoes on their sides for better viewing.

While organizing my bones, I mutter, "Are there no secrets around here? It's not like I'm jealous. Devi and I weren't girlfriends."

"You could have fooled me. The energy between you two is electric. Deadly electric, but still electric." Nicole scans the table. "Who has the double sixes?"

Nedra tosses the double six in the center of the table to start the game. "In small, close-knit communities, there are rarely many secrets."

"Well, then to set the story straight. Devi might have a crush on me, which I find baffling, but I'm not looking for a relationship." I glance at my bones, not one six in the bunch. "Pass."

Nicole slams down the six-three and collects fifteen points. "Devi's never acted like an idiot for anyone like she does with you. The sooner she gets over you, the better."

Nedra plays a six-two off of the sixes.

Being a virgin when I turn forty next week has me a little worried, not only because of the societal stigma, although I'll admit it's part of it. I'm also curious about what it would feel like to sleep with a woman. Perhaps I should travel to a place where nobody knows me and give sex with a woman a try. Nedra said sexual orientation can be fluid. What if it is for me?

"I'm thinking of taking a vacation to a far-off land," I say. "Or perhaps a cruise to Spain, or a week in New Zealand. Did you know the Spanish national anthem has no words?"

"Come to Punta del Este in Uruguay with me?" Nicole shoves a domino in the mix.

Curious, I ask, "What's in Uruguay?"

"Lesbian Paradise. Devi and I visit every year, but she doesn't want to go. Her flight and hotel room are paid for. You'll have your own room, and the best beach view in the whole joint if you decide to go."

Sunshine and walks along the ocean are exactly what I need. "Won't Devi be upset with you for inviting me?"

"Hmm, she might, but a sapphic vacation is something you shouldn't miss, and Uruguay is hella gay. Virginia helped Devi signed up for some online college courses. She's more interested in studying and making extra money than partying with dozens of women." Nicole lifts her palms in the air. "It's like, who is this girl? I barely know her anymore."

I'll analyze why I'm thrilled Devi isn't interested in going out with women later when I'm alone. I also make a mental note to ask Virginia what school and courses Devi is taking so I can help financially.

"When is this fabulous trip you're going on?" I ask Nicole.

"Day after tomorrow," she replies. "I get that it's short notice, but there'll be a lot of single and very horny lesbians staying in the same hotel with us. And what happens in faraway countries stays in faraway countries." She winks, then takes off for the bathroom.

After the restroom door clicks shut, Nedra asks, "Are you considering going with Nicole? Why would you want to continue this charade of being a lesbian?"

I lean in and whisper, "I tried to be with Devi when we were trapped in the garage last week."

"You were stuck in a garage?" Nedra laughs. "Goth is right. You two are destined to be together, whether you want to or not."

"We weren't stuck. The lights went out and Devi stayed with me. She was being her tender self. I wanted to give her something for her kindness."

"And you didn't think saying thank you was sufficient?"

Pinching my nose, I try to analyze the reason I became wet for Devi. Why did I shove her hand down my pants? Why do I want her? Still, no answers come.

"I wasn't of sound mind. You know I have severe nyctophobia. Fortunately, Devi gave me an out."

"Were you aroused? And what do you mean she gave you an out?"

I don't want to answer Nedra's first question because admitting how wet I was will entail a long conversation. "When she asked if I wanted her, I panicked."

Nedra tilts her head toward Nicole, who is returning from the restroom.

Nicole sits and gives us both an odd look. "What are you two talking about?"

"Devi, who else?" I reply. "Now, tell me more about Uruguay."

"Well, a bunch of us singles plan a trip every year. This vacation is one ginormous orgy waiting to happen, and trust me when I tell you, Uruguay women are sexy as all get out."

What a perfect opportunity to test the waters. I can have sex with a woman from another country. A woman I'll never see again. And if I don't enjoy the sex, I can quit without reprisal.

Perhaps in a different country, away from places and particulars that remind me of Candice, I'll want to pleasure myself again.

"I'm in! I'll go to Uruguay with you."

Nedra looks stunned, then slams down a domino. "Ten points!"

27 - Devi

Nicole is helping me move my things from her place to Devitron, but I'm so upset with her, I can't look her in the eyes.

"I can't believe you invited Joel to Uruguay. Shit Nicole." I throw my shoes into a black garbage bag. "You know how I feel about her and so you invite her to Sierra's orgy? Thank you very much, my friend."

"Calm down Devi. This is Joel we're talking about, the owner of the most elite nightclub in Los Angeles. She can have more action at The Tenth Muse in one night than she'll get all week in Uruguay."

"Don't give me that shit." I scoff. "The Tenth Muse is her business, not her playground. You're taking her to another country where she has absolutely no ties to people."

"Whatever, you both need to move on. I'm doing you a favor by helping Joel hook up with someone else. Anyway, I'm guessing her stuffy ass has to be wasted to have sex, and as you know, she doesn't drink anymore."

Nicole is wrong about Joel. Joel pushed my hand down her pants in the garage. After being a hermit for so long. Sierra's harem of women will be too much for her to resist. As incredible as Joel is, there's no way she'll stay celibate or single for long.

Nedra walks in and hands me her cell. "I lost the key. You'll have to take my spare phone to start the truck. Do you need help? I can come with you."

Nicole rubs the back of her neck. "You better come along. Devi's pissed off because I invited Joel to Uruguay. We'll need a mediator."

Nedra swats her hand in refusal. "I'm not getting in the midst of your spat. Jealousy involves intense emotions and I'm off the clock."

She's right, I am jealous. I should be grateful I have people in my life who love me. I should be ecstatic about moving into the most awesome place on the planet. I should be excited about starting online business management classes tomorrow.

We moved a lot when I was a kid. We stayed with Mom's many boyfriends and I never felt safe. When I was eight, I was tossed from one foster family to another. They weren't bad people, but they never loved me, they never fought to keep me. This is why the word family means little to me.

I wanted nothing more than to become an independent adult so I wouldn't have to live with people who didn't give two shits about me. "At your age, you're lucky we took you in," they'd say.

I wanted to make it on my own so badly I ran away several times. Even though my independence thus far has been a disaster, I'll never stop craving it.

Someday I'll own a thriving business and pay everyone back who has helped me along the way. Without my modeling career, it'll take a decade or two, but because of the fabulous gift Goth and Virginia gave me, what was once impossible and truly unattainable is now probable.

Joel will only ever love me in my dreams and it's time I focus on reality.

28 - Joel

It's a gorgeous day on the fabulous peninsula of Punta del Este in Uruguay. The view from my room is magnificent. The ocean is dark with ripples of white dancing under a bright blue sky. Nicole is in the next room. We have reservations for dinner at Floréal in an hour and I'm taking a shower before we go.

There's a knock. At least I think it's a knock. I turn off the water to hear better. Nothing, it must have been my imagination. I return to washing my hair and hear the bathroom door open. Through the foggy glass, I see a blurry figure and my heart stops. "Who is it?"

"It's me, Sierra. I brought your favorite coconut lotion. I'll wait for you on the bed."

The woman with the slight Latin accent is apparently a masseuse.

I hurry out of the shower and toss on a Grand Hotel robe.

A wide-eyed woman stares at me from the edge of the bed.

"Who are you?" she screams.

Alright, so she's not my masseuse.

"Shouldn't that be my question? This is my room."

The woman rattles off a bunch of Spanish phrases, none of which I understand—although I'm sure she's using expletives—then sprints out of the room and pounds on Nicole's door. By the time I get into the hallway, the crazy woman is yelling at Nicole.

"Where is Davy? Why is some strange woman in her room?"

Davy? Oh, she means Devi. Great, another admirer of Deviant Wallace I have to deal with.

Nicole grabs Sierra's hand. "Didn't she tell you? She's working overtime and can't get away."

Sierra glares at me and stomps her foot inches away from my left toe. "Davy is the only one I want."

Nicole attempts to explain who this woman is to me. "Sierra is why we have so much fun here. She organizes this affair."

"Splendid, but what does this have to do with me?" I ask.

The woman who broke into my room eyes me up and down, then she peers at Nicole. "I'll pay for this one, but only if Davy calls me. You have thirty seconds to get her on the phone."

Frustrated, I jump in her face. "Excuse me. You're not buying me. I'm not some gay-for-pay whore."

Nicole frantically taps her phone. "Devi, you need to talk to Sierra. She's losing her cool with Joel."

Sierra snatches the phone from her. "Davy, why are you not here instead of this rude bitch?" She listens for a while and says, "You promise?" There's a long pause then she says, "I can't wait to see you. Yes, okie dokie. I love you too."

I love you too? How many women is Devi in love with? I dart into my room, wishing I hadn't come here. There's a knock at the door and before I can answer it Sierra barges in.

"I forgot my bag." She slides past me and sits on the bed by her purse. With her spine erect and chin pointed out, Sierra says, "Davy told me to do with you what me and her do together. To do everything exactly the same way."

"Thank you, but I'm not interested in sex at the moment. I need to get dressed for dinner." Sierra is attractive in an athletic sort of way, but I'm not in the mood to try having sex with someone right now. Certainly not this unhinged person.

She raises a fist. "You are a stupid woman."

Sierra has long, wavy brown hair, dark skin, and dark eyes. My guess is she's in her mid-thirties. Wearing a sleeveless button-up shirt and shorts, she flaunts her lean muscular arms and legs.

I pull the tie to my robe tighter around my waist. "I don't know what you want, but I'm not interested."

"Look, silly woman, my father owns this hotel. I pay for Davy's room and discount the other rooms for the American women. In return, Davy and I spend the day together."

"Well, I'm not Devi. So, what do you want with me?"

"Nothing, I don't like you, but Davy insists I do with you exactly what I do with her and I love Davy." Sierra lowers her chin to her chest. "I cannot refuse Davy anything. I promise you many orgasms—an orgy if you want, but tonight you must go to sleep early. Promise me. We leave before the sun rises tomorrow."

I want to know what it's like to have sex with another human being, but if this woman thinks I'm getting up while it's still dark outside, she's out of her mind. "Why so early?" I double check to make sure I packed my flashlight.

"You'll see. Your steak and lobster will be here in"—she looks at her smartwatch— "three minutes. I'll send a bodyworker to you but you must finish in a hurry and get to sleep early. Okie dokie?" Sierra swings her purse over her shoulder and stands by the door, waiting for me to acknowledge our date tomorrow.

All I need is for a bunch of single women from LA who are most likely customers at The Tenth Muse to spread rumors about me being the cause of them not getting a discount on their hotel rooms in Uruguay.

I came here to let go of my inhibitions. To be with a *bodyworker*, as Sierra calls them, and experience what it's like to have sex with another human being. I'm glad it's not her I'll have sex with tonight. I've already been with one person who was obsessed with Devi and it ended in disaster.

I walk closer to the snooty woman by the door. "Tell me why so early in the morning?"

Sierra rubs her eyebrow. "To view the sunrise and to stroll the boardwalk before breakfast. What else?"

Viewing the sunrise will be nice. However, I'm not mentally prepared for whoever Sierra is sending to satisfy me tonight. Should I tell her I'm a virgin? No. It's none of her business. I'll discuss it with my bodyworker. Famished and craving the steak and lobster she says is on its way to my room, I agree with this princess's demands.

"Fine, Sierra. I'll go with you in the morning. Now, if you'll excuse me, I need to cancel my dinner date with Nicole."

29 - Devi

I meant to call Sierra earlier, but I forgot my phone when I left for work this morning. Hopefully, she'll keep Joel busy. I don't know why I'm worried Joel might meet someone in Uruguay. What difference will it make? She'll never want me. But, hanging out with Sierra might get her out of the funk she's in.

Enough ruminating about Joel. Virginia will be here any minute to support me during my first online class. She's an ace at business management and is teaching me the ins and outs of being a college student. I suck in my lower lip and power up a seven-year-old laptop crammed with too many files. The struggling device may take several minutes to load.

The sound of footsteps on sand builds as Virginia walks into my new digs at Devitron.

She removes her thin beige sweater and sits next to me on the leather sofa Nedra donated. "Are you excited about starting school?"

"Yeah, and a little nervous too." I place the tea I made for us on the coffee table.

"You seem out of sorts. What's on your mind other than school?" Virginia curls her hand around the glass of raspberry tea.

I'm out of conditioner and my hair is fuzzy, but we have fifteen minutes before class starts. It will settle down by then. This is a good time to ask Virginia about her friendship with Joel.

With an anxious cough, I say, "Goth said you and Joel were friends, but you had a falling out. Can I ask what happened?"

"Joel's doting and extremely wealthy parents sheltered her on such a high level, it was difficult to steal moments alone with her. The family bodyguards followed us everywhere. Joel said I was her first and only friend so I endured the people in black suits for her sake." Virginia wipes the side of her face, covering an adorable dimple.

"Wow, that's hardcore, and it explains a lot." I reply.

"Indeed, I don't know what her parents do, perhaps something political, but they feared Joel would get kidnapped and rarely let her out of their sight. I assume you're aware I suffered from a lengthy bout of depression two years ago."

I nod. "Nobody mentioned what was going on with you, but I guessed as much."

"Joel tried to reach out, but her many protectors nosing in my business affairs, while I battled demons in my head, was overwhelming. To keep the body guards away, I had to stop seeing Joel."

"I thought you quit hanging out with her because of Candice?"

Virginia takes a drink of her tea, then says, "Predominately, it was her security detail that detoured me, however, my disdain for your roommate wasn't a secret. Alright, turnabout is fair play. How did you meet Joel, I suppose it was through Candice?"

She deserves the truth and I'm going to give it to her. "Candice's birth name was Cain and Cain was a cis man."

Virginia scoots her empty glass of tea to the side. "So, this is how you met Joel. Your roommate Cain introduced you to her?"

"No, I met her the day before they met, but I was wearing sunglasses and a face mask. I also had green hair and wore a ton of gritty makeup. Till this day, she doesn't know it was me. I was a cosmoholic, going through a goth stage back then. I wish I had told her my name and given her my phone number before I left for Manhattan to work for Chase Janice. I'm such an idiot. I never thought Cain would have swooped in and taken Joel like the vulture he was. Sadly, my roommate got to the woman who still occupies my dreams first, and he did everything in his power to keep us apart."

Virginia stands up. "I don't like to speak ill of the dead, but what a little prick."

Not used to Virginia talking this way, I laugh and swipe at my unruly hair. "Yeah, my so-called friend was a conniving asshole."

Virginia pushes her glasses, the rims resting on plump cheeks, further up her nose. "You're pretty as always. This is only an orientation." She types in the university's URL.

I pat my hair down again to no avail.

"Wow, this thing crawls. Ah, here we go." The page finally loads for Virginia.

A man with a gray beard greets us on the video screen. "When I call your names, I want you to share a little about yourself and explain why you want to take my business class."

After he calls on several other students, he says, "Deviant Wallace?" The professor osculates his head, searching for any reaction from the video conference gallery.

I unmute myself. "Hi, I'm currently a barista and hope to own a business someday—maybe even a swanky coffee shop." I wink at Virginia, who smiles.

The professor rubs his fingers through his beard, thanks me, and moves on to the next student. When introductions are complete, he discusses the supplies and textbooks we must buy and how much they'll cost.

My heart races and I blow out a puff of air. "What the fuck? I can buy a new laptop for that amount."

Virginia quickly mutes the screen, but everyone is laughing on the monitor. She squeezes my wrist. "This semester and your textbooks have been paid for. Don't stress."

I shake my head. "No, you and Goth have already given me a home I hope to reimburse you for someday. This is way too much."

Virginia releases my arm. "It wasn't us. She clicks on the college's financial page. Because of your low income, your bill was picked up by some big charity giver in New York. See? Paid in full." She points to my zero balance.

I know damn well the so-called charity is Hudson Inc. This is most likely another one of Goth and Virginia's anonymous charities. I'm grateful, and once I own a business, I'll pay them back for everything.

After class, I hug Virginia goodbye and hurry to call Nicole to find out what's happening in Uruguay.

She picks up on the first ring. "Devi, I'm sorry. Now that it has happened, I feel bad."

"What's going on, Nicole?"

"Joel canceled our dinner plans and when I came back to my room after I ate, I saw a sweaty man in shorts come out of her room. I'm sorry, but she came here to get laid. It's not like I could stop her. I'm not a babysitter, Devi."

"Fuck!" I end the call with Nicole and collapse onto my bed.

Okay, okay, so Joel had sex with someone and she's obviously into men. Fucking men, not women. Not me. Dammit. She isn't into my dumbass. I turn on the music full blast and pull the covers over my head. "Fuck, I hate my life."

30 - Joel

Sierra is here before six a.m. and demands I wear a jacket. She opens her backpack, takes out a beanie, and hands it to me. "You will thank me later. Now, let's go." She points to my head, silently ordering me to put on my beanie and I obey. "Did you get your massage last night from the bodyworker?"

It's frightening how incredibly naïve I am. A bodyworker is a masseuse, not a sex worker.

"Yes," I say, "Bruno did a great job getting the kinks out. Thank you."

She nods and reaches out to me. "Devi holds my hand, but you don't have to."

"That's good because I prefer not to if you don't mind." Bruno's neck massage was more human contact than I can handle in a twelve-hour-span.

Sierra drops her hand. "No, I don't mind."

The moment we step outside, I'm thankful for the beanie she gave me. "Brr. It's cold." I turn on my flashlight.

"Oh no, that is too bright. You'll wake up everyone with that crazy thing."

"I'm sorry, I'll try to keep if lowered but I must use it."

"You are too much." Sierra hugs herself. "Uruguay's summer is December through March. The mornings are chilly in November, but it'll warm up later today."

We walk in silence along a sidewalk lit by solar lanterns, but it's not enough light to see who might be in the alleyways, so I keep my flashlight on. As we pass the last building on our way to the beach, a freezing gust hits us. My guide pushes against my back, encouraging me to hurry across the sand to a lifeguard tower.

"The beach on this side of the peninsula is windier, but this is where you see the sunrise." Sierra tilts her head toward several steps leading to the small hut. "It's warmer in there."

Inside are two chairs. She's correct. Without the frosty wind, it's more comfortable in here. She sits next to me and we listen to the ocean currents as we wait.

As the first rays of the sun show themselves, I wish Devi were here to share this extraordinary view with me. To curb my craving for someone I can't have, I murmur, "This is breathtaking."

"Yes, you have the same face Davy does when she sees it." Sierra smiles.

Curious about her and Devi's relationship, I encourage conversation. "How long have you known each other?"

"Five years. I send her a plane ticket every November. This is my favorite week of the year, but don't tell my wife."

Trying not to act shocked, I scratch the side of my neck. "Does your wife get jealous about you being with Devi?"

"Yes, I think, a little, but not any more than I am of her mistress."

So, Devi is Sierra's mistress. Why then does she want me if she already has a rich lover?

The woman from Uruguay faces me with pleading eyes. "How well do you know Davy?"

"Not well. She was a friend of my girlfriend's."

Sierra's eyes narrow. "Is your girlfriend as pretty as Davy?"

"No one is as pretty as Devi." Needing to deflect the conversation, I gesture toward the crest of the sun, which is now peeking over the water. "This is truly magnificent."

"It's nice, but I only come here for Davy. I hate the cold."

I'm taken aback by her frankness and although I think the sunrise is worth enduring the chilly morning for, I say, "We can go back to the hotel if you like."

"No, we have to do what Davy and I do. Exactly the same way. I promised her. When you see the full sun, we'll go for our walk." She sits with her elbows resting on her thighs and her chin in her palms—disappointment etched across her brows.

"Hey, if you want, I'll tell Devi we did everything she asked you to do and we can go our separate ways."

Sierra stares at me as if in wonderment. "Davy is the only person I can never lie to."

"You must love her dearly."

"It's not about love. It's because it's impossible for Devi to lie without her eyes flapping like the wings of an angry goose. To have such an advantage over her makes me feel bad if I don't tell the truth."

"Ah, yes. Her eyes twitch when she lies."

"I made her lie to me once to see how funny it looks." Sierra snorts.

The honking coming from her nose is hilarious and I can't help but laugh with her.

When the sun is in full view, Sierra takes me on a promenade along the beautiful *Rambla*. The boardwalk is, as she said, on the windy side of the peninsula. We pull down our beanies and stuff our hands in our coat pockets as the waves crash on rocks and the seagulls soar against the frigid air. About four miles in, we cross the middle of the peninsula and walk to a much calmer beach on the other side.

Sierra reaches for my hand and I let her take it. However, I'm not getting a sexy vibe from her. Her holding my hand appears to be a dominant trait of hers, but it's not uncomfortable.

"Over there." She points to a small restaurant. "We'll have breakfast."

Sitting at an outdoor table near a portable heater feels fabulous. The sandy beach of *Punta del Este* is stunning. I understand why Nicole and Devi come to Uruguay. After several miles of walking, I'm famished and scan the menu. They have a variety of pastries, and I'm dying for some hot coffee.

Sierra grabs the menu from me. "No, you will eat what Devi eats."

"Wait a minute. This is getting out of hand. I'll eat what I want. Thank you very much."

"So, you cheat on our deal? Okie dokie, but tell me what you want to order because Aleko doesn't speak English and will get it wrong."

Not sure whether to trust Sierra when our server comes, I point on the menu to an omelet and coffee. Sierra rattles something off in Spanish. Aleko nods and scurries off. I can't wait to get back to the Grand Hotel to take my shoes off. I didn't expect to walk so far this morning and these Lucchese Baron boots are new.

The server returns in record time with our breakfast. He puts a cake along with a gourd filled with what looks like hot water and tea leaves in front of me. Whatever it is, it's wrong. I tap on a metal straw sticking out of the gourd. "What is this?"

"*Bombilla*," says Aleko. Sierra jerks her chin, and he rushes off.

She smirks. "I told you he doesn't speak your language."

"Did you tell Aleko to bring me sugary cake topped with peaches and whatever the hell this is?" I point to the organic bowl with a *bombilla* sticking out of it.

"It's yerba-maté tea, and the sponge cake is *chaja*. It's Devi's favorite breakfast. Don't argue. We need to get back to the hotel soon," Sierra snaps.

Too tired to debate with her, I reluctantly eat and drink Devi's favorite breakfast. I prefer coffee to the yerba-maté and I rarely eat sweets, but the *chaja* is delicious. Devi is missing out on a fabulous vacation.

"Mm, they have excellent coffee here." Sierra sips from her cup and bites into her scone, getting jelly on her top lip.

She's fucking annoying.

The walk back to the hotel is brief and the moment we enter the room, Sierra orders me to take off my clothes and lie on the bed.

I suppose this is how the sex part of my *Davy's* day goes. A bossy Sierra will be the top no doubt. Good, because I have no idea what to do with her. A tinge of nervousness strikes, but this is the best chance I have to find out if I can be with a woman or not.

Wanting a drink, I ask, "Is there a minibar in this room?"

Sierra averts her eyes as I undress, which I appreciate. "Do you need alcohol to sleep with me?"

"No," I lie. "But will you be offended if I don't touch you?"

"Touch me?" Her thick eyebrows sink into each other. "Oh, you won't touch me. Alright, good." She sighs and dashes for the bathroom.

After taking off my clothes and hanging them over the back of a chair, I slide under the sheets. My body is nothing like Sierra's. I have wider shoulders and more sinewy arms, and my stomach isn't as flat. My tummy is what I hide most from others. Still, I roll on my back and wait for her to fuck me. I'm calmer now that she's agreed to a lack of reciprocation on my part.

The woman who loves Devi, but is settling for me, comes back into the room. She tosses her clothes onto the same chair mine are hanging from. Her dark skin and even darker eyes are beautiful, so why am I not excited about her getting under the covers with me? Why do I even care if I'm sapphic or not? I can never be with Devi, not without telling her who I am, and once I do that, she'll never want to see me again.

Sierra scoots onto the mattress. Our arms touch. Her skin isn't as soft as Devi's. It's easy to tell Sierra subjects her fit body to the elements. I should stop Sierra. Tell her I changed my mind. However, I would hate to go home without achieving my goal. Being the madam of a harem, Sierra must be an expert at giving orgasms. She's the best person for me to try having sex with.

Maybe if I close my eyes and just let it happen.

Sierra is tapping my arm.

I cross my arms over my bare tits. "I'm sorry. I don't know what to do."

"Roll over. This is what Davy does. You must do exactly the same." She points away from herself.

I turn onto my side. Getting fucked from behind is better. This way I don't have to think about gender. Her cool body presses against mine. Her tiny breasts and hard nipples push into my back, and her unshaven legs tickle me. This feels strange and I'm not getting aroused, but I'll give her a little more time.

She nudges her face into my neck. "You are not as feminine as my Davy. It takes a lot to pretend you are her."

I'll be goddamned if I'm going to apologize to this woman for not being *her Davy*. Sierra is doing the opposite of turning me on. There's no chance I'll get wet for her.

"You don't have to touch me if you don't want to either," I say, hoping Sierra will get the hint.

"We'll do everything Davy and I do. So please, be quiet and take your nap."

My nap? What nap? I'm too embarrassed to ask, and I'm also trying to suppress a laugh. Are we only taking a nap? Perhaps sex is an activity Devi prefers in the evenings.

If Devi were here with me instead of Sierra, we'd—well, we wouldn't be here together because we are keeping our distance. My preoccupation with her is why I came to Uruguay. If I could wave a magic wand and make these peculiar feelings vanish, I'd do it.

31 - Devi

I call Sierra. The phone rings over a dozen times. What are they doing that she can't answer her cell?

"*Hola.*"

"Sierra, it's me."

"Davy!" she says with excitement. "I miss you, and Joel is boring."

She must be outside, I can hear the wind blowing into the phone, but I need information and stat. "Who did you send to Joel last night?"

"Bruno, same bodyworker as I send you."

"You didn't send her a sex worker?"

"Not yet."

Instant relief puts a smile on my face. "Nicole said she saw a sweaty man in shorts leaving Joel's room."

"Yes, Bruno was in the gym when I sent him up. He had no time to shower first."

"Where is Joel now?" I ask.

"She's still asleep. I'm on the balcony."

"Ah, it's nap time. I forgot about the time change. The sun hasn't even risen here yet. Did you take her to view the sunrise?"

"Yes. She had a face like yours when she saw it." There's laughter in Sierra's voice.

"I'm glad you talked her into going. I'm shocked she agreed." I'm relieved Joel didn't have sex and is instead enjoying her time there in other ways.

"Your friend agreed because I promised to give her many orgasms if she'd hang out with me. She'll have an orgy tonight."

My heart drops back into my gut. So, Joel still wants sex. A reverse harem no less. I can't go through another night like last night, I just can't. "No, um, no Sierra. Please don't hook her up with anyone."

Sierra is quiet. We both are for a few minutes. Then she says, "Why am I keeping Joel Hunt busy for you? Do you love this woman?"

"No." My eyes are fluttering so ferociously; I'm worried Sierra can hear them flapping through the phone. "Yes. I love her."

"Oh, Davy. You crazy woman. This Joel person is strange. She carries a big flashlight with her. She's too much trouble. She's not even nice."

Hearing Sierra say this makes me want to defend Joel, although, to do so would be a waste of breath. The truth is, she is strange. She's also a pain in my ass. Still, I can't take back what I just said.

Finally, Sierra says, "No sex for Joel—I promise."

Gratitude flows out of me and I laugh out loud. "You never offered me an orgy when I was there."

"You never asked for an orgasm like Joel has." She giggles. She doesn't understand how hurtful the idea of Joel wanting to have sex with somebody else is to me.

My visits to Uruguay are about spending time with Sierra. I don't normally allow women to pay my way, but I like Sierra and look forward to seeing her once a year. The other women from Los Angeles are intent on hooking up, but staying up all night drinking and having sex isn't conducive to watching magnificent sunrises over the ocean and walking several miles along the beach in the early mornings with Sierra.

"Davy?"

"Sorry, my mind went adrift. I hate to ask, but did Joel want a harem of women or men or both?"

"She didn't say. I don't think she likes men or women. She's very stiff, this icy woman you love."

If only that were true. Joel wants sex or she wouldn't have seduced me in the garage. "Okay, my friend. Thank you."

I'm grateful Sierra will make sure Joel doesn't get her wish. I'm interfering with Joel's social life. It's wrong, yet I cannot stand the idea of someone else touching her. Tonight, the brilliant constellation manufactured by Goth is Lupus, the wolf. Virginia visited Madagascar, a beautiful island off East Africa. She fell in love with the wolves she saw there and named this community of ours after them. Amboadia means wolf. I bet this is a tidbit of knowledge Joel isn't aware of.

    As I lie in bed, I reminisce about working long hours for Chase Janice in New York. Who knew modeling could be so draining, but wearing sexy clothes was fun. I was in New York for weeks but visited The Tenth Muse the very night I returned to California. My temporary green hair had washed out several shampoos before, and it was apparent when I spotted Joel and we made eye contact, she didn't recognize me in my pitch-black hair. Not that she would. I was minus a face mask, sunglasses, and green hair. By the time I maneuvered through the crowd, Cain reached her first. He ignored me and dragged her off to the DJ's booth.

    Oh, how I wanted to punch the little turd for kissing the woman I've been dreaming about. They clearly knew each other. Both were oblivious to my presence. All the joy and hope of connecting with Joel again died a fleeting death. Cain was dressed in glamorous drag and Joel, who did stare at me before being pulled away, was in a tailored leather suit and sexy combat boots. She was so hot with her mohawk.

    When Cain announced to the crowd that *her* name was Candice and Joel was her Dom lesbian girlfriend, stomach acid made its way into my throat. Then Joel whipped the new and fabulous Candice with a flogger and dragged my ex-roommate to her office. They locked the door, refusing to let me in, leaving me to wander the club by myself. A stinking slap to the face would have felt better. I imagined they were fucking in her office. Seemed crude then—seems even more disgusting now.

    I miss the bookworm who invited me to sit in her SUV to freshen up. Little did I know the closing of her office door on the evening of the Diva Bi Night performance was the very moment our lives unraveled. Joel would get to know me as her girlfriend's slutty drug-pushing buddy and Candice continued to blind us both with a clusterfuck of misinformation.

~~~~~

 The phone buzzes. It's a text from Kayla, Nicole's sister. She's looking for volunteers to come to a town called Tehachapi for two months to help her start an in-house LGBT center there and wonders if Nicole or I would be interested. The timing is perfect. The only way I can get over Joel is to leave for a while. I can study from anywhere, but if I agree, I'll need to find someone to work at Writerly while I'm gone.

32 - Joel

I'm barely awake when Sierra grabs my clothes off of the chair and tosses them at me. "Let's go."

I must have fallen asleep and I'm grumpy when I wake. "Where were you?"

"On the phone on the balcony. I didn't want to wake you. We have to hurry if you want to eat lunch. Siesta is in twenty minutes."

"I thought we just had a siesta," I tease.

"If you aren't hungry, we can go to Point of Four Seas. It's located on the thinnest part of the peninsula. There's a street with a four-way intersection. If you stand in the center, you can see the sea at the end of all four streets."

Sierra sure is acting strange, almost as if she wants to hang out with me. Everything shuts down from one p.m. to three p.m. in Uruguay and a walk sounds nice.

"Wherever you want to go is fine with me," I say with an unfamiliar excitement.

After a lovely day of sun and fun and lots of food for dinner this evening, we end up back at the hotel.

"Shit, I'm late," she says, standing at the door. "I promised to meet my father at ten tonight."

"I don't understand. Are we going to have sex? Or are you sending someone else to my room tonight?"

She crosses her arms in front of her chest. "No."

"If you don't want to have sex with me, it's fine. I don't think I'm into women, anyway, but you promised me an orgasm tonight." My face warms. Crap, I sound like a horny woman desperate to get laid. Which, in the realm of things, is no longer at the top of my list of things to do. I had a fantastic day. This trip is already much more than I hoped it would be.

"Are you in need to come?" Sierra asks with a frankness that is disconcerting.

"Well, look, you certainly don't owe me sex. I'd decline if you offered, but I'm a little hurt that you had sex with Devi, but won't even set me up with someone." Can I sound any more pathetic?

Sierra gives me a confused look. "I never had sex with Davy. Who told you this lie?"

"I'm sorry." Crap, here I go assuming again.

"Everyone knows I'm ace and my wife is poly. She spends the weekdays with her mistresses and the nights and weekends with me."

"You're ace?"

"Yes, and I'm late, I have to go." Sierra sweeps a strand of long brown hair from her face and gives a loud sigh "I was going to bring men and women to you tonight, but it would hurt Davy if I do this, so I cannot."

Sierra thinks my sleeping with someone will hurt Devi. Was it Devi she spoke on the phone with on the balcony earlier? I bet it was. I can't prevent a smile from forming on my face, and Sierra notices.

"You'll have to self-pleasure if you get aroused." She grins.

Sierra shared intimate details with me. I want to be honest with her as well. "I haven't been able to masturbate for almost two years. I was hoping someone here could snap my libido back into place."

"I don't understand your desire for sex. If you don't feel like it, you don't feel like it. So what?" Sierra tosses her hands into the air.

Before I can answer her question, she puts up her hand to stop me. "Okie dokie." She walks to the nightstand. Picks up a pen and writes something on a notepad. "Thank you for sharing the day with me." Sierra kisses me on the forehead, swings her Gucci purse behind her shoulders, and flees the room.

The number Sierra left is probably an escort service. If I don't call them, I'll probably never be brave enough to hook up with someone again. Stripping naked, I climb into bed and grab the note off the nightstand. It's a number with Devi's name above it. Sierra is leaving it up to her to decide if I have sex with someone or not. What utter bull. Asking Devi to approve a hookup for me is out of the question, but it would be nice to hear her voice.

I punch Devi's number into my phone and nibble at my fingernails as I wait. One ring, two rings, three, four, five, six...

"Hello." Devi's voice is raspy.

Then it hits me. It's two a.m. in Los Angeles.

"Who is this?"

"Sorry, I forgot how late it is there," I whisper.

"It's okay. What's on your mind?"

Great question. Why did I call her? I have to say something. "Um, I'm alone tonight thanks to you." Oh, my fucking gods. Why did I say that?

There's a long pause, then Devi says, "Sorry, I'm a jealous asshole."

Devi being jealous shouldn't make me feel this good.

"I'll call Sierra and ask her to send you several ugly-ass men if you want?" she says.

I would snort aloud at her green monster if I weren't so saddened by the pain I hear in her voice. Getting laid tonight was supposed to be the portal to me becoming well, a breakthrough, the end of my sexual hang-ups.

"Joel?"

"Yes."

"I miss you."

It's easy for Devi to share her emotions. She's fearless. What would happen if I were as brave? What if I tell her how much I wish she was here enjoying this amazing vacation with me? What if I tell her how much she's on my mind?

"Joel? Are you okay?"

With my voice cracking, I prepare myself for the proverbial hammer of doom to come crashing down on my head. "I miss you too."

I can hear Devi make what sounds like a sigh of relief. "Did you enjoy your time with Sierra?"

"It was fantastic. I loved everything about our day. The same can't be said for Sierra." I giggle. Crap, I giggled. What has come over me?

Devi laughs. "She hates getting up early, and the cold. Even the strolls along the beach are not her thing—too touristy. She's sweet to do those things."

"Love makes people do stuff they otherwise wouldn't do." Ugh, I need to keep my mouth shut.

Devi clears her throat. "Love is making me do things I otherwise wouldn't do, too."

"What do you mean?"

"I don't find anyone sexually attractive anymore. I mean, other than you." She pauses, then says, "Which is a problem since you can't stand me."

My breath catches at her confession. Once I gather my thoughts, I say, "I'm not sure what love is, but I'm getting better at creating friendships and I am fond of you."

Devi doesn't respond, so I continue. "We seem to communicate better over the phone. We can't see each other, or touch each other. We don't have physical distractions. Do you mind if we chat for a while?" Apprehension settles in my gut and I need to end the call. "Never mind. I'm sorry."

"It's okay, Joel. I want to talk to you."

Oddly, there's nothing I want more than to hear her snuggly voice. "It would be great to get to know you better, Devi. What are your dreams? What do you need or wish for? What style of clothes do you like? If you had a vehicle, what model would it be? Are you interested in going to a university or—"

"I'll never forgive Candice for what she did to you. You can't love me because of her. I don't expect you to ever feel the same way about me as I do you." She lets out a long breath. "I wouldn't be going to Tehachapi if I had delusions of you ever wanting to be with me, Joel."

Tehachapi! Isn't Devi living at Amboadia? Where in the fuck is Tehachapi? My adrenaline pumps through every vein in my body at the thought of her leaving. I should offer to pay her to be my companion again. Sweeten the pot. Hell, what am I thinking? She can have any woman she wants, and she knows I'm incapable of loving anyone. She'll never agree. Crap. *Think, Joel, think.*

"Thing is," Devi continues. "You may not be sexually attracted to women or people in general, and the aro rumors about you might be legit. But I think you have sexual feelings for me."

I can't lie to her. I stuck her hand down my pants in the garage for fuck's sake. "I uh, I wish you were here. Uruguay is lovely."

Devi sobs, "Me too. Missing you sucks."

Although I can't see them, I know Devi's eyes aren't twitching. I want to tell her I'm hurting too, but I can't lead her on. We have no future, not even as friends.

After a period of silence, Devi stuns me with a change of topic. "I still think about your finger inside me. Your touch was the only thought I needed to arouse me, but fantasizing about you is too painful now. I can't even masturbate. We're two pitiful peas in a pod. We're too mentally fucked up to have orgasms." She lets out a laugh and blows a sigh through the phone.

Someone finally falls in love with me and it's Devi of all people. The last person on earth who would love me if she knew I was the one who had her fired from Chase Janice.

Needing to push her away, I growl, "That wasn't the real me who fingered you. I was high. I can't fathom doing such a thing."

In a desperate tone, Devi says, "I've racked my brain trying to figure out a way to get you to want me. My past is off-putting to you, and I'm a woman, but I'm not ashamed of who I am."

Listening to Devi blame herself is disheartening. "I'm not ashamed of you either. It's not about your gender or who you are. It's me. I have so many issues."

Devi sniffles. "I should have fucked you in the garage—endured the heartache I knew would follow. You were so wet and hungry. I could have satisfied your thirst, and maybe, if I were the luckiest woman alive, I could have sucked your clit into my mouth." Her voice deepens. "How soon would you have come if I brushed my tongue over your sweet bud and shoved my fingers inside you? How loud would you have moaned when I made you climax? I already know your smell, but I dream of tasting you. Whatever you want, I will do, Joel. Let me please you."

If I had any sense, I'd hang up on Devi right now. However, my clit is throbbing. I press it with my fingers to soothe the pain. I'm swollen and in need. Unbelievable! I'm aroused! Devi's words piqued my hunger!

Her voice turns smooth and sensual. "Spread your legs. Please open your legs, Joel. Touch yourself. Are you wet, Joel? Do you want me to make you come?"

I spread my legs and dip my finger into my soaked entrance. I can't believe the heat Devi is creating inside me. Fuck yes, I want to come. Rubbing my slippery warmth to the beat of her voice, I wait quietly for her next request.

33 - Devi

I can hear Joel breathing heavily into the phone. Talk of my yearning for her has Joel aroused. She's not capable of loving me, but her moan proves I can excite her. Phone sex isn't something I've done before, but the sound of Joel's desire has me turned on.

"If I was with you, Joel, I'd place my mouth over each of your hard nipples, licking and sucking them until they turn red and tender. Mm, I want to stick my tongue inside you, taste you, fuck you. Do you want me to... Joel?"

"Yes."

Is she answering me calling her name, or saying yes to me virtually sticking my tongue inside her?

She moans and I can hear her panting. We're really doing this. I pull off my blankets and easily stick a finger inside my soaked slit and moan.

"I bet you're wet, and your gorgeous clit is aching for more, isn't it? Damn, you're so fucking hot, Joel. You are in control. Tell me what you want. Do you want to pinch your nipples hard while you fuck yourself?"

There's a sloshing sound on the other end of the phone. Can she be that wet? I want her to come for me, so I up my game. "Spread your legs wider, gorgeous. I'm going to stick a finger inside you. I want to feel inside of you. I want to go deep—make you come. Mm, yes, Joel, ride my hand. That's it, take another finger. Take them all."

Joel mumbles something. It's too jumbled to understand, and I continue to work her with my words.

"All I care about is you, Joel. Your pleasure. I want to make you come so fucking hard your toes curl. Pick up the pace, baby. Pound that perfect opening of yours."

My breathing is erratic, and I whimper as I circle my entrance, desperately waiting for Joel to have an orgasm so I can get some release as well. I'm too close to the edge and have to move my hand out from between my legs. "Oh, Joel." I moan and thrust my hips. "You're making me so hot. I want to come for you."

Joel must be penetrating herself because she speaks in staccato. "Oh. Yes. So. Good."

The sound of her pleasuring herself has me wanting to come, even though I'm not touching myself. I groan uncontrollably. "Uh, I'm going to—"

Joel grunts with enough force, my phone crackles, sending a glorious surge of elation throughout my body. "Oh Joel, I'm going to come."

"Yes, come for me, Devi," she murmurs.

At her encouragement, I press down on my clit and experience an orgasm intense enough to shake my entire body with release. My screams for Joel are loud, as are her cries of ecstasy.

"Devi, oh yes, that's it. Mm."

Holy fuck, we're coming together.

With my palm pressed between my legs, I whimper with each extra ping of pleasure until my brain becomes blissful mush.

I hold the phone to my ear as I recover. Thump, thump, thump, thump. Joel's cell must be laying on her chest.

The phone becomes silent. Joel may have fallen asleep. Unable to end the call, I adjust my pillows, one under my head, and the other between my legs. With my phone tucked near my ear, I wait, and wait some more. Will tonight be the forming of something new and special, or will she freak out and ghost me? I'm not superstitious, a believer in gods, superheroes, or magic, but I cross my fingers and ask all these higher powers to show mercy.

"Devi?"

"Yes, Joel?"

Joel sniffles and before I can ask what the problem is, she says, "Thank you."

34 - Joel

Someone is screaming, "Why are you asleep? They'll be here any minute."

"Huh? Who are you talking about?" I wipe my eyes with the back of my hands.

Sierra stands next to my bed, fully dressed in a bumble bee jacket and pink beanie. I pull the covers over my exposed breasts. "How long have you been staring at me? For fuck's sake, you need to stop coming into my room without invitation." Rolling to one side, I search for my phone on the nightstand but can't find the damn thing. "What time is it?"

Sierra plops her hands onto her hips. "It's 8:30. I have a special surprise for you." She grabs my blanket and yanks it off me.

Not being the exhibitionist Devi is, I roll over concealing my breasts. "Get out of here, Sierra."

She slaps my bare ass. "You're going to miss your plane if we don't get going with this."

What I'd rather do is stay in bed and daydream about the magnificent sex I had last night. I don't know what Sierra's hurry is. My flight isn't until this afternoon. "Will you please turn around?"

There's a knock on the door. Sierra's purse swings across her back as she rushes to answer it.

I scamper through the room, gathering whatever clothes I can, and put them on as Sierra, three men, and four women watch. Sierra stands in front of me and wipes a tear from her cheek.

"Why are you crying? Is my body so ugly, or are you going to miss me?" I say lightheartedly.

She huffs as if exhausted by my stupidity. "I don't like you enough to miss you. But Davy must love you too much. She wants you happy. She wants you to understand your sexuality, even if it hurts her." Sierra turns to the crowd closing in on us. "Select one, or as many as you want."

Bewildered, I stare at seven strangers of different shapes, sizes, and genders, then back to Sierra. "What's going on?"

"No need to hang out with boring little me this morning. You're free to have gross sex instead."

Sierra's yanking on whatever compassionate strings she thinks I might possess. Well, today is her lucky day. I had the best sex of my life last night and it's put me in the greatest of moods. I don't need any of these people. I find my phone under the covers, put on a windbreaker, and walk past the small group to the exit.

At the door, I wink at Sierra. "Let's have breakfast together. I'm starved."

A big smile forms on her face. "Hmm, this is why Davy loves you. I understand now."

At the cafe, Sierra expresses her desire for us to be friends. "Next time you come, I must take you and Devi to Buenos Aires on the family yacht. We can go shopping. We'll do what you want next time."

Devi could have quite a luxurious life if she wanted to be with any of the wealthy women who salivate over her, but she's stubbornly independent, and I find this trait extremely attractive. The woman is magical.

This morning, I feel like a new woman, not just because I have my libido back, but because I allowed someone to crash through my protective barrier. It's as if we have a unique attachment. Volatile as our relationship once was, a connection between us always existed. Still does. Only now, we're evolving into a more profound duo.

Unlike the rest of the women who are going back to Los Angeles, I'll fly to Manhattan tomorrow to celebrate my fortieth birthday with my parents.

Sierra jabs my arm and gestures toward a limo. "My chauffeur is prepared to take you, Nicole, and the others to the airport. Finish your mate." She hugs her purse to her chest. "Our weekend is over and the Grand Hotel doesn't run itself." She wipes her eyes.

"Thank you for everything, Sierra. It's been fun."

"Yes, it was fun, even though neither one of us got to be with Davy. So, what kind of person do you want for yourself? Someone like me, who you never have to touch?"

"You would be perfect, and you have a yacht," I tease.

She kisses my cheek. "Don't be silly. We're both too bossy."

35 - Devi

We're evacuating Writerly after a leak from a sink behind the bar caused an electrical shortage. Virginia wants Writerly rewired, and the plumbing updated. The coffee shop is out of commission, which means I'm out of work for some time.

Nicole taps my arm. "You look like shit. Let's go to my place for a beer."

Sierra told me Joel declined to have sex with any of the people she brought to her room, but I haven't heard from Joel since our night on the phone.

Once inside Nicole's condo, we plop down on her sofa and I vent my frustrations. "I left her a text, and she's fucking ghosting me. Why didn't she come home with the rest of you?"

Not needing me to tell her who I'm talking about, Nicole says, "I don't know, but hey, Kayla asked if I could go to Tehachapi to educate the community on queer issues and fundraise for an in-house LGBT-plus center. I'm too busy and declined, but she said you agreed."

"Yep, I did. It's only for two months. Spending time in the mountains with plenty of fresh air and places to hike sounds fun, and I need to get away for a while."

Nicole leans back and presses her fingertips to her temple. "Tehachapi is in Kern County, the bible-belt of California. People who are different from mainstream Americans aren't welcome there."

"Times have changed."

Nicole huffs. "Times haven't changed enough, or we wouldn't still need safe spots and centers to protect our community from the haters."

"Nicole, I'll be fine. Now can you please ask your sister how soon she needs me to volunteer?"

She sighs. "Alright, I'll text Kayla."

While Nicole is chatting with her sister, I call Virginia to inform her about my leaving for a while. She expects Writerly will be closed for two or three months during the remodel. She'll keep me updated.

Nicole peers up from her device. "Okay, you're set. You leave on Tuesday. My sister is putting linen on the Murphy bed in her guest bedroom as we speak."

I'll use the next few days to celebrate my new digs at Double Ds before I take off for Tehachapi. It's still hard to believe I own a home. Chase Janice tossed me out for no reason, but screw them, I have a fantastic Rainbow Cavern to live in. My new home is better than any house I could have imagined. A large part of my dream has come true, so why aren't I happy? Why, because Joel is ghosting my ass.

At the Amboadia Store, I feel the weight of shopping baskets pull at my arms as I fill them with food and drink.

"Wow, Devi. Are you throwing a going away party?" Goth eyes my bottles of booze and mojito mix then grabs one of my baskets and skips down the food aisle.

"If I were having a party, I'd invite you." I run to catch up with Goth.

"No, Dotty, not now." Goth slaps her head to jostle her inner voices. "How long will you be gone, Devi? A month, two, three? Why do you have to leave your homeland? Droopy is still missing and the other brainbugs need caring for." My best buddy is manic and might need to up her meds.

"I'll only be away for a month or two. You and Virginia have gone on vacations for almost as long. Plus, it's for a good cause."

"Hey, I don't get involved in other people's problems, but if you ever want to talk about things, I'm here." Goth's turquoise eyes sparkle with the making of tears.

I squeeze her in a strong embrace. "I'm in love with someone who doesn't love me back. I need to get out of Amboadia for a little while. It's not forever."

197

"We're your family, and Devitron is your home. Go for as long as you need, but promise me you'll return to us when you're ready."

I take in a deep breath. "I promise and I'm grateful to you for building a place I can always come back to."

Goth sets my basket on the counter. As the cashier takes each item and scans it, Goth reaches for her wallet. "Let me get this as a going away present."

"I'm not moving away, dork." I take money from the pocket of my shorts and pay for the groceries.

Goth offers to carry the baskets to Double Ds. "I'll drop these off at the entrance for you. Virginia is cooking dinner, or I'd stay."

"You're fortunate to have a woman who loves you."

Goth pokes me in the arm. "Remember how long it took my wife to realize she loves me? An eternity, but she was worth the wait. Give Joel time."

"Virginia is sapphic. I have to respect Joel's choices. She's not sexually attracted to women or any gender. As a lesbian, I understand what it feels like when people refuse to accept me for who I am. Hell, why do you think she's ghosting me?" I answer my own question. "Because I pushed her too far. I'm such an asshole."

My buddy sets the groceries inside the Detronian entrance door. "You're not an asshole. And hey, if I don't see you before you leave, remember I love you. We both do." Goth gives me a quick hug and I ruffle her hair before she jogs off toward Amboadia-East.

I put the food away, open a bottle of rum, and dance to King Princess's *"Let Us Die"* playing on my phone—only a few days before I hit the road. I can do this.

36 - Joel

Back at Amboadia, Virginia reminds me Deviant Wallace is going to Tehachapi to work with the LGBT community there. I need to thank her for helping me with my sexual issues before she leaves. Letting go of the hatred I had for her is a tremendous weight off my shoulders. Still, I'm riddled with guilt for ruining her career. While Devi's gone, she'll most likely fall for someone else. Hence, I'll wait until she returns before telling her the truth about me so it won't hurt her as much.

I give a light knock on the glass entrance of Double Ds, but Devi is nowhere in sight. Next to the door is an intercom. I push the button. "Devi? It's me." I wait a while, then try again. "I want to say goodbye. Please let me in, Devi." Still no response.

I call Goth. "Has Devi already left Amboadia?"

"No, she doesn't leave for two more days. I'm going to miss her, Joel."

"Can come let me inside Double Ds? Devi isn't answering the intercom and I need to see her before she leaves."

Goth's voice sounds muffled. "She bought a buttload of liquor yesterday, and she isn't much of a drinker. Punch my mum's name in at the door and let me know if my buddy was abducted. The alien lesbian snatchers are on the hunt again."

I can't help but inform Goth of the inaccuracy of her statement. "Did you know the word buttload was a unit of measurement for wine in medieval times? A buttload of wine was about 126 gallons. I doubt Devi purchased such a vast amount."

"Yeah, well, we live in the twenty-first century, and I'm going to kick you a buttload of times if you don't go check on my buddy." Goth laughs.

"Right, right. I'll text you after I check on her."

After typing *Stephanie* at the entrance, the glass doors slide open, and I walk to Devitron. Inside is a newly constructed ramp leading down into the bright Rainbow Cavern. In awe, I pause for several seconds to take in the incredible sight, then proceed through the tunnel.

The Sky Viewing Cave has been converted into a small apartment with state-of-the-art appliances, fixtures, and eclectic furniture. Under the stargazing ceiling is a queen bed. Devi's lean body is sprawled naked on the mattress. Her tiny ass is sticking in the air and her hair is a shaggy mess. Two small bottles of rum and an uneaten sandwich sit on the floor below her head.

The white sand lightly crunches with every step I make until I enter a sliding glass door to her new place, but Devi doesn't move. I pick up the liters and dried sandwich and toss them into the trash before texting Goth.

Joel Hunt: 5:47 p.m. *She's knocked out. One liter is full. The other is over half depleted but she'll live.*

GOTH: 5:47 p.m. *Please take care of my buddy, Joel.*

Joel Hunt: 5:48 p.m. *Will do.*

I brew coffee, clean Devi's grotto, and search her refrigerator to gather ingredients to make soup.

An hour passes when I hear Devi stir. She rolls on her back and her small firm breasts jiggle with the movement. Her neatly trimmed mons arches as she stretches and dizzily glances up at the Night Sky.

She spots me staring at her and pulls a blanket over herself. "Joel?"

I let out a little laugh. "Are you hungry?" I pour a mug of water and walk over to her.

Devi's head is bobbing with drunkenness. "Only for you," she says as her head drops back onto a pillow.

A sense of humor is a good sign. She'll be alright if I can get some food inside her. I perch on the foot of the bed and poke her leg.

She props the pillow up and smiles. "Hi, Joel."

"How are you feeling?" I ask.

Her voice is hoarse. "Okay." She licks her pale lips and combs fingers through her shoulder-length black hair.

I put the cup to her mouth, and she places her hand over mine, eagerly slurping down half the contents.

"I made some chicken soup. Want some?"

She pushes her face into the pillow and mumbles. "I don't want you to see me like this."

"I don't blame you. You're a mess, and you stink." I pinch the bottom of my nose.

She wraps the sheet around her and tries to get up but falls back onto the bed. "I need a bath."

I lift Devi into the sitting position. "I'll help you bathe if you promise to eat some soup when you're done. Agreed?"

"Okay," she burps.

"Oh, ick." I swat her nasty breath away.

After drawing the bath water, I return to the bed and pull her into my arms.

Devi giggles. "Mm, you're so strong. How sexy." She squeezes my biceps as I aid her to the bathroom and sit her on the edge of the tub. Having her in my arms is phenomenal. She reeks and her hair is sticking up everywhere, but I think of her words when she made me come over the phone and I don't want to loosen my grip on her. What I feel for her is genuine, and I'll miss her. The pain I'll endure from her absence, serves me right. It's time to pay the piper.

Devi twists out of my arms and dips one of her feet into the water, then immerses herself in its warmth. "Oh yeah, this is fucking euphoric."

She splashes water on her face and clears her throat. "Uh oh. I got dizzy."

What a featherweight. I kneel next to the tub to make sure Devi doesn't fall under. Her eyes are hidden by tresses the color of midnight. She looks rather disheveled.

Noticing pink toilet paper by the commode, I ask, "Did your toilet paper come from France?"

Devi furrows her brow. "No, why?"

"Toilet paper in France is almost always pink, and not a pretty pink either."

"Oh, no, the ass-wipe isn't from France. I accidentally dropped a bag of them in the pond. They're finally drying." She laughs.

I can't help but chuckle. Only Goth would come up with a pink pond, and only Devi would clumsily drop toilet paper into said pond.

"Do you need help washing your hair?" I ask.

Devi tilts her head. "No, you'll just make my clit hard."

Her bold sex talk normally irritates me. Not today. To hide my smile, I kiss the top of her head. "I'll change your bedding and gather you some clothes. Try not to drown while I'm gone."

Devi waves me off. "My skirts and blouses are to the left of the closet, but any dress will work."

37 - Devi

Instead of returning with the dress, Joel places pajamas and fuzzy slippers on the bathroom counter. She helps me out of the bathtub and wipes me down with a towel. As much as my head hurts, my nipples harden when she touches me. I cover my breasts with my arms and say, "I can handle it from here."

When she leaves the room, I slip on my PJ bottoms and button the cotton shirt before scrambling for the bed.

"Oh, no you don't. Get over here. You said you'd have some broth." Joel beckons me over to the table.

The food smells delicious. She must have used the chicken and carrots I had in the fridge. As promised, I sit at the table.

Joel scoops hot soup from a pot and sets a bowl with cute cows on it and a lavender spoon in front of me.

"Why did you drink so much last night?" she asks.

I take a sip of the broth and moan as it warms my tummy. After a few more swallows, I answer Joel's question. "I was trying to stop loving you."

Joel sighs. "You don't know me. You can't possibly love me."

Putting down my spoon, I stare at Joel so intensely, she averts her eyes. "I know you're inquisitive and recite bits of trivia when you're emotional. I know you used to wear eclectic clothes and drive an SUV. You didn't care what people thought of your mismatched attire. I know you love to read books. You like many of the same things I do, such as watching the sunrise and walking along the beach. You're an only child and your parents are strict, but you love them anyway. I know my asshole of a friend betrayed you. I also know you're amazing at phone sex and you're compassionate. Ask me any questions about yourself. I'll know the answers."

Joel rests her chin on the back of her hand. "Is what you feel for me a simple crush that will dissolve soon? Please explain it to me?"

"It's not infatuation or a crush, I'm in love with you."

"Don't hide your batting eyelashes," Joel says with a laugh.

I drop the spoon, and it hits the side of the bowl with a clank. "I'm not kidding. Don't you know the influence you have on me? I would do anything for you. Shit, I as much as killed Candice because of you."

Joel stares at me in astonishment. "What are you talking about?"

I lean back. "I didn't *kill her*, kill her. It's just that Candice couldn't deal with how I felt about you."

Joel shakes her head. "I don't understand how you could have had feelings for me. Are you a masochist or what the hell is wrong with you? There's no way you should have even liked me. We never spoke, and I hated you when I was with Candice."

"It wasn't the *you* who was with Candice I was fond of. It wasn't the fake lesbian Dom persona you two cooked up I dreamt about. It's the *you* before you met Candice I yearn to be with."

Joel rubs her eyes. "Candice introduced us. We didn't know each other before I met Candice."

Should I tell Joel how we met? Why not? If she tarnishes my precious memory by telling me our hug inside Writerly meant nothing to her, it will make it easier for me to leave. Easier to forget her.

Daring to find out if she felt anything that day, I ask, "Have you ever hugged someone who made you feel special? Someone who made you feel so content in their arms you didn't want to let go of them?"

Joel is quiet for a while. Her eyes water, her chest rises and slowly deflates, then she nods. So, she has had a connection with someone before. Was it with me, or someone else? Joel's eyes shine as she stares at me.

I take her hand. "Talk to me, Joel. I know you have experienced the feeling of being home in someone's arms. Tell me who she was. Please?"

Joel wipes her eyes. "I'm confused. How do you know she was a woman?"

I walk to my bed, lift the mattress, and pull out a small piece of paper. "Do you remember this?" I place the paper in her hand.

Joel visibly gulps as she reads, *"One free pass to Joleen Hunt's club, the Tenth Muse."* She combs her bangs back with her fingers and smiles. "She called me gorgeous."

With my head bent forward into my bowl of soup, I mutter, "*I* called you gorgeous. You still are gorgeous. It was me sporting green hair, a rainbow mask, and dark sunglasses. It was me you hugged in Writerly."

"Oh, crap." Joel stands and her breathing grows heavy. "Your voice was muffled by the mask, but you do sound like her."

I get out of my chair and lean on the table. "It was me who sat in your SUV. It was me who gave you the free matcha tea for your parents."

Joel holds a hand over her chest. "But when I asked Cain about you, he said he didn't know you."

I slam my fist on the table, spilling soup. "Cain was my fucking roommate. Of course, he knew I had green hair before leaving for Manhattan the next morning, and I told him I couldn't stop thinking about you and that your face replaced that of the faceless woman in my dreams. I didn't realize the jealous bitch wanted to steal you from me. You both tore my heart apart little by little as I watched you get wooed by my friend. I thought you meeting my roommate was just a horrible coincidence."

Joel closes her eyes and her hands tremble as she dishes out another dose of trivia. "Did you know the heart of a blue whale is so enormous, large fish can swim through their arteries, and their heartbeat is strong enough it can be heard two miles away? Another certitude is that love at first sight doesn't exist. Well, not unless you're a mother seeing her newborn for the first time."

I sit back down in defeat. "Oh yes, I forgot you're the expert on hearts, love, and relationships. The geek with ice queen aspirations doesn't believe in insta-love. Tell me about the day we held each other, Joel. How did I feel in your arms?"

"No." She slumps into her seat. "Now, goddamned you, what was your involvement in Candice's death?"

Great, she doesn't give a shit about me being the woman in green hair. I wish I hadn't told her. I've been dreaming about her for two fucking years and all she wants to talk about is what I did to Candice.

"Okay, fine! Cain knew I had a crush on you. I talked nonstop about you the night before I left to work for a fashion company in Manhattan. I didn't put it together at first, but the night of Candice's death she boasted about how she played you for the sole purpose of keeping us apart."

Joel stares at the free pass to The Tenth Muse in her hand. "Why did you keep this note? Didn't Candice fill your head with negative crap about me?"

I shake my head. "Candice rarely talked about you. Sure, she told me a few lies, like you transitioned into a man with a big penis. She always bitched about how greedy and unloving you were. But for the most part, she didn't speak of your lives together or what you did behind closed doors. She spent most of her time trying to make me happy. Bringing a smile to my face with her fantastic wit and charm."

Joel scoffs. "She could be charming when she needed to be."

I don't want to think of Candice flirting with Joel. I don't want to think of them together at all. My hands feel damp and I wipe them on my shirt. "The night you broke up with Candice, she ranted on and on about how you were putty in her hands and how she'd have you sucking her cock by daylight. I wanted to punch her fucking face in. Instead, I went to get a drink at the bar. On the way, I peeked into your office through an opened blind."

Under the Rainbow

D.A. Hartman

I wipe the fabric of my pajama pocket in an attempt to reach a normal tone, but my voice is cracking. "You were crying with a half-empty bottle of Scotch in your hand. I knew it was because of Candice that you were drinking heavily. The sight of you in pain made my blood boil. I returned to our table and told Candice the thought of you sucking her off nauseated the fuck out of me and I never wanted to see her again."

Joel rubs her chest. It's obvious she knows how much my words hurt Candice. She stares at me for a long time then says, "Look, we can debate over who's at fault, but the authorities deemed her death accidental. Neither of us are to blame for her addiction."

Moisture builds in my eyes. "Remembering how tormented Candice was over my unrequited love reminds me of why I must give up on you. But just like her, I don't know how to do that. I'm incapable of letting go of you."

Joel rubs the back of her neck. "I remember having an indescribable bond with the green-haired woman, with you, and when I took you in my arms…"

There's a deep sadness in Joel's eyes as if she has lost the greatest possession she's ever owned.

"But my vagina is as undesirable to you as Candice's penis was to me, isn't it?"

She doesn't answer, but lowers her eyes.

"Isn't it, Joel?"

When she nods in agreement, I swallow my tears and smile. "You'll never fall in love with me no matter how at home we are in each other's arms, and having to give up on loving you is fucking gut-wrenching. When I told Candice, I never wanted to see her again. I understood the pain I caused her that night, and still, I walked away.

"She was such a goddamned manipulator." Joel rubs her hand on my shoulder.

Her touch burns with pity. It's bad enough she doesn't love me, but I can't tolerate her knowing how pathetic I am, and rush to conceal myself in the bathroom.

Under the Rainbow   D.A. Hartman

38 - Joel

Devi is the only person I have ever felt a connection with. I'm not surprised she was the green-haired woman I embraced inside of Writerly over two years ago. She's the only one who can melt me with her hugs. Now this woman who has a significant place in my heart is behind a locked door.

Attempting to twist the doorknob to the bathroom, I yell, "For fuck's sake, you didn't kill Candice!"

Devi speaks through the thin barrier. "I'm sorry for trying to force you to love me."

"Come out of the bathroom. Please."

The door slowly opens and Devi practically falls into my arms. She wipes her wet face on the collar of my shirt. "I'm going to miss you."

How can this heart of mine, which has forever been entirely devoid of love, feel so much for this woman? And why, after a life of not wanting or caring, am I falling for her, a woman I can't have? I guide Devi to the bed and she flops on her stomach. With the lack of a headboard, I scoot against a clear glass wall and sit beside her with my legs crossed at the ankles. I should go home, but I don't want to. I want to stay with Devi as long as I can before she leaves.

She curls into a tight ball and whines, "I'm destined to be alone. This is such bullshit."

It's difficult to feel sorry for the most beautiful woman I've ever met, but I rub her head and smile. "Many women want you, and you're still young." As I reassure Devi, the thought of her with someone else has me grinding my teeth. This is ridiculous. I can't allow my jealousy to prevent her from being happy. I'm responsible for destroying her only chance of making it big, and keeping quiet about who I am is becoming more difficult every day.

Devi rubs her nose against my thigh and sniffles. "I don't want to be here to witness you having sex with people in an attempt to cure yourself."

I smooth my palm over her arm. "I'm back to my old self and masturbating again, thanks to you. I won't be dating anyone. I promise."

Devi jumps out of bed, grabs a cracker off the table, and stuffs it into her mouth.

Without a doubt, I crave Devi's touch, but when she learns what I've done to her, she'll hate me as much as I once hated her. There can never be anything between us.

Devi needs to go to Tehachapi and forget about me. And while she's there, I'll put my condo up for sale and move back to Manhattan. Then when she returns to Amboadia, she can get on with her life. Virginia can keep me up on any needs she may have. That's the plan, anyway.

I get off the bed, walk to her, and wipe a piece of cracker from her cheek. "I should go. I'll call you later to check on how you're doing."

Devi lifts her head. There's anguish on her face as she wipes her nose.

I feign a smile. "I'll contact you when you return from Tehachapi."

"Whatever." Devi trudges toward the bathroom. "Have a great life." She closes the door and once again locks it.

I lean on the door and whisper, "I'm sorry. I'm sorry about everything. Please stay safe in Tehachapi."

When I turn to leave, the ground jolts with such force I swear my brain taps the top of my skull.

Devi opens the door, her eyes wide. "Earthquake!"

I push her back inside the bathroom and into the bathtub, then place my body over hers. Devitron creaks and rumbles. A bottle of shampoo drops from the top of the stall and hits me on the shoulder. I shimmy up her torso to cover her face. I won't let anything hurt her.

The bathroom shakes and roars. I've never experienced a quake lasting this long.

The potential of us dying today exists and I embrace Devi tight enough, the pounding of her heart penetrates my chest.

Devi kisses my chin. "We aren't going to make it and I never got my dream girl. But you're on top of me just like you are in my dreams."

Double Ds stops shaking.

"We're not going to die and you said in your dream you fell onto a dancefloor. This tub is the smallest dancefloor in the world." I joke.

"It's close enough, Joel. You're still gazing into my eyes as you have hundreds of times before."

She wants her dream to come true so badly, she's grasping at straws and willing to accept a distorted outcome. Devi's pleading face has me wanting to make her dreams come true. I owe her that much, but I'm so damn tired of lying. To say I love her would be another lie. I can't do it.

Once again, the ground shakes. Devi's body stiffens and I swear she stops breathing. The grinding of metal and the sound of broken glass has my heart beating out of my chest. This quake may very well kill us. The rumbling continues and the fear in Devi's beautiful hazel eyes turns to a sad gray as she holds me tighter.

Three words slip from my mouth, and I'm amazed at how comfortable I am at saying them. "I love you."

A smile forms on Devi's face and she places her warm, soft lips on mine. Instinctively, I push my mouth against hers, wanting more. The tip of my nose presses into her cheek and I can't breathe. Gasping for air, I lose contact with her mouth. For fuck's sake, how do people kiss and breathe at the same time?

Devi whispers, "Thank you. You're much more than I ever dreamed possible."

I get off of her and out of the tub. I shouldn't have said what I did, nor should I have kissed her.

We walk into the living area. Other than a fallen ceramic plate splattered into pieces, the Sky Viewing Cave has gone unscathed. Devi takes my hand and leads me to the bed. She picks up her phone off the nightstand, dials a number, and punches the *speaker* button.

"Are you and Virginia, okay? Have you heard from the others?"

Goth replies. "Yes, they're okay, and Christine in Manhattan with Javier for a medical conference. We're checking on the Amboadia residents and had to turn off the outdoor water at the condo buildings. I may need your help in the morning to fix the lines."

"Call me when you're ready. I'll be there."

Devi sets down the phone. She's visibly shaken and I take her into my arms. "We'll be alright."

39 - Devi

I'm trembling, but I'd go through dozens more quakes if it meant kissing Joel again. I'm in her arms and life is fucking amazing right now.

"You know I love you, right?" I whisper to Joel.

"Devi, let's not talk about what we did. People act irrationally when faced with the possibility of death."

"It's important you know how lovable you are. Please answer the question."

Joel pushes me away. "So, you think you love me, even though it breaks the three-month rule? Did you love me the night I kicked you out of my club?"

I'm not sure what Joel's implying, but I say yes to her question.

"But you allowed a young stud to fuck you in the alley behind The Tenth Muse. Yes, I saw you two. Worse yet, I heard you coming. Goddamnit Devi." Joel stares at my eyes, daring me to lie. "You can't help yourself. Hell, I bet you've already bedded the woman who worked with you at Writerly. What is her name, Bo-bette? Did you have sex with Bo-bette too?"

Something sticks in my throat. I can't swallow—of course it was Joel who was walking in the alley when the Korean butch was fucking me. Who else would carry around such a large flashlight. My eyelashes are running amok, and I slap my hand over my eyes as my lashes flap against my palm.

"Right, and you loved me when Sapphic Cream was drooling all over you, but loving me didn't stop you from flirting with her."

I throw my hands in the air, frustrated at her asinine excuse to argue with me. "Sorry, I had no idea we were in a committed relationship. You should have said."

Joel turns toward the kitchen. "I noticed earlier that you have ingredients to make sandwiches. Would you like one for dinner?"

Is she kidding me? She starts a fight, and when she gets called on her bullshit, she changes the subject to food?

"I can make my own fucking sandwich." I shove her to the side with my hip, open the refrigerator, and toss ham, lettuce, and cheese onto the counter.

We won't see each other for months and she wants to fight with me? Does she want to make sure I stay away long enough for my feelings to disintegrate? Or is she hurting? Will she miss me? Is this her not understanding what to do with her emotions? Whatever the fuck is happening with Joel, I'm not going to allow her to ruin the last day we have together.

"Would you care for a yerba-mate tea?" I ask her.

Joel's looks as if she has swallowed a bug.

Concerned, I place my hand on her shoulder. "What is it? Are you okay?"

She braces herself against the counter with both hands. "It's clear you're unable to quell your feelings. This leaves me with no choice but to tell you the truth."

I place my hand on Joel's, and she jerks hers from under mine. "Let me get this out, Devi." She takes a napkin from a holder, tears it, and lets the pieces fall on the island counter. "If I believe someone has harmed me, I have the means to make their lives miserable."

No joke, she kicked me out of my favorite club. Maintaining distance, I smile to encourage her to keep talking.

She takes in a deep breath. "It's clear Candice pitted us against one another. She never told me you were the green-haired woman. She said you were a drug dealer and you were sleeping with her. I thought you two were in cahoots to steal my money. As Candice's addiction worsened, so did my home life. I wanted you both to stop making a fool out of me, and I wanted her the fuck out of my goddamned house."

Wanting—no, needing for Joel to continue, I mutter. "I'll make us some mate tea."

Tears flow down Joel's blotched face, and it's easy to tell she's struggling to speak. "I'm not attracted to any gender," she finally says. "Regardless of what Candice told you, we never had sex. I have never slept with anyone—excluding myself. I am, however, into masturbation, and various toys." She tilts her head, cracking her neck. "I regret everything I did to you. I'm more flawed and morally corrupt than I ever thought you were. My horrible actions and ignorance are why we can't have a relationship."

"We can work through anything, Joel. Don't push me away."

My heart drops along with the *bombilla* that plunges into the hot cup of brew, and I slide it in front of her.

She wipes her runny nose, stirs the tea, and gives me a fragile smile. "I've acquired a taste for this earthy slush, thanks to you."

Her swollen face flushes with defeat. She bends over the counter and her cries of anguish make me disturbingly aware that whatever chance existed for us to stay in each other's life has been annihilated by a secret so appalling, Joel can't bear to share it with me.

40 - Joel

I can't divulge the details of my unethical behavior to Devi because I'm a coward and because she's adamant about us having a pleasant evening before she leaves for Tehachapi. She takes my hand and leads me to her bed where I agree to watch Thelma, a lesbian paranormal film, in which the main character coincidently is more blemished in personality than I am.

We have a few more aftershocks, although nothing drastic enough to make us flee from the comfort of Devi's soft mattress. When she falls asleep, I gaze at her stunning face. Her gorgeous hazel eyes are closed. The cleft in her chin, her dainty nose, and plump lips absent of her favorite purple lipstick keep my interest.

Why she wants a frigid, imperious snob such as myself, when beautiful people endure long queues to dance with her at my club, is beyond my comprehension. The fondness she feels for me will breathe its last breath once I muster the courage to tell her what I've done, but that isn't tonight.

Feeling drowsy and knowing I'll never see Devi again once I leave Double Ds, I take my bra off from under my shirt, drop it to the floor, and scoot under the covers to snuggle with her. Tonight, Orion brightens my dreary mood as I watch the twinkle of stars on the ceiling of the Sky Viewing Cave. My devotion to her will hold no bounds, even though all we have remaining of us is tonight.

~~~~~

I wake to the pressure of Devi lying on top of me. She's wearing a thick flannel shirt and kisses my neck just below my ear. In a husky voice, she whispers, "I want you." Devi spreads my legs apart with her knee and presses her thigh against me.

My clit twitches with thirst as she nibbles and sucks my earlobe, but I must decline. "Devi, I've never—um, this isn't a good idea."

I'm bewildered as to why I haven't shoved her off me yet, but her body pressed against me is exhilarating and her kisses along my neck are making me feel things I've never felt before. I'm not interested in people sexually and it's difficult to give up control of my body. When I self-pleasure, I fantasize about the variety of toys I'll use. I don't fantasize about being with someone else. Hence, the gratification I feel from Devi's touch puzzles me.

"Don't you want to come again, Joel? Like you did on the phone with me? You were so hot. I could hear you whimpering." Devi's soft temperate lips brush across my neck and she kisses her way to my chest. "Say yes, Joel. Let me make you feel good."

My breathing becomes heavy as Devi licks my collarbone with her tongue and her hands work their way up my sides. It's then my traitorous body succumbs to her touch and I murmur, "Yes. Alright."

Devi dips a hand under my shirt while she stares into my eyes, searching for any resistance. There is none. She caresses my tits. Her movements are considerate, yet eager. And when she takes my nipples between her fingers and pinches them, I moan. "Yes, Devi."

She presses her other leg between my thighs and glances up at me again, waiting for me to give her the go-ahead.

Unaware of what she is asking, but not giving a damn, I nod my consent.

Her only intent is to please, and she gives me complete control at every turn. This is a novel experience. I don't know what to expect, but I know I'm being cherished and this shatters my defenses. I can't refuse her valuable offer, although I know I should. Only Devi can show me what it's like to be with someone. She is the only one I've ever wanted.

Devi lifts my shirt. "You're so damned sexy, Joel." She kisses one of my breasts, making my clit throb with need. She laps at my nipple, then takes it into her mouth and nibbles at the tip with sharp teeth. Her movements feel desperate. I can tell she's fighting to be gentle. To have someone else touch me is new and unfamiliar, but I'm too excited to analyze what I'm feeling.

She sucks me harder, and her moans arouse me. I need nothing more than what she is doing—grinding her pelvis against mine and devouring my tits.

"Oh shit, this feels so fucking good." My mouth parts as I lean my head back and close my eyes.

Devi mutters, "Open your eyes. It's just me wanting to take care of you."

Doing as Devi asks, I focus on the stars above and let go of all my fears. Devi's voice is soothing. She has been with lots of women. If anyone on this planet can give me an orgasm, it's her. I nestle my head into the hollow of her neck and squirm against her. "Please make me come."

"I will. I promise you." In one strong swoop, Devi pulls off my sweatpants and panties and tosses them to the floor. Devi is wrapped in layers of masculine clothing, yet I know she's a woman. A woman whose only desire is to satisfy me.

She plants tender kisses down my belly. Normally, I'm self-conscious of my pudginess, but Devi is whimpering with such delight as she licks and tastes my sensitive skin, I don't feel ashamed.

With my arms still at my sides, I feel guilty for not participating. "What should I do?" I ask.

"Nothing. This is for you, Joel. Only you." Devi lowers herself and presses my thighs further apart with her shoulders. When she brushes her wet tongue over my clit, the feeling is shocking, yet euphoric. Her mouth covers me with pliable warmth. Her lips excite me more than my fingers ever had. They're soft and wet, yet full of determination as they work to gratify me.

Devi takes my clit into her mouth and the sensation sets my body on fire.

Oh fuck. With a primal groan, I press my fingers into her shoulders and succumb to her completely.

Devi swipes her tongue up and down my slippery opening, sucking on my hard clit with each finished lap. Her mouth stays pressed against my wetness as her fingers dig into my inner thighs.

"Mm, sweetheart, yeah, so good." I valiantly spread wider for her and press my hand on Devi's head to dominate her movements. *She's an extension of me* I repeat in my head. "Right there," I mutter. "Harder. Mm, yes."

Devi hums, sending vibrations deep inside me. She licks and sucks per my instructions and I arch my back, wanting more. Devi reaches under my ass, squeezing and pulling me closer to her mouth.

"Mm, yes, now fuck me," I plead, not knowing exactly what *fucking* to her might entail. How do I tell Devi I need penetration? A finger, a toy, something. I don't care what she fucks me with as long as the inside of me gets attention soon. I press my hips firmly against Devi's face and she plunges her long, stiff tongue inside me.

I let out a whimper and spread my legs even farther apart, but Devi goes back to sucking my clit and pinching my nipples. Damn, I want her tongue inside me again. Although there's a good possibility, I'll burst with pleasure regardless.

Not knowing what to do, I beg, "Please. Please, Devi."

Please must be the magic word, because Devi immediately thrusts her fingers inside me. The intense pleasure forces a cry of delight from my mouth. With her skilled fingers, she prods and strokes. I'm about to explode. I dig my nails into Devi's hair and order her to fuck me harder.

She presses her tongue against my clit as her fingers curve and hit the upper wall of my vagina. She lavishes me with such precision I'm about to soar over the edge. Then, to my dismay, her proficient fingers slow.

What the hell? Tired of being teased, I pull her hair and press her face so hard against me, she gasps.

Devi squeezes my ass cheeks, making me squeal in surprise, but if her goal is to persuade me to pace myself, her strategy fails. I'm closer to an orgasm than before. "Please Devi, make me come."

Obeying my plea, she cups my ass with one hand and shoves her fingers in me with the other. First shallow and fast, then deep and slow.

The sound of my juices pushes me over the edge and my body becomes rigid with ecstasy. "Fuu-uuck," I scream as my walls expand and contract around her fingers. Pure elation gushes from my core to every part of my being. "Oh shit. I'm coming so good."

"Yes, Joel." Devi's voice is barely audible as my orgasm rushes throughout my body.

The magnitude of my release is almost overwhelming. "I can't go again," I tell Devi so she'll quit touching me, but she leaves pressure on my clit with her tongue, creating more undulating currents of euphoria.

After the final wave of pleasure, I let out a sigh and relax my arms and legs.

Devi rolls off my body, leaving me in peaceful bliss. Everything that confused me before, is now crystal clear. Life is incredibly glorious and I've never felt so content at being me.

~~~~~

I'm awakened by the sound of someone approaching from the bathroom. It's daylight. Devi is wearing a tan buttoned-up shirt and, oh holy shit, she's carrying what looks like a triple rabbit dildo. I've used many dildos while self-gratifying, but none like this.

"Joel?"

"Yes, Devi."

"You mentioned you're into toys. Want to give this one a go?" She flops it around in her hand, almost dropping it.

I cover my eyes and laugh. "Come here so I can get a closer look."

Devi smiles as she outfits her harness and aligns her body next to mine on the mattress. The tip of the biggest dildo on the rabbit is glistening with a dollop of lube, and my vagina sprouts with need.

Devi wipes the gel up and down the massive silicone rod, then adds lube to the anal plug below and some more to the clit massager above. The thought of being entered in both openings while getting my clit hammered has me so wet it's embarrassing.

Upon closer observation of the toy, I shake my head. "The girth is too big. Don't you own something smaller?"

She climbs over me on all fours and rubs the tip of her silicone rod up and down my slit, making me so hot I almost don't care what size her dildo is.

"If you can't take it, I won't enter you. You can trust me."

Aching with need but still wary, I say, "Alright." She has proven time and time again that I can trust her.

She kisses my neck. "I'll just put the head in and we'll see how it goes, okay?"

"Alright," I say again.

On her knees and between my legs, Devi gently slips in the head. We both moan in unison. She pushes her pelvis against me a little more and the anal plug enters me as well. Dipping in both places, she slowly rocks and pushes deeper and deeper inside me.

"Hell, you're so hot, Joel. I'll try not to come too fast," Devi whispers.

I can't help but smile at her. "I want to hear you come with me again."

Devi swallows and her eyes turn a dark gray. "Are you sure?"

"Yes." The thought of her coming already has me on the edge of release.

Devi pulls out completely, then places her hand on my mons and brushes her thumb over my clit. "Spread your legs wider."

I'm surprised when I, the autocrat, do as she demands.

Devi stuffs a pillow under my ass. "Are you ready for me to fuck you?"

"Yes, please." I remember the magic word.

She presses the enormous shaft inside me, easing it in and out, deeper and deeper. Devi is sliding back and forth with ease now as she pulls out and pushes in, harder and harder, forcing her pelvis to hit me each time.

"Oh, shit. Yes." I squeeze Devi's shoulder and dig a heel into her back. The simultaneous hits on my clit and the pressure of fullness in both of my openings is pushing me to the edge.

Devi bends over me and tugs on my nipple with her mouth as she glides in and out, slow and steady now. She quivers and I kiss her temple.

"Use me to make yourself come." I place both of my hands on her back, ready for her to fuck me in whatever way will make her come best.

"Are you sure?" she asks.

"Yes. I want you to come while you fuck me, Devi."

Her arms tighten at my sides, and she thrusts her body against mine, again and again. Juicy sounds of want and smells of sex fill the room. Each time our bodies bump, Devi's whimpers grow louder.

Now grunting, Devi fucks me like a feral beast and sweat streams down from the side of her face. The movement plunges our heads closer and closer to the glass wall, but before we hit, her body tenses, and her loud groan reverberates into my neck and down to my core.

"That's it, oh, yes." She's very vocal and her sounds of rapture cause me to explode with such intensity a white flash of energy races through my brain. I scratch Devi's back, knowing I'll leave marks on her delicate skin, but my climax strikes with such force I lose control of cohesive thought.

Together, we ride the untamed current of our orgasms. Her face glistens. Her mouth remains open, and she cries out her love for me.

She collapses on top of my chest, and I squeeze her tight. Our smooth bodies, soaked with perspiration, slip against each other's with each breath we take. The movement is sensual and bonding. What I wouldn't do to keep her with me forever, but I can't deceive her for another minute.

As if reading my mind, Devi kisses the corner of my mouth, and lifts enough for the dildos to plop out of me. Her eyes meet mine and she whispers, "Please don't push me away, Joel."

The intimacy of the moment is potent. I want to give her everything she asks for. I want to be with her over and over again, but loving Deviant Wallace means heartache, and my falling in love with her is poetic justice.

The buzz of her phone sounds like a siren to my ears as Devi rolls off me to answer it. Apparently, Devi is volunteering to help Goth repair broken PVC sprinklers over at the condo buildings this morning.

She gathers her clothes and quickly dresses, leaving me splayed and spent. The wonderful soreness between my legs will stay with me for a while, but I can't help but worry about what we've done. A night of incredible sex with another person, let alone Devi, wasn't something I planned, and yet, she gave me the most precious gift I've ever received.

41 - Devi

Goth and I are digging in wet earth to mend pieces of broken pipe this morning. The dull pulsation between my thighs reminds me of the amazing time I had with Joel. She not only wanted me, she begged me to please her, not once, but twice. Last night I didn't have sex, like I've had sex with many women, I made love. Each touch of her body was profound and meaningful. All I have yearned for over the last two years converged in one mind-blowing night and I don't know if I can ever turn back. I don't know if I can leave her, but if she doesn't want me, I'll have no choice.

My buddy kneels in her muddy white T-shirt and khaki shorts, to shove her tiny shovel into the dirt, and reveals a GPS bracelet. Virginia suggests she wear the monitor in case she has a psychotic episode because Goth prefers to take a lower dose of her medication than what is prescribed by her doctor.

"We're almost done, Devitron."

Still looking at her bracelet, I ask, "Is everything good with you and Virginia?"

"Oh yeah, we not only embrace each other's imperfections, they knit us closer together." Goth gestures to her GPS watch and grins. "She swears only she, not the authorities, can track me with this new device and I believe her."

I glance at the ground where I glued a coupling to connect two pieces of busted PVC pipe. "That's the last one. We're done! I better get packed. I leave for Tehachapi tomorrow morning."

Goth grunts. "Stay here. Don't let Joel chase you off. I don't know what is going on, but it's easy to tell you care about each other."

"I know she has feelings for me but she hasn't asked me to stay." I don't think she wants me to because of some dark secret she's hiding. As I kneel by the hose to spray dirt off my hands, Goth throws her arms around me. "Your relationship with Joel is as tight as mine and Virginia's. I wish you two could see it."

I turn off the water and mutter, "We don't have a relationship. That's the point." Right as I say this, Joel passes by and I break free of Goth's hold to dart after her.

"Hey, Goth was only hugging me goodbye."

Joel stops and turns to face me. "I know. You don't have to explain yourself."

"Really? Because it's clear you don't trust me."

"I don't trust anyone, not even myself, but I trust you more than most." Joel combs her fingers through her short dark hair. "I appreciate the great sex we had. You've helped me in ways a therapist never could. I'll be forever grateful." She rubs the back of her head. "The thing is, I'm not good for you. I promise to explain everything when you get back from Tehachapi."

Joel turns and walks off.

I run in front of her and plant my feet in a wide stance. "Nothing you've done in your past matters."

"You can't say that. There are things you don't know about me, Devi."

Grabbing Joel's hands in mine, I say, "You gave me yellow tulips at the hospital, just like the woman I told you about in my dreams did. You bent over me on the smallest dancefloor in the world and said you love me."

Joel flinches, forcing my hands to let go of hers. "It was a bathtub. Dreams aren't real. They don't come true simply because you have them." Her bottom lip quivers. "We can't be together." She glances at Goth, who appears worried, then takes my hand and pulls me along with her. She's taking long strides down the sidewalk toward her condo building and I struggle to keep up.

"Where are we going? Do you want me to stay now? We can make it work." I ramble on. "Sex with you is awesome. I don't mind being on top. It's all—"

Joel interrupts with a frown. "Stop it. You deserve someone who appreciates your body, all of it. You need to be who you are, not the person you think I want you to be."

Of course, Joel is right. But I love her and if that means never being on the bottom, so be it, our sex is great as is. There has to be more to our story—and I'm waiting for her to get on the same page as I am.

At the entrance of Condo Building Three, Joel lets go of my hand. "If you don't mind, I'd like to hug you goodbye before we enter my home."

I give her a questioning look and step back. "No, I'm not hugging you goodbye."

Joel's eyes dim. "More than you want to know about me is locked inside my condo."

Locked? Okay, now I'm a little nervous.

She taps in the code. A buzzer sounds off, and we walk down the hallway to unit number nine. Joel opens the door and we step inside a cookie-cutter living room slash kitchen area. Its furnishings are minimal and appear new. There are no personal objects—nothing to remind me of Candice, or Joel for that matter. The place is clean and nondescript.

"Did you just move into this unit recently?" I ask.

"I moved here just days before I met you—the green-haired you," Joel says. "Candice stayed here for the year we were together. I disposed of everything, including the furniture after she died. It's all new."

We reach the hall closet and she grabs a key card from a cigar box, then we step down the hallway to another door. With an unsteady hand, she swipes the card to open the lock. After a few failed attempts, the key drops to the floor.

"Crap." Joel hits the door with her fist.

"Let me try." I pick up the card, step in front of her, and with one swipe, the door clicks open.

Joel steps back with the look of sadness and a tinge of fear on her face. I'm curious about what hides behind this door. Visions of everything from a walk-in closet of Joel's favorite clothes to a room full of self-help books crosses my mind.

I turn the knob to enter the room. The slight crack of the door allows the smell of leather, metal, and dust to escape. Pushing further inside, I can tell from the light shining from the hallway that the walls are painted red. Thick chains draped from a wood beam above hang motionless. Wiping my hand against the wall, I search for a light switch. Once I find it, I turn it on. An assortment of floggers and paddles hang on the wall to my right.

"Cool!" I blurt out, even though I'm getting an eerie vibe from this place. It's dusty and stale.

To the left of me is a giant wooden X with leather tethers and steel cuffs at the top and bottom of both long boards. A few more feet away is a black padded bench. Next to it stands a majestic four-post bed with a harness hanging above the mattress. In one corner of the room is a rack of women's clothing, probably freebies given to Candice by the fashion industry. In front of the outfits is a cage large enough to trap a human. Whoa, I've visited a few BDSM parlors before, but never a dungeon.

"This place has a torture chamber vibe, but I can get into it." I can't figure out what the window on the right side is sealed with. I'm guessing aluminum foil.

When I look above the rack of outfits, my breath catches. "What the actual fuck?"

The side wall is plastered with photos of me. Dozens of pics from modeling gigs I did with Candice. One is of me posing in front of the Dolby Theatre on my twenty-third birthday, another of me wearing a tutu in our old apartment. There are photos from the time I met Candice, right up to last year—hundreds of them. An entire wall, smeared with photos of me. My heart pounds in my chest and I'm afraid to make eye contact with Joel.

On a coat rack in the middle of the shrine, hangs my Giorgio Armani leather jacket. It was a gift from Sierra. I lost it the first night I visited The Tenth Muse during the Diva Bi Night drag show. The night I tried to introduce myself to Joel, but Candice prevented us from meeting. She must have stolen it.

Black wigs, cut in the same style as mine sit on several Styrofoam heads on top of a dresser drawer beside several tubes of my favorite purple lipstick. I steel myself and glance at Joel.

She's staring at the bed, and in a monotone voice, says, "This was her room."

Of course, this was Candice's room. Who else would tack this many pictures of me to a wall? Some are magazine cutouts secured with tape, although many have fallen to the floor. A lot of time and thought went into this collage.

Joel cringes as she searches the room, and her eyes always stop short of the shrine. "Candice begged me to wear the jacket and the wigs. I thought they were just props she used to teach me how to act like a dominatrix." Joel points to the wall behind her but doesn't turn to face it. "Candice had an enormous tapestry covering those images. Several weeks into our relationship, the flimsy veil toppled down while I was flogging her. It was then comprehension struck. Candice tricked me into dressing like the woman she was obsessed with. She conned me into being her Deviant Wallace substitute. I said all the words she wanted *you* to say to her. After whipping and talking dirty to Candice, she'd tell me to leave so she could jerk off."

How demeaning. How fucking twisted. No wonder Joel hated me. "I'm sorry. I didn't know."

Joel sighs. "I haven't been in this room since the tapestry fell to the floor. Candice said she had videos of me playing the role of you and often threatened to post them online. I found camera equipment in here, but no evidence of the recordings."

Joel refuses to view the photos, my jacket, or the black wigs. She won't look at anything in the room that has to do with me. She gulps, and to my dismay, she averts her eyes from me as well. To think Candice duped her into becoming me. The bitch asked Joel to wear my clothes, my style of hair, my lipstick. I feel sick, and if Candice wasn't dead, I'd fucking kill her.

The sound of Joel's delirious guffaw snaps me out of my thoughts. "Things I did in this room keep me awake at night. The night Candice died I finally chose one punishment over another. While Candice was with my bouncers and dying from an overdose, I searched tiny islands for sale. Someplace I could hide while she made good on her threat."

I walk to a tall pink upholstered chair and plant my hand on its back to brace myself. A clicking sound has my heart pounding and I spin to face Joel. "What was that?"

In a low-key voice, she says, "Don't be scared. The door is programmed to lock once someone passes this point. I have the code."

My pulse is thumping against my neck when I motion to the shrine. "I need to get out of here."

Joel's eyes water as she glances around the room, again, everywhere except the side wall where hundreds of images of me are on display. "Yes, you should leave, Devi."

I walk to the door and twist the doorknob, but it won't budge. I turn to Joel. "How do I get out?"

She stands beside me and presses her palm to my chest. "I can tell by how fast your heart is beating, you're frightened."

"It's a lot to take in," I say.

"This is why you can't love someone you don't know."

I brush my bangs to one side with my fingers. "I don't think less of you for what Candice conned you into doing. You don't scare me, but this place creeps me out." I reach for her. "Let's get out of here."

Joel's chest expands, and she refuses to take my hand. "There's no escaping this place for me. If you want out, push the blue button next to the bullwhip and type two thousand eighteen."

I punch the button and type 2018. The door clicks open and the knob moves when I rotate it. Turning to Joel, I smile. "The code to unlock this door is the year 'Pussy Is God' came out."

"Yes, a King Princess song." Joel covers her eyes. "As it turns out, I couldn't stop thinking about the day we met, or our hug." She places her hand over her heart. "You made such a big deal out of being a lesbian that day. I contemplated how wonderful it would be if I were one too."

The irony of this isn't lost on me. After all, Joel became a lesbian dominatrix when she met Cain just days later.

Joel tilts her head. "Why didn't you tell me you were the woman with green hair? Eighty-eight percent of all misunderstandings are due to a lack of communication."

Sometimes I wonder if Joel makes these stats up. "It was impossible to communicate with someone who glared at me with disdain whenever you saw me at the club. Cain made it clear I wasn't to speak to you, ever. I didn't want to get kicked out of The Tenth Muse. You know how much I love that place. Plus, you hated me so much, I feared if I told you, you would tarnish the best day we ever spent together."

She takes a step closer. "I experienced a bond with the green-haired woman—with you. I went to Writerly looking for you but I didn't know your name. Instead, I met Cain, and we, well, we—" Joel cups my chin with a trembling hand. "What happened in this room will haunt me forever. Don't you understand?" She leans in for a kiss and between her soft lips, whispers. "You must go to Tehachapi and forget about me. When you return to Amboadia, you can start fresh with someone who wants all of you."

"You won't be here when I get back, will you?" I ask with a shaky voice.

"There are other reasons we can't be together. I have done things you'll never forgive me for."

"I don't care what you've done. We can get through anything together," I insist.

"I can't. Dammit, this would be easier if I still hated you," Joel yells. Her body becomes stiff and her hands squeeze into fists. Her face becomes one of defiance, and in one quick turn, she covers her eyes and faces the horrific shrine Candice dedicated to me.

42 - Joel

With my hand over my eyes, I brace myself to relive the same horror and regain the same hatred of Deviant Wallace that I had the first time I saw the collage of Candice's obsession. If I can return to the uncaring and hateful person I once was, I'll have the strength to help Devi and tell her who I am.

The fear in my chest pounds, fierce and without mercy as I remove my hand from my face and open my eyes.

The first photo that comes into view is of a stunning Devi standing on a catwalk in a spring design by Chase Janice—an outfit, I know well.

Next to the picture of Devi on the catwalk is a photo of her at The Tenth Muse, dancing seductively by herself.

Another image shows hordes of people vying for Devi's attention as she sits sipping a cocktail, also at the club. She seems happiest when at my nightclub. In every photo, she's wearing sexy clothes, all worthy of the front cover of fashion magazines.

When I look at these photos now, I'm not filled with anger or jealousy. I'm not feeling shameful or foolish. The woman on the wall is not Cain's Deviant Wallace. She isn't who I once thought she was. The woman on the wall is the only person who has ever loved me.

Viewing these photos doesn't make me hate Devi as it once did. I thought it would, but I can never hate her, not ever again.

Then I see it, a picture of two women through a glass window. One has green hair and is hugging me inside Writerly. Her big round sunglasses are pressing into my neck. Candice must have taken this photo from outside of the coffee shop window. The love in my eyes is unmistakable. Candice was aware of our connection before Devi even had a chance to tell her about me.

The beautiful photo shows two women who are very comfortable in each other's arms. They are safe, loved, and even a little hopeful. I focus on the picture of Devi and me in a perfect moment in time. How different things might have been if Candice had allowed Devi and me to travel a natural trajectory.

"Are you okay, Joel?" Devi's voice sounds fragile and troubled.

I walk to the clothes rack and squat on the floor, pulling one of my dead fake ex's dresses into my lap. Candice was obsessed with Devi. She did everything in her power to win over the striking Deviant Wallace. She even pretended to be someone she wasn't, just as I had. Desperation is a powerful influence.

Allowing the dress to fall to the ground, I get up and walk to Devi and brush the back of my hand across her cheek. "How can I hate an addict who was in love with such a beautiful woman as you?"

With a new understanding of love and its power of persuasion, it's easy to forgive Candice, and I do forgive her. I'm tired of storing hate in my heart. I'd rather let it go to make room for someone else.

Devi follows me as I flee out the door, down the hall, and to the comfort of my living room. She sits on the sofa and murmurs, "Are you going to ask me to stay now?"

"You're relentless." I rub my forehead, knowing there's only one way this day ends.

"Be with me, Joel. I mean, why can't you? Is it really because I'm a woman?"

"Your gender isn't the problem." Vocalizing this makes me realize how accurate my statement is, but it doesn't matter now. I have to tell Devi the truth. A fiery volcano erupts in my stomach and I mutter, "There's something I need to tell you."

Devi's eyes crease as she picks up bills from my coffee table and peruses them. Her eyes widen. "You paid for my hospital stay, to fix my motorcycle, and my schooling?"

"It wasn't much. I didn't mind." I grab the receipts and toss them in a nearby trash can.

"You don't care about me enough to ask me to stay, but you're paying my bills? Why, Joel?"

On the brink of hyperventilating, I stutter, "There's something you need to know."

"I'm listening, but we can—"

"You don't know me because who I am is a well-hidden secret. My overly protective parents made me promise not to tell anyone I was connected with their fashion company. They received a lot of threatening calls back then and it scared them. Anyway, in return for my silence about being their daughter, they called off their security guards and gave me my freedom."

"What are you talking about?" Devi sits back on the couch and crosses her legs.

I attempt to steady my breathing to no avail. "My dad's name is Chase and my mom is Janice."

She recognizes their names immediately. The distress in her eyes is unmistakable. "Your parents terminated me and wouldn't tell me why. Fuck, they somehow blocked my ass from the entire fashion industry. I was on top of my game and they pulled the plug on me." She rubs her legs and the veins in her neck are protruding. "Your parents are fucking assholes."

My eyes water with contrition. "My parents weren't responsible for firing you, nor did they have anything to do with other fashion companies denying you employment."

"Bullshit." Devi's hands ball into fists.

Tears gush from my eyes and a lump grows in my throat. My hands are shaking so severely, I have to place one over the other to stop them from moving. I gulp for air. This is worse than death. Worse than living because I want to die. I plea for physical pain to take over my body to relieve my breaking heart.

Devi's eyes flare as comprehension sets in. "No. Not you, Joel."

Holding back a whimper, my bottom lip trembles, making speech impossible.

Devi stands. "Tell me you didn't do this, Joel. Tell me you didn't fuck up my career, my life?"

When I find my voice, I stutter, "I'm—I'm CFO of Chase Janice. I had you fired. I also informed as many fashion companies as I could about your drug dealings."

Devi paces in a circle. "Fuck, fuck. FUCK!" She falls to the floor and pounds the carpet.

I drop next to her and wrap her in my arms from behind. I press my face into her neck. "Candice said you were a whore who sold drugs. I'm so sorry."

"You stole my independence because of hearsay? How could you?" Devi rolls from me and holds her belly.

I reach out to her again, but she slaps my hand away. Her entire body is trembling. All I want to do is comfort her—touch her, but my touch is the last thing Devi wants.

"New York's Fashion Week starts next month. You can do the catwalk at a few houses as one of CJ's substitute models." I grab my phone from the kitchen and return to Devi on the carpet. "I'll get you on a plane tomorrow for Manhattan. The designers can fit you and—"

Devi swats the phone out of my hands. "I don't want anything from you or your shitty family." Her face pales. "You let me make love to you last night, knowing you cut my throat, then happily watched me bleed out."

Devi's inability to look at me, and her words bite through to the bone. A sudden falsehood spurts from my mouth, "I can fix this. I'll get your career back. You'll be a supermodel. I promise."

This is a lie. A model's career is never guaranteed and Devi is heavier, older, and I've tarnished her name beyond repair. I'm embarrassed by my desperate manipulation—my defective character—because I know damn well no matter how hard I try, Deviant Wallace will never be the supermodel she could have been, and it's all my fault.

Profound wrinkles grow between Devi's eyes and she doesn't utter a sound as she plods through my condo toward the exit. Her trek is slow, resembling a wounded bird wading in thick mud. She twists the knob and pulls the door open, leaving me with a somber view of a hallway as empty as I am.

43 - Devi

The reprehensible things Joel did to me preoccupy my thoughts. She's the CFO of Chase Janice. Her parents are Chase and Janice. I cry daily on the phone with Goth. Joel killed my dream, a dream she's still a part of. I'll never forgive her.

She's a lot more powerful than I realized, a lot richer, and she's incredibly messed up in the head. Her sex issues are minor compared to her callousness. What happened to the woman who wore mismatched clothes and drove an SUV? What happened to the bookworm who didn't care what others thought of her?

Did her parents pressure her, or did she buckle under the stress of not living up to cultural norms? Who cares? Joel broke. She caved, and she's not my problem. I have zero fucks left to give. Screw my manipulative dead friend, screw Joel, and screw Chase Janice.

Joel must have known the consequences of telling me the truth. She knew I'd run away from her as fast as I could. It's what she wanted after all. Joel believes she isn't deserving of my love, and she's right, she isn't. And now, I'm Tehachapi-bound to forget her deceiving ass!

I can be a model again, Joel said. What a crock of shit. The last two years have been hard. Days I sold my soul to get by, and it's her fucking fault.

I'll never accept her offer to go back to CJ. When I got the job with her parents' fashion company, I did so on my own merit. If I went back to Chase Janice, it would be her doing, not mine. It would be more of her charity.

Luckily, I'm not desperate. Goth has not only created my forever home she gave it to me. Who would have thought two years ago the first woman I ever slept with would become the most important person in my life? I don't want to think about where I'd be without her. Maybe headed to Fresno with Nicole, working two jobs again, or back in Chinatown living behind windows with bars on them. I've got to keep focused on how good things are. How great my life has become and how awesome it will be without Joel.

Currently, I have time to take business classes and when the plumbing and renovations of Writerly are done, I'll go back to work. My plan is to have enough money to open a small business within a decade.

Strutting down a runway in fancy clothes was fun, but my ultimate goal was always to own a business. A fantasy I thought had died until Amboadia became my home. I'll never be able to afford a place as grand as The Tenth Muse, but a coffee shop or a bookstore in a trendy neighborhood like Silver Lake will suffice. Being rich isn't my goal, being independent and living in a safe environment is.

Goth, not only gave me freedom from worry. She gave me what I've always craved, my independence. I will forever be grateful. Now that I don't have to save for a place to live, I can save to buy a business.

I should be deliriously happy, and I will be as soon as I get Joel out of my dreams. After everything she's done to me, my feelings for her should diminish in a snap. Soon, she'll be a distant memory, and owning a business will become my only focus.

My dream of having a relationship like Virginia and Goth's is dead. Joel killed it. She was right all along. Dreams really don't come true. They're just mental fabrications that disintegrate from existence once we wake the fuck up.

Now, I understand what Joel meant when she said I don't know her enough to love her. Hell, I don't know her at all.

44 - Joel

One month later...

I'm certain Devi hates me as much as I once hated her, and it's killing me. I had intended to follow through with my plan. Sell my condo, move to Manhattan, and give Devi the peace she deserves so much here at Amboadia. But I've had no desire to get out of bed since she left several weeks ago. Now, I'm too weak to walk and my spirit for life has perished.

It's poetic irony. I neither wanted nor thought it possible to give my heart to another person. Now that I have, I'm being punished with rejection for my misconduct. Self-sabotage at its finest. *Well done, Joel.*

There is a pounding on my door I'm trying to ignore, yet the banging persists. I toss the covers over my head, wishing whoever is disturbing my solitude would fuck the hell off. There's a faded voice. Someone is in my brain, or more logically, in my bedroom. It takes a minute for me to open my eyes, and when I do, I see Nedra barge in, kicking the door closed behind her.

"You get your ass up and visit a therapist or I'll drag you to one," she says emphatically.

"Nedra, for fuck's sake, calm down. I was asleep."

"It's three-thirty in the afternoon." Nedra backs up. "Oh, my gods, you reek. When was the last time you bathed or washed those pajamas?"

Before I can tell Nedra it's none of her damn business. Goth, Christine, Nicole, and Virginia come scampering in. Wonderful—an intervention.

Virginia, forever the glue of our community, is carrying a bag of groceries. "It took me a while to remember you gave me a spare key when you moved here in case of emergencies. I'm going to prepare a meal and you'll eat it."

Next thing I know, Goth and Christine pull me out of bed and lead me into the shower while Nicole gathers clothes. If this isn't proof of how impossible it is dominate people, I don't know what is. No matter the path I lay down, there will always be the inevitable fork in the road where others, not me, will decide what route I'll take.

When my friends finish bathing me. They help me into the kitchen. The smell of what I assume is vegan garlic hummus and some sort of veggie stir-fry turns my stomach.

Nedra collects empty bottles of Merlot from around the house. "We haven't seen you for a month. Are you planning on hiding out here until you rot and die?"

With a shaky hand, I wave her off. "I just need some alone time to gather my thoughts, Nedra."

Nicole finds a bottle with some wine still in it and gulps it down. "I'm going to need a buzz to deal with this drama queen."

Nedra pulls a chair from under the kitchen island and tugs at my sleeve. "Sit before you topple over."

I plant my butt on a chair and rest my head in my palms. "I'm going to need a timeline of how long I'm going to be depressed, Nedra. My parents think I'm on a camping trip with very little Wi-Fi access. Dad has taken over my job for a while, but he won't for much longer, and Mom wants to visit. She said she made willy warmers for everyone."

Nedra replies, "A broken heart can take years to mend. The healing process depends on many variables."

Goth yells from the hallway, "Does your mom know I'm a lesbian?"

"Please do not ask questions concerning my mother. There are no reasonable answers." I prop my head up with my hand and moan.

Virginia hands me a fork and smiles when I take a bite of tofu. "My doctor is on her way. You've lost too much weight. She may want to admit you into Cedar Sinai."

The last thing I want to do is see a doctor. When I shake my head in refusal, I become dizzy and watch the floor rise to my face—or am I falling to the floor?

~~~~~

After a two-day stay at the hospital for malnutrition and dehydration, I'm being released. Everyone is here visiting, 'To make sure I don't do something stupid again.' Those are Nicole's words, not mine.

"I feel fine. You can all go home. I promise to eat and stay in contact. Truly, I don't know why you guys are worried. I'm much better now."

"We're worried because"—Virginia pulls her phone from her pocket and swipes at it until a photo of Devi helping Goth in the yard shows up— "you have chased the one and only person you've ever loved away. Frankly, I'm perplexed."

I poke at the fast food Christine brought. "I messed up. Devi will never forgive me, and she shouldn't."

Nedra takes a bottle of water from her purse and swallows almost half of it. "You can right your wrongs. Why are you pouting? Why isn't the mighty Joel Hunt resolving this mess and going after the girl?

I can't fix our relationship, not even the grandest gesture will, but Nedra has a point. I have the power to make Deviant Wallace's life easier.

I text Devi to ask if she'll allow me to visit her, but my phone doesn't verify the message was sent. I try texting her a second time. "Goddamnit, I think she blocked me."

Nedra smiles. "You are pining over someone, much like Candice and Devi did." She squeezes my body close to hers and brushes her lips across my damp eyelashes. "Do something. Make a move, my friend."

"I have everything under control, Nedra." This time, instead of texting, I call Devi and anticipate hearing her sweet voice, but it goes straight to voicemail. "For fuck's sake, she's ignoring me."

Nedra rolls their eyes. "Oh yes, you're the picture of self-control. It's what you strive for, isn't it? To manage your life to a tee. Keep your ducks in a row. Stifle your emotions. What good has micromanaging and anger done for you? Let your heart usher your decisions for once."

My friend's words hit like bright flashes of comprehension. Devi's absence is too much for me to sit with. I must see her, if only for a few minutes.

I hop out of bed and put on my clothes. "Nicole, I need your help."

Nicole leans forward in the chair she's occupying. "What with?"

"I need your sister's address. Devi has blocked me."

"Hello, dumbshit! She blocked you because she doesn't want to talk to you." Nicole is quiet for a few seconds, then mutters, "Devi won't tell me what happened between you two. Would you care to fill us in?"

I can feel my friends' eagerness to learn the truth. Nobody knows I'm the financial pulse of Chase Janice. Virginia and Nedra have never asked where I worked. Why would they? I have rich parents and I'm the owner of The Tenth Muse. I still don't feel safe telling people who I am, or who my parents are. I was taught to keep quiet about family matters and our company.

My hand wasn't on the hammer of today's hip culture, but being CFO of CJ is my only win. It's the one thing I'm great at and proud of, and these are my friends, they'll keep my secret.

Goth steps in front of me. "Well? Are you going to answer Nicole?"

"Right, right. Well, the truth is, I'm a meticulous number cruncher for a fashion company in New York."

"A fashion company. You?" Virginia giggles as she glares at my beige and crimson plaid shorts and blue polo shirt.

"Yes, I am CFO of my parents' fashion company, Chase Janice."

Virginia slaps her forehead. "Your parents are Chase Janice? I thought they were politicians concealed with boho chic disguises."

I press my tongue to the roof of my mouth, trying not to cry. "No, my parents design clothes, and as you may know, Deviant Wallace worked for Chase Janice for a short time. She'd still work for us if I hadn't fired her. I also schemed tirelessly to get her expelled from the entire fashion industry."

"You're the reason her life got fucked up!" Nicole glares at me and gets up to leave.

Christine flanks her, then turns to face me. "No wonder my poor girl wants nothing to do with you."

Goth is still standing next to me and addresses the others. "Hold up. It's not as if we haven't done things we regret." She eyes Christine. "We've all made mistakes, and if you can't tell how much Joel and Devi love each other, you're blind."

"I don't have ugly ass skeletons in my closet and I for sure don't lie," Nicole snaps.

Virginia steps in front of the door, blocking Nicole. "Well then, you belong in the Guinness World Records because you are the only human on the planet who doesn't."

I give Virginia a weak smile. "I was lied to. I believed I was doing what was best for my parents and their company, and for Candice, who ironically was the person who concocted the lies. I feel horrible about what I've done to Devi."

Nicole lingers by the door. "You need to stabilize this oncoming disaster your stupid ass created. Then I'll give you Kayla's address."

"Just give it to her, dammit," Goth yells at Nicole with an ire I've never witnessed in the benevolent woman.

Nicole hands me her phone with Kayla's contact info showing. I type the address in my GPS app, and without the need to ask, Virginia offers to drive me to the garage of my condo in Amboadia.

The SUV was serviced a few times in the last two years. Still, I'm worried it might not start. Once inside the car and at peace, I feel myself morph into the old me. The me I like. The me I miss terribly. I glance down at the passenger seat where the green-haired woman once sat. If only we could return to that day and start over. The air between us back then didn't contain the pollutants it does now. I turn on the ignition and the Bentley roars with gusto. Whatever hill Devi is on is the hill I'm willing to die on.

45 - Devi

Tehachapi is beautiful and Nicole's sister has been a gracious host for the month I've been here, but nothing compares to Double Ds and I miss my friends at Amboadia. Everyone keeps in touch. None mention, *you know who*. She has moved to Manhattan for all I know. Kurt is watching over Double Ds for me, but I can't wait to get home again.

My phone buzzes and I accept Virginia's request to a video chat. Her hair is messy and she has bags under her eyes.

"Are you okay?" I ask.

"Joel was in the hospital for dehydration." Virginia raises her hand before I can react. "She'll be fine. I brought her home yesterday. I just thought you'd want to know."

Part of me wants to go home to make sure she's okay. The other part of me refuses to care. Loving someone who has hurt you is bone crushing. Joel stole my profession from me, which is equal to her robbing me day after day until the day I die. She annihilated my dream, all of it, even the part she played.

Just like Joel, I don't dream anymore. My sleepless nights are uneventful. The only chance I had to have a lucrative career is long gone and as of last month, so is the woman who gave me tulips as I slept.

Virginia's kind and patient eyes watch as I process what she just told me. Joel must not have been eating or drinking enough. She's agonizing over my absence more than I imagined possible. Hell, who misses someone so much they starve themselves? I mean I've lost a few pounds, but not enough to be admitted to a hospital. Joel is fucking crazy.

But then I'm the one who shamelessly begged her to be with me, and now I'm pleading with whatever powers may exist to turn my heart into stone.

After a few minutes of pondering, I ask Virginia, "Is Joel still at Amboadia?"

Her adorable dimples deepen and she answers, "Yes. She never left her condo until the ambulance arrived to take her to the hospital."

Fuck, I don't want Joel to suffer like this. Why doesn't she go to Manhattan and forget about me? I'll have to return to Amboadia eventually and I'm not sure what will happen if I see her again.

The thought of Joel in the hospital has me crying. I'm sick and tired of wiping my soggy face. So what if she misses me? She's a fucking liar. I can't trust her. I've held on to this broken and unattainable dream for too long, and I need to let it go.

I ask Virginia another question. "What would you do if someone you loved took Amboadia from you? Could you forgive them?"

Her chest expands and she averts her eyes by looking at her keyboard, then looks back at her screen. "If someone tried to take my home away, I'd fight tooth and nail to keep it. Now if someone tried to take my wife from me, I'd never forgive them and I'd wish them dead, and once they were dead, I'd bury them twelve feet under Double Ds where they'd never be found."

Okay, that's precise. Creepy-as-fuck precise. Why is it I never have a clue to what Virginia is trying to say? "Does this mean you think I should forgive Joel?"

Virginia sits taller, as tall as her short form allows. "No, it's not my place to suggest such a thing, but Joel is filled with remorse and will do anything to make amends to you. She was hooked to an IV not caring if she lived or died. She simply gave up on life." Virginia closes her eyes. "I don't want to think of what might have happened if we didn't storm into her condo."

My heart flutters, and I rub my chest to calm myself. "I'm glad she's better, and I forgive her for what Candice conned her into believing, and I don't hate her for what she did to me in what she perceived as an act of self-defense, but her plan was to abandon me and once she was far enough away—what? Was she going to fucking email me the truth, or not even tell me at all? I've had more than enough people toss me aside as if I were garbage. Joel is weak much like my mother was. She won't fight for me, and I can't—I just can't."

Virginia lowers her head but still looks at me when she says, "I'm not here to twist your arm, only to inform you. Call us if you need anything and please stay in touch."

"Okay. Love you. Tell Goth, I miss her."

"We love you too, Deviant."

~~~~~

Kayla, who divorced her husband three years ago and swears never to remarry, loves to have fun. She slaps my back with vigor. "Wake up Cinderella, we're going to a house party at the vineyard tonight and I won't take no for an answer. My sapphic friends want to meet you."

"I don't feel like partying. It's too soon," I mumble.

"It will do you good to get out. Like I said, these women are sexy. They'll take your skinny ass for a ride if you know what I mean." She winks and drags me to the closet to help me choose what to wear.

Kayla and I are both sporting skirts, although hers costs ten times more than mine and is short enough to show her butt cheeks. I'm in a lacy, strapless blouse with crisscrossed backing. Kayla's wearing a cream see-through blouse with a black bra underneath. We're dressed for action.

We arrive at a vineyard too small to view from space, with music loud enough to hear from another planet. A bunch of people are gathered outside the wine-tasting house. It's a warm evening and Kayla drags me to where a few women are drinking in the orchard. Kayla directs me to a green umbrella. Under its shade sits a couple of other women.

"Devi, this is Loca and Tatiana."

I shake the hands of two women, both are butch. Tatiana has long hair, and Loca has a buzz cut. They're in khaki shorts and t-shirts like most of the people here. Yep, I feel overdressed.

"It's nice to meet you." I smile.

Tatiana hands me a beer from a nearby cooler. "Kayla tells me you're in need of a good time, and my friend and I are always geared to help a beautiful damsel in distress." She winks.

So now I'm a damsel in distress? I feel my face wince. "Thank you for the beer." I take the brew from the sexy soft butch, but don't wink back at her.

Kayla's girlfriends scoot apart and she places an empty chair between them. It's a setup, but then I expected as much. I doubt these two gorgeous players can take my mind off Joel, but I'm desperate to feel better. I chug half of my beer and take a seat between them.

Tatiana wastes no time and kisses my neck. She maneuvers her hand up my blouse and I try to enjoy her touch—*get into it, Devi, let these hot butches make you come.*

But I can't stop thinking of Joel and get out of my seat. "Sorry. Maybe some other time." I pull away from their grasps and kiss both butches on the cheek before excusing myself.

Sneaking away is easy. It's total chaos here with all the drunk people and the loud music. The four-mile trek back to Kayla's house is a warm one. There aren't many street lights and I step in a pothole about a mile from Kayla's place and fall to the ground. "Fuck you, Joel. Fuck you." Yes, every woe I encounter is now her fault.

I sit on the soft dirt, not wanting to advance forward or backward. Joel has all she ever wanted—her pricy shit. She never wanted me, not enough to fight for me. She's probably on her way to Manhattan to whine to her parents. Let them take her under their wings. She's too much of a chicken-shit to live her own life.

Voices come from down the road, and I jog the rest of the way to Nicole's sister's house.

When I near Kayla's place, I see a shiny white Bentley SUV in the driveway under the garage light. It's like the one Joel used to own when she was dull, yet interesting. I make my way closer and stumble over a plastic flamingo into a flower bush. "Fuck."

The door to the SUV opens and someone rushes to pull me to my feet. I'd know her smell anywhere, even though she's wearing a muskier perfume than usual.

"Joel?"

She lets go of me and corrects her short hair, which is in a tuft as if she's been pushing her fingers through it. "Did you know there are more plastic flamingos in the world than there are real ones?"

"What are you doing here?" I snap.

Joel straightens her posture. "Deviant Wallace, as CFO of Chase Janice, I must make good on the enormous debt my company owes you. This is little compensation for the harm I caused, but it's all I have." She hands me a check.

Lifting it closer to my face because it's still rather dark under the garage light, I'm stunned to see the amount is in the millions. My heart leaps into my throat. Hell yes, I'm going to accept this check. Deviant Wallace *can* be bought. But what springs out of my stupid mouth is, "I'm not taking your filthy money. You can't buy me. How many times do I have to tell you the same shit?"

Joel tilts her head as if in shame. "I don't want to purchase you, Devi. I don't want your forgiveness either. This amount is what I estimated you could have earned in the last two years and in years to come via sponsors and advertising campaigns. It's every penny I have."

"Hold on, Joel. I mean." I let out a huff. "I know how manipulative Candice was. I know the torment she put you through and I have already forgiven you for your mistakes, but you kept a secret from me, which is the same as fucking lying." My face heats and I know I'm blushing. "You let me taste you the night before you told me you were the one who killed my career. What kind of sick person does that?"

"Right, right. I was selfish. I'm incredibly flawed. You'll get no argument from me. I did include pain and suffering as part of the package."

Why is this nerd so fucking insane? She has lost a lot of weight and her face is sunken in. Truth be told, Joel looks like shit—still, her eyes are beautiful.

"So, you're giving me all your money to avoid a guilt trip for the hell you put me through?" I jab my finger into her boney chest, daring her to say something to piss me off.

Nervously, Joel mutters, "My aim is only to give you what you have earned. There are no strings attached to this check. It certainly won't appease my guilt. Once I leave here, you'll never see me again." She hunches as if punched in the gut, then straightens herself. "If you prefer to take me to court, you will win the lawsuit because make no mistake, Devi, I will go to battle for you. I'll admit not only to defamation of your character but to an abuse of power for aggressively ruining your career. If you sue me, you'll be awarded a similar sum to what I'm giving you, and I'll most likely have to step down as CFO of Chase Janice. The decision is yours."

I take in a deep breath and stare at the check. "It's not like I would have made this much." I would pay myself to shut up right now, but Joel's presence makes me anxious and evidently, when I'm nervous my mind turns into tossed salad.

Joel shuffles from one foot to the other and shoves her hands inside her front pockets. "Devi, I've been in the fashion industry along with my parents since I was a teenager and I've never seen a model as stunning as you are. I'm trying to pay for my mistake but I can't afford to pay you as much as I think you're worth. I don't have the money my parents have."

I kick the plastic flamingo with enough force it almost hits the house. "I don't want your fucking money. That's never what I wanted."

"For fuck's sake, Devi, what then?"

Why is she giving me anything? She doesn't have to. She must know I'd never sue her.

I hand her back the check. "If you think this is what I want, you don't know me at all."

Joleen dips inside her SUV. She opens the glove compartment, snatches a pen and notepad, then scribbles something. "How about I give you this instead?" She rips a sheet from the pad and hands it to me.

I accept the consolation prize and read what she wrote. *I Joleen Hunt gift my club The Tenth Muse to Deviant Wallace.*

I stumble back. Fucking A! She does know me! There is nothing in the world I'd like more than to be the owner of The incredible Tenth Muse. Joel Hunt is giving me more than I dared to dream for.

I should thank my lucky stars. I'll own The Tenth Muse! This blows my mind. I should be elated, and I will be, eventually, when it sinks in. The smart thing to do now is get away from Joel before she changes her mind. Owning my favorite club, her club, is the ultimate prize. I'll be happy soon. Once I'm over Joel.

She stares at my mouth. "You're wearing a different shade of lipstick."

There's no way I'll wear the purple lipstick Candice tricked Joel into wearing ever again. I don't hate Joel. I'm in love with her, but I don't think either of us can get over the pain we've caused each other because of Candice's lies. The mountain is too steep to climb.

I tilt my head toward the house and say, "Blue matches my mood better these days. Now, if there isn't anything else, I have studying to do."

With a weak nod, Joel says, "Of course. I'll send the deed to you via your Amboadia address." She noticeably struggles to put one foot in front of the other, but eventually reaches the driver's door of her vehicle and slips inside.

Relinquishing ownership of The Tenth Muse will hurt Joel and her dignity is fragile at best. I almost don't want to walk away from her, but she didn't come here for me. No. Joel wants to live on a tiny island where she won't have to interact with people, or me. She's a fucking candy-ass.

Joel rolls down the window. "I apologize for all the trouble I've caused." Pain is evident in her eyes. "I wish you the best, Devi."

My eyes well up. She believes I'm better off without her, and I am. I mean dammit, she's not even brave enough to love me. And hello, I'm rich now. I own The Tenth Muse! I can dance every night and hire more DJs and get Diva Bi Night to become a permanent resident. Oh yeah, nightly performances at the club and all the women I want in my bed—a free ticket to utopia!

The SUV's brake lights come on, and Joel slowly backs out of the driveway. That's right, go. I don't need a girlfriend. Especially one who doesn't have a damn clue about what she wants.

I don't need Joel. Screw this dream-girl bullshit. I don't, ugh—

As if my body has a mind of its own, I dart behind her SUV and kick the bumper with all my might, and fall on my ass. The brake lights flickers and the car stops.

Joel dives out of her vehicle and her lower arms scrape against the pavement. Then she jumps to her feet with a grunt. "Have you lost your damn mind, Deviant Wallace?" She struts toward me with her eyes narrowed and her glimmering lips pursed, reminding me of the studly dominatrix whose sporty BMW Roadster I rammed into at Amboadia.

Damn, why can't I leave well enough alone?

When her eyes reach mine, they soften, and she takes my stretched-out hands and lifts me up on my feet.

She scratches her chin. "If you wanted to get my attention, you could have tapped on a side window instead of putting yourself in peril."

"Yeah, well, I panicked." I gasp at the sight of a broken heel on my sandal. "Why are you here, Joel? You could have sent one of your lackey lawyers to do your bidding."

Joel rubs her hands together and steps in closer. "I'm sorry, I hurt you. I guess I went to extremes."

"You guess. You fucking guess. Joel, you turned into a cutthroat ninja mercenary."

"A what?" Joel's eyes furrow.

Panting in frustration I yell, "Just tell me why you are here."

Joel combs her hair back with her fingers and gazes at me with her compassionate brown eyes. "Oddly enough, um well, evidently, I don't know how to let you go, Devi." Tears gush down her cheeks. She attempts to wipe them away, only they keep coming. "I can't eat, or sleep, or fucking breathe correctly without you in my life. I don't know what's happened, but you have me pining for you."

'Pining for you?' Who talks like this? Joel. Joel talks like this. I tighten my arms across my chest, trying not to melt into a puddle. I want to hold her, but if I do, I won't be able to let go.

Again, my mouth runs before my mind can catch up. "Just so you know Joel Hunt, I'm rich now. I have a business, a business you gave me because your privileged ass seriously hurt me."

She cringes. "Right, I can confirm you are rich and I'm a privileged ass." Concern is etched in Joel's face, along with perplexity.

To drive my point in, I add, "As you said, I could dismantle Chase Janice if I were so inclined. I could destroy you much like you destroyed me a couple of years ago."

The big shot CFO winces. "Yes, and you'll have my full support through it all."

Returning my hands to my hips, I say, "I don't have to put up with your bossy ass anymore."

Joel scratches her head. "You never listened to me, anyway."

I take in a deep breath. "What I'm trying to say is there is no reason for me to have you in my life."

Joel takes a step back. "None. I agree, and just so you know, I'm moving out of state. It's all set up. I won't be there when you return to Amboadia."

My breath hitches as I fight the fear of never seeing Joel again. "So, you're going to take refuge on an island like a scared rat?"

"It's for the best."

When she turns to leave, the garage light shines on her shirt. I giggle in delight when I read the words across her chest, *SLUTS RULE* in all caps!

"So, you're into sluts now?" With a grin on my face so wide it hurts I step in front of her. "Well today is your lucky day. I just happen to be the sluttiest lipstick femme in town. I also have soft vagina folds and other girly parts."

"Soft vagina folds?" Joel bites her bottom lip. Most likely in an attempt not to laugh.

"Whatever they're called, labia, folds, lips. The point is I have them, and other girly parts. You know this, yet you still want me."

My knight without shining armor loses her footing and falls against her SUV. Is she still weak from not eating? I stand between her legs and say, "I'm going to need one more thing from you."

Joel reaches into her pocket and pulls out the now wrinkled check. "Take it, there isn't anything I won't give you."

Pressing my palms against her car on both sides of her, I lean in and whisper against her mouth, "I don't want your money. I want someone who cares about me enough to fight for me, to do everything in their power not to lose me." I wink at her. "That and a permanent dance partner."

"I, don't um. I can't—" She sputters, "I've never danced in my life."

Pulling Joel away from the car, I squeeze her waist and press my body into hers. Joel moans as her arms circle around my neck, and unsurprisingly, my desire for her is as strong as ever. Without moving our feet, we sway to my very off-tuned humming of *"Dear Insecurity"* by Brandy Clark.

A stiff Joel soon relaxes as we continue to move in sync.

"I've missed you so much," I say, as I adjust my lacy blouse which is crawling above my pink skirt.

Joel notices what I'm doing. "You're beautiful tonight."

"Really? You think so?"

She rubs the side of my face, leaving a finger under my jawbone. "You look prettiest in sexy clothes."

"I'm glad you think so because now that I'm rich I plan on buying a few La Perla negligees and Versace bustiers."

Joel intertwines her warm fingers with mine and frowns.

I peck her cheek. "What? Too much too soon?"

"No, it's that I'm still uncertain if I'm worthy of having you in my life."

Feeling feisty and somewhat hopeful after Joel said she'd battle for me in court, and gave me The Tenth Muse, I grind my pelvis into hers. "We both have a lot of healing to do, but if you are still at Amboadia when I get home next week, we can date for three months to see if what we feel for each other is real and if we work as a couple."

Joel smiles. "Date? Alright. Yes, we'll abide by the three-month rule! Fabulous idea, but what if at the end of three months you don't like me?"

"Just be yourself, Joel. I liked the geeky bookworm I met at Writerly who dared to hold me because she cared and I like this Joel—" I press my finger into her chest — "the one who is willing to do anything to keep me."

46 - Joel

Three months later...

Devi has been putting in a lot of hours at *her* club for the last three months. The Tenth Muse has been packed nightly. She has live bands booked every Saturday for the next several months.

She hired Nicole as the manager and Sapphic Cream who has excelled at DJing, is now a regular on Fridays. Danni and her wife lead the security team and Goth is painting a mural of sapphics on the ceiling. She rents out the space to a dance instructor on Mondays and Tuesdays. Devi and I take dance classes there, even though she doesn't need them. Who would have thought I would love to dance as much as I do, but then any excuse to have Devi in my arms makes me happy.

After meeting my parents who adore her, she agreed to allow Chase Janice to have a Sneak-Peek fashion show at The Tenth Muse tonight. She also volunteered to walk the runway when one of the models mysteriously became ill.

What Devi doesn't know is I'm the one who planned this event. I'm going to turn her dream into reality.

She hasn't asked to have sex with me. Not yet. We promised we'd wait until we got to know each other better and agreed to give the Three-Month-Rule a try. Our date nights are every Monday and Tuesday, and like smitten teenagers, we text each other dozens of times a day. On Mondays, I choose what events we'll attend at places like museums, art openings, theatres, and music venues. On Tuesday, Devi chooses where we go, which is generally out to dinner, movies, long hikes, or a day at the beach. Sometimes we do nothing but lie on the couch together reading books.

I'm making progress with a therapist Nedra referred me to. With desensitization therapy I've become less fearful of the dark and carry a much smaller flashlight with me at night. I also talk to him and Devi about everything, my fears, wants, dreams, and goals. The secrets that once made me vulnerable are no longer secrets, and with each reveal, I grow stronger and more confident.

Trusting someone as fully as I do Devi is amazing. I've never felt so protected and loved. I never thought my life as it is today was possible.

"Hello, handsome." Devi smiles as she strolls inside my condo tossing a fob in the air and catching it.

I'm undecided as to why I like it when she calls me handsome, even though I'm wearing pink sweats and yellow polka-dotted slippers.

"Shouldn't you be studying?" I ask.

"I borrowed Nedra's truck to take a load from the dungeon to the dump." She sniffs my neck. "You smell so fucking good. What are you wearing?"

"A cologne Mom gave me during her last visit."

"Mm." Devi sniffs my neck again. "Tell your mom you want another bottle of this."

I wipe a smudge off her face with my thumb. How we have changed. When I met Devi, she covered her face with a mask because of smudged makeup. Now, she doesn't worry about her appearance as much. And I'm not only dating, but constantly thinking of someone other than myself.

We dismantle and wrap most of what we load onto the truck with blankets so the neighbors can't see what we're disposing of. We tear down the bondage cross, flatten the human cage, and toss all of Candice's belongings out of the house in less than an hour.

The photos of Devi on the wall still need boxing up. The bed frame and headboard need to go as well. I want to put in flooring durable enough to handle gym equipment once we clear everything out.

I take the magazine clippings and photos of Devi down and put them in a pile. To think I once became enraged by these pictures, now I want to keep them.

"Hey, I'm taking off for the dump—be back in an hour." Devi walks in front of me. "I'll throw these creepy photos in the trash before I go."

I rub her small but firm ass. "Honey, don't wear your new sundress to the dump. Grab an old pair of my corduroy pants and a shirt from my bedroom."

"Yes, boss lady." She laughs.

My phone rings and I push the *speaker* button. "Hi Mom, I'm in the middle of something. Can I call you back?"

"No, it's your adorable girlfriend I need to speak to. She isn't answering her phone."

Devi leans in. "I'm here, Janice. What's up?"

"Pineapple wants to know when you can meet her at the club for your fitting. You're the first model to walk the runway tonight. She needs you ready."

"I'll be there after lunch—in plenty of time, I promise."

"Alright, love you girls. See you soon!"

Mother ends the call and we return to cleaning up the guest room.

"Perhaps I'll buy a scrap album to keep these in. What's the harm?"

Devi rests her hands on my shoulders and kisses my nose. "I'm glad these photos of me don't haunt you anymore, but I'd rather you toss them. We'll have our own collection of pictures, bondage equipment and kinky toys."

Her implying that we'll have sex someday makes me smile.

"Sounds like a plan, sweetheart."

Using terms of endearment feels odd, but to hear myself say them is delightful. I take the picture of the green-haired woman and me hugging inside Writerly to the living room, so I can have it framed later.

Devi returns from my bedroom wearing my clothes and says, "We conquer the three-month rule of dating tomorrow. What do you say we move to the next step?"

My heart is somersaulting with excitement. "You want us to become girlfriends?"

"I meant sex," she grins. "But becoming official sounds good too. Are you ready for us to be a couple?"

"Yes!" I run to Devi and I have her moaning within seconds, with my kisses. I'm ready to have sex right here, right now.

But Devi pulls back. "Mm, you taste good, but I only have Nedra's truck for a couple of hours and I'm in desperate need of a shower. I'll return as fast as I can, promise." She sprints outside and I can't stop smiling. At forty-years-old my life has flipped a one-eighty. I'm in a loving relationship with a woman and I cannot wait to have sex with her! What a concept. What a reality.

~~~~~

By lunchtime, we have Candice's room all cleared out and invite Nedra over for Mexican food to thank her for the use of her vehicle.

"These burritos are amazing," Nedra mumbles between bites.

I scoot another one her way. "Take one home. Devi bought enough from the food truck to last a week."

"I wanted to help with whatever you were moving today." Nedra points to Devi. "She declined my offer."

I smile. "We cleared out the dungeon and my girlfriend insisted she had everything under control."

Nedra's eyebrows raise. "Your girlfriend?" She turns to Devi, who is beaming. "I'm thrilled for you both."

"Yes, Joel begged me to be with her and I didn't have the heart to say no. Didn't you gorgeous?" Devi winks at me.

"On bended knee," I agree.

Devi kisses my temple. "Are you coming to my club to watch the Chase Janice fashion show?"

"Yes, I wouldn't miss it."

I feel Nedra staring at me as I gaze at Devi's ass when she exits the house. She leans back into her chair. "How is your sex life?"

I face Nedra. "If you are asking if I've topped Devi, I haven't. And yes, her body arouses me—big time, but she hasn't asked for sex or made any moves, and I won't push her."

Nedra takes her extra burrito and heads for the door. "Oh, she wants you, and if the way you drooled over Devi's cute behind is any indication, it won't be long before you take the dive." She laughs, then says, "Your mother stopped by the other day to give me a sock she crocheted. Not a pair mind you, just one sock."

I cover my eyes and sigh. "It's a willy warmer."

"Ah! Well, tell your mother I'd like to purchase a few more socks. Preferably in different sizes." Nedra waves goodbye.

"Wait, aren't you ace?"

"They're not for me. Nicole's niece is opening up a costume shop in Santa Monica."

"Kayla has a daughter?"

"Yes, her name is Laguna. She says her customers ask for all kinds of quirky things. She'll get a kick out of your mom's creations."

"Alright, I'll tell Mom we need more socks! And hey, my dear friend, next time we get together. It will be I who asks you the questions, and you who answers them."

Nedra smiles. "I promise to share more of myself with you in the near future."

~~~~~

Fighting the crowd at The Tenth Muse and wearing my *SLUTS RULE* T-shirt, I proceed to the temporary catwalk created by Chase Janice's crew for our fashion show tonight. Carrying a huge bouquet of yellow tulips makes it difficult to find my way, but I've worked tirelessly with my parents to ensure today goes off without a hitch.

I've been plotting how to reenact Devi's dream since I visited her in Tehachapi. Everything will happen as it did in Devi's dream except the falling-off-the-stage part. Danni, the bouncer is here with me to gently lower Devi from the runway to the floor.

My heart races when Chrissy Chlapecka's voice booms out of the speakers singing *I Am Pretty*. My beautiful girlfriend throws one of her very long legs through the curtain and we get a good look at her silver stiletto. When she pushes through the drapes dressed in a metallic evening gown and walks toward me, I can feel myself quivering at her beauty. I cannot believe Deviant Wallace is my girlfriend. A large white scarf floats and swirls around her and the crowd goes wild.

Devi struts down the runway and the cheers grow louder. She doesn't smile. She's a professional and keeps her cool until she stops at the end of the catwalk, and her wide sparkling eyes meet mine and her skilled mouth drops.

With trembling hands, I reach out to give her the bouquet of yellow tulips and Devi bends on her knees. Tears stream down her cheeks and she smiles. When she stretches her arm to take the flowers, our fingers touch and—oh crap.

Devi is falling.

"Danni, catch her!" I scream.

Danni flings her arms in the air with such force she knocks me over and I land on the dancefloor.

Through the chaos and people, I see Danni grab Devi saving her from the fall. My girlfriend's eyes widen when she sees me on the ground and breaks loose from Danni.

Kneeling over me, she takes my hand, "Are you okay, babe?"

Crap, this isn't how her dream is supposed to end. I failed her. I messed up again. I quickly pull her down with me and roll on top of her.

"I love you. I fucking love you, Deviant Wallace."

We both laugh and cry in each other's arms. The tapping of another model's heels on the runway above us distracts most customers, yet the very protective Danni continues to ensure nobody steps on us.

Holding one another, we try to stand but we're, laughing and crying so hard we can't get up. Yellow tulips are splattered all around us, and I stop for a minute to take it all in. The sound of Devi's delightful laughter is beautiful and the world goes silent as her happiness reverberates through my body and fills my heart.

Overwhelmed by the vast amount of love nestling inside me, a revelation strikes with such force it sounds like thunder. To love her, to love others, is to love myself. I've never felt this powerful, this self-aware. I'm enough. I'm more than enough, and I'll never allow self-doubt to sidetrack me again. I want nothing more than to be who I am and to take in Devi's beautiful blue-gray eyes every day for the rest of my days.

Epilogue - Devi

Waking up with the woman of my dreams in my arms has me whimpering with glee. I own The Incredible Tenth Muse, and my girlfriend proves over and over again that she'll do anything to keep me. I don't think of myself as an orphan anymore. I have an awesome family here at Amboadia.

When Joel and I left the Chase Janice After-Party at sunrise, we were exhausted. I fell asleep as soon as my head hit the pillow, but this morning I want to make love to my girlfriend.

As I gaze at the gorgeous woman who made my dream come true, I want nothing more than to give her an orgasm. Sadly, it's almost noon and I have an important date with my bestie.

Trying not to disturb Joel, I take a quick shower and leave to meet with Goth. I promised her I'd help hunt for the missing Detronian today. Her other brainbugs are safely in the cavern on Devitron or so she says, but one is being stubborn. Of course, there are no such creatures, but Goth texted me for backup and I'm here for her.

Walking through the tube, I spot my bestie with Amboadia-West's security guard, Kurt Hartman, Virginia, and Christine.

I kneel in the grass under a tree beside them. "Any luck?"

Goth huffs. "I saw Droopy a minute ago, but the little stinker is playing hard to get."

I brush my hand through the grass. "Detronians resemble ladybugs only they're lavender. Oh, and, their spots are on their black bellies instead of their shells, and they walk on their hind legs, right?"

"Yes, and they have very long antennas—double the length of their bodies, but Droopy is clumsy and fell out of my head, bending theirs beyond repair." Goth scrapes loose bark off a nearby tree. "Not in there either, dammit. We need to find them before the bats do."

"Them? Is it non-binary, or is there more than one missing?" I pretend to scan the area for the nonexistent creature.

Goth runs her fingers through her short, blond hair. "Didn't you read the pamphlet, Devi? They're hermaphrodites. Each has both male and female organs. They don't need a mate to reproduce."

Scratching my head, I concede I must have skipped that section. Then, incredibly, I see it. A funny little bug with a lavender shell running, or more like wobbling, on its hind legs. Its bent antennas are waving about excitedly as it nears my best friend's foot.

"Don't move Goth. The Detronian is by your left boot."

Goth tilts her worn Italian hiking boots ever so slightly to get a better view, then stretches forward. "There you are, Droopy. You crazy shit." Goth scoops the tiny critter into her cupped hand. "You've always been the troublemaker." She scolds her brainbug as she gets onto her feet. "Oh, and before I forget, you have to feed them Fruit Loops or they'll invade your kitchen seeking scraps of food."

"Okay, I'll buy some today." I'm still stunned by what I'm seeing, and follow everyone to take Droopy to Devitron.

Inside the Rainbow Cavern, I spot Joel heading our way wearing striped pants and a plaid sweater. When she nears, she kisses Virginia and Christine, then stares at my buddy's closed hand. I'm confused by my disappointment at her for not noticing Kurt Hartman, the man people are only supposed to see if they're in love. It's not like I believe in the superstition, but still.

"Hello, Goth," Joel says. "What do you have, there?" she leans in to kiss me. "Morning cutie."

Goth opens her hand. "A naughty little Detronian. It was foolish of me to think they could survive in Detronia. There are too many predators there." She places her brainbug on a multi-colored glass mound near the stream. The tiny bug expands and flutters its wings but doesn't fly off.

"Droopy is calling for their friends using the vibration of their wings. Hopefully, they'll come and welcome the little brat."

Goth looks around as if pleading for the other Detronians to accept Droopy.

Within seconds, several other lavender brainbugs fly to the glass mound and land next to the misfit with bent antennas.

Joel's eyes widen, and she stares at me with questioning eyes.

I take her hand. "Goth's brainbugs are fucking real and they eat Fruit Loops!"

Joel bends to get a closer look. "Did you know even though Fruit Loops are different colors, they all taste the same?" She directs her gaze to Goth. "Your mind creates wondrous things."

Joel turns to Kurt Hartman. "I apologize for not introducing myself. I haven't had coffee yet. I'm Joel, Devi's girlfriend."

My lips stretch so wide in a smile they hurt. Maybe there is magic in our universe.

"The Detronians will be safe here with you and Devi." Goth lets out a sigh of relief. "Now that Droopy is safe, we,"—she points to Kurt and Christine— "can go bowling. They hurry up the steps and out of the Rainbow Cave.

Joel turns to Virginia. "Alright what's up? Where did these bugs come from?"

"What are you talking about?" I ask.

Virginia smiles. "Droopy and the other Detronians were a birthday present for Goth's thirtieth birthday. She always speaks of her brainbugs with such love, Stephanie Courtenay had them created in her entomology lab. The harmless critters are Mutant Spotted Ladybugs."

Joel sighs. "I figured they were mutants but I rather believe they come from Goth's mind."

My rich friends are outlandish, but there's never a dull moment in Amboadia because of them.

~~~~

Within seconds of returning to the Sky Viewing Cave, Joel orders me to take off my clothes.

"What?" I stand in shock. Does this mean she wants to touch me? What happens when she touches my breasts and finds them disgusting? "Are you sure?" I croak.

Joel rolls onto her side and leans on her arm. "I'm not very good at showing my emotions, but Devi, you must know when I am with you the rest of the world slips away. You're everything to me, and I want to love every bit of you."

Warmth wells in my eyes. This isn't just about sex. It's about love as well. I want to jump on Joel and kiss her all over, but I'm immobilized with fear. Will she love all of me? Or will she not? What happens next will either solidify us as a couple or put a wedge between us.

Aware of my hesitation, she says, "Trust my love for you and undress for me. Let me see all of you."

When I was hungover the day of the earthquake, Joel saw me naked. She knows what my body looks like, but she has never touched me intimately except for the time she was on mushrooms. She's asking me to trust her and I do but she can't help how she feels. What if she becomes repulsed by my girly parts? What if she doesn't like my smell? What if so many things.

With weakened knees, I manage to take off my clothes. Naked in every sense of the word, I gaze at Joel, silently pleading for her to like my body.

"You're as stunning as I remember." She says as her eyes drop to my feet and slowly rise until they meet mine. Joel is checking me out, and she's smiling. She's fucking smiling!

She pats the bed, beckoning me to lie next to her, and so I do.

Joel cups my breasts and with a curious glance, says, "They're much softer than I expected."

I'm not sure if she thinks this is a bad thing or a good thing. I don't know if the sight of my boobs excites her or if she's merely examining them, but then she places gentle kisses on my neck and pinches one of my nipples, then the other.

Joel gazes at me with heavy-lidded eyes. "Your nipples are so hard."

"Well, yeah, you're turning me on." I grin, as I plead with all the powers in the universe for her to not be repelled by my girly parts.

She furrows her eyebrows, leans in, and takes my nipple into her mouth. She brushes her tongue over the tip, making my clit throb.

"Mm, that feels good, Joel." My body shakes with need. "Fuck, I want you inside me." I realize saying this might put too much pressure on her and I add, "Not that you need to do anything. I can take care of myself." I place a hand between my legs and slip a finger inside my slippery opening. I thrust it deep and whimper at the pleasure I'm giving myself.

Joel pulls on my wrist. "No, sweetheart. Let me take care of you. Please."

Under the Rainbow   D.A. Hartman

Joel

Sucking and nibbling at Devi's round breasts is the most sensual thing I've ever done. Her silky and warm skin arouses me as I kiss down her firm stomach to rest my cheek on her clean-shaven mound. I feel soft stubble, but what grabs my attention most is her smell. She's cool ocean air and sweet peaches. I watch myself as I wipe a finger along her slick slit. "My gods, Devi, you're so wet."

I want to top the woman I love, and I want to go slow, and experience as much as I can while I please her for the first time.

Taking her clit between my fingers, I gently pinch to see what Devi will do. She lets out an indecipherable word, more of a squeak really.

"Did I hurt you?"

"No. I like how you're touching me, babe. Do whatever you want."

I dip a finger inside her slippery warmth and move it around, stirring her juices. "Have you been thinking about fucking me all day?"

Devi grabs my shoulder and moans, "Yes."

And now you want me to fuck you, don't you, sweetheart?"

"Yes, Joel, please."

"Good girl. You know the magic word, don't you?" I whisper, and yes, I want to fuck her and feel the depths of her passion.

I push another finger in and press deeper to explore the walls of her vagina. "You're so beautiful, Devi."

Her hips sway and grind against my hand. "I'm going to come too fast," she says.

Not wanting her to come yet, I remove my fingers. "May I taste you?"

Devi stills and her eyes tear up. With a face filled with concern, she nods.

Placing my head between Devi's legs, I take in the view. Her legs are trembling. Perhaps she fears her taste will turn me off and I wonder the same thing. To shorten our angst, I hungrily take her clit into my mouth and the fabulous feast has me moaning in contentment. I not only love the creamy taste of Devi; I'm becoming aroused as her clit thickens in my mouth.

"Oh, fuck," Devi moans.

Fearing inadequacy, I try to follow my plan which is to move my tongue as fast over my girlfriend's girly parts as I would my fingers when I pleasure myself. However, Devi is backing away, trying to free herself from my over-eager tongue.

Alright, so that plan doesn't work—got it.

Slowing down, I inhale Devi's scent and allow myself to feel her—to feel us, together. My heart warms as I enjoy her taste and the sensation of my tongue sliding with delicate intent up and down her sensitive wet slit. With each rotation, I swirl around her bud, and suck her clit into my mouth.

When I stick my fingers back inside her, Devi hums her approval. Taking the woman I love into my mouth while I fuck her has me whimpering with need. I regret wasting so much time not doing exactly this—experiencing the most intimate connection of my life.

I revel in her heat and allow myself a much-needed cry—a cry of joy.

"I love you so fucking much," she whispers.

Wanting to savor every part of my girlfriend. I slip my fingers out and dig them into her ass cheeks. Pulling her closer to my mouth, I plunge my tongue inside her.

"Oh, shit, I'm going to—oh Joel." Devi presses her hand on my head.

I want nothing more than to drink her up. It doesn't matter that I can't breathe. I desperately want her.

The movement of her hips are in sync with my tongue and her body becomes tense.

"Uh, yes." she groans.

I push deeper inside her, and she tightens her thighs around my head as she explodes. Her liquid warmth surrounds my tongue as she periodically jolts with aftershocks until she releases my hair and falls limp on the mattress.

With as much tenderness as I can manage, I kiss her clit before wiping my damp face on Devi's thighs.

Between her legs, I murmur, "I don't want to stop looking at you. I want to kiss every bit of you."

Once again, I cry happy tears.

Devi tucks a pillow under her head. "I've never been topped by someone who loves me before. Nothing compares. You've made me the happiest I've ever been, Joel." She taps my shoulder and asks for me to lay on top of her. It's then I realize she's crying too.

Her taste, smell, and the sounds of her arousal are things I want to experience again and again. I'll never get enough of Devi. I wipe the tears from her face with kisses and think of the day we met over two years ago. This beautiful woman who had green hair and wore a mask and oversized sunglasses now lays naked beneath me. Our bond, even while tainted by hatred, never completely broke.

I wrap my arms around her neck and lift her head so she can see the words form on my lips. "I love you, Devi."

~~~~~

We stay in bed the rest of the day and I familiarize myself with every part of her body as we lie bare under the constellation of Cassiopeia.

"Now that you've topped me several times today, do you have a better idea of your sexuality?" Devi asks.

"Yes, I've decided I'm Devi-romantic."

She laughs. "You're Devi-romantic and I'm Joel-sexual."

I giggle and squirm as Devi kisses me all over my face and body.

"Did you know my favorite planet is Venus?" she asks.

"Did you know the planet of love is the only known planet that spins counterclockwise?" I reply.

Devi snorts into my neck. "I love you, ya big dork."

There is nothing better than cuddling with my girlfriend beneath a prismatic galaxy of twinkling stars. A glorious rainbow of colors shines on us tonight and hopefully every night for the rest of our lives.

I want to fall asleep and end this perfect day with these exquisite thoughts marinating inside my brain, but my girlfriend insists on uttering the corniest statement before we do, and because I'm absolutely pussy-whipped, she'll get her wish.

"Joel?"

"Yes, Devi."

"I have to say it."

"No, I beg you, please don't."

"I can't help it. I feel compelled."

"It's so trite and mawkish."

"True, but I won't be able to sleep unless I say it."

I press my palms over my ears. "Right, right, well do what you must."

With sparkling eyes and a smile as wide as the constellation Hydra, Devi whispers,

"Dreams, if you dare to dream them, really do come true."

THE END

Thank you, readers, for sharing the lives of the many sapphics who live at Amboadia with me. Please leave a review and share your journey under the rainbow on Amazon and Goodreads, or a rating is good too. <3

If you would like to read/listen to Goth and Virginia's love story, check out Round Trip by D.A. Hartman.

Made in the USA
Las Vegas, NV
29 April 2024

89292547R00151